Louise Kean is 27 and grew u[illegible] the University of East Anglia, she works as a marketing manager at an international film company in London. *Toasting Eros* is her first novel.

LOUISE KEAN

TOASTING EROS

Some loves start wars,
change whole worlds,
span lifetimes. Apparently.

HarperCollins*Publishers*

This novel is entirely a work of fiction.
The names, characters and incidents portrayed in it are the work of the author's imagination. Any resemblance to actual persons, living or dead, events or localities is entirely coincidental.

HarperCollins*Publishers*
77–85 Fulham Palace Road,
Hammersmith, London W6 8JB

www.fireandwater.com

A Paperback Original
1 3 5 7 9 8 6 4 2

A catalogue record for this book
is available from the British Library

ISBN 0 00 711463 X

Set in Garamond 3 and Futura by
Rowland Phototypesetting Ltd,
Bury St Edmunds, Suffolk

Printed and bound in in Great Britain by
Clays Ltd, St Ives plc

Acknowledgements

Massive thanks to wonderful Ali, Doug, Carol, Emma, Diana, and all at Curtis Brown. Just as much to all at Harper Collins, especially Jennifer, Maxine, Fiona, and Sarah, for being lovely and working so hard, and to Jane Harris, Martin Palmer, and Nick Sayers. Also, and very important, huge thanks to Katherine Ball, for shouting about me before anybody else did.

To Mummy, Daddy, Laura and Amy, for their love, and to Nanny, whose singing and clapping I miss more than anything. To Jase, for stupid amounts of encouragement and enthusiasm, to Watson for filth and sales support and to Lisa, for picking up her canvas that day, and telling me I should too.

And thanks to my girls: Clare, Alice, Nim, Nix, Kennedy, Karen, Jules, and Nat, for inspiration, but mostly for fun.

For JP, and his dedication to the cause . . .
And for Laura, just because.

Contents

Where Am I?

I'm standing in the sun.

The inside of my eyes is a red colour-wash, and as I tilt my head back, my neck heats up. Henry stands behind me, arms on the doorframe, tall enough to catch his own rays, not in my shadow.

I am exhausted. It is 3 p.m. on a cold sunny Sunday, and I've had enough sleep, but still. I'm drained. This unexpected sunlight on an overcast day feels like it will pour through my body as I breathe it in, and wash everything away. Soothe me.

Why am I so tired? I'm tired of it all. Of the doubts, and the almost certainties. Of the search, and the hope.

Of what could be versus what will be. I'm not just talking about my dress size.

I'm worn out with my own ambition and my battle with laziness. Of the need to constantly go back to bed, sleep a little longer, and postpone it all. Of other people's expectations and assurances that I will be 'something', when all the evidence points in the opposite direction.

In so many ways I just want to be told, and not have to make my own decisions any more, but by all accounts people don't like that in the end. Take South Africa. But I really feel like I don't want a vote, just speed me where I'm going and leave me there, don't tell me I can change it.

It's depressing to be such a cliché, fighting through this mid-twenties war zone. But I am at that point where you decide what you're going to do with your time, before the time runs out and what you end up doing just happens to you, and you get on with it. It's too much responsibility for me, though, I feel too young, and I have the hopes of others resting on my shoulders. But of course, I'm on my own here. They'll surf the wave, but I have to get the momentum going first.

And I am not talking about careers here. Those things are rarely enjoyable. They are a means to an end; they are rarely the end in itself. Few people have the luxury of an enjoyable working day. This is why the other stuff becomes so important. Marx called romantic love a misleading distraction from the reality of toiling for someone else's benefit, not realizing our proletarian power. But who has the time for an uprising? I'm free Wednesday lunchtime, but I have to be back in the office for a meeting at three.

It's the curse of education I suppose, when they show you something allegedly better, and they force you to think. I should never have started it, should have been confused by my thoughts and ignored them, rather than seeing them through to the end. The end being here, or so it seems right now.

But there is too much to live for. Coke is not the drug of your average twenty-something. It's not a joint either, or a pill, or a tab. It's hope and it's dread. What you could be versus what you might be. I know you've managed it, and you've mostly survived. I'm bitching about the obvious, and dwelling unnecessarily. But where is your manual, your pass notes? Show me how to make it through this stage, and I will stop all this terrible introspection.

Yes these are the wilderness years of drugs, and doubts, of laughs and sex, of a new independence, and bills. And clock watching. You see time for what it is at last, and you realize that it owns you. It's not quite running out – nothing that dramatic. But it'll tick, and it'll tick and you won't even realize it, and another five years will have passed with which you've done nothing. For the first time I can hear the clock ticking faintly, somewhere back there.

And my God, you do not have to tell me it's trivial for me to know it. I know I'm not starving, not dying, not fighting some cause that's not even my own, not experiencing anything new. I see how easy I have it, I see the luxury of spending time with my twenty-something crisis, I see all of that. But don't tell me this is not important, just the whinging diatribe of a spoilt twenty-first century western princess.

Because this is my twenty-fifth year, and it is the only one I'll have. Once it's over, I cannot claim it back. I am allowed to worry, I have the right to doubt the future, even if I haven't lost a leg, or my home, or my livelihood, or my freedom. I would never be so terrible as to say 'give me one of these, give me my disadvantage to dwell on, and take my mind off the rest of my life'. But until my life stops being so trivial and I get knocked for six by something I cannot control then let me have this. For now at least, it seems a hard enough burden to bear. I don't expect your sympathy, and I won't court it, but do not pass your fucking judgement on me either. Not this early at least.

I think I know what I want.

I want it to be in his eyes.

I want to be able to hold his gaze, surely and honestly without feeling anything else. Without irony, or jokes, or any fraudulent feeling. I find it hard to see anyone, or anything, without a joke in mind.

I don't want it to be lust, just lust. I don't want to have to say anything. I don't want to be thinking anything, or be distracted by my own embarrassment. To be absolutely and utterly silent and awake, and only looking in those eyes, with honest confidence. I want to fall asleep still looking.

And I want to be able to rely on myself, and on him, completely, to do all that we can to absolutely fulfil our lives, and not get disappointed, or worse, bored.

Move your mind through space and time. I read that somewhere. It's what I want to do. I want to see myself in the context of tomorrow, and last week, and ten years' time. I want to see it all and map our lives from there. I want to know that everything is going to work out for the best, for the both of us. I want to know that we won't ruin it for each other.

I just don't want to be the cause of somebody's disappointment. I don't want to be the baggage that weighs their life down. I just want to remember to look at the big picture, always. Move my mind through space and time. Live my life like I'm fifteen and eighty all at once.

So maybe, the answer in not in his eyes, but mine.

The sun is clouding over, and I turn and walk back into the house, but Henry stays and catches the last rays.

It's time to go, or we'll miss our flight.

The Morning After

His shoulder, a massive shoulder, is pinning me down. His leg, still in his jeans, is curled around me, keeping me in place. His head is turned away, his hair in my eyes. I think I could move, but do not try, I'm still half-asleep. I am also very aware that the slightest movement of my head will fire my hangover out of his blocks. Hangovers are little bastard men in Lycra and trainers living just under your skin, constantly in training for the slightest morning after.

Give them just a couple of glasses of red wine, and they will allow you one misleading night of sleep before they sprint a thousand crazy laps around the inside of your head, mercilessly smashing a brick baton against your skull every few paces. But there is nothing slight about this hangover. No, alcohol has been well and truly abused in the last twelve hours. And the little running sadist of pain inside my head is flexed and warmed up, and ready to go, as soon as I quite literally give him the nod.

I also know that I've been drinking by the taste in my

mouth. It feels like the last resting place of some random rodent with a forty a day habit that got the little fella in the end. Besides, the smell of alcohol from the night before always hangs on me more than any other, including all the nice smells that you pay a fortune for.

Even without the hangover, I still don't want to move. I could stay like this for hours, not forever, but hours at least. No part of me aches, or itches, no part of me wants to go anywhere, or stop looking at this sleeping form beside me. There is no talking, no discussion, no before or after, no post mortem. There is no future to be confronted, it can last as long as I can make it last, by just doing nothing. I don't want to bolt although I suppose I should. I don't want to run. I just lie here.

But he moves, raising himself up on his arms, one of which uses my left breast for support, which is incredibly painful I wince, but say nothing. He shifts his body around, and then his arms give way and he slams down onto me, his makeshift mattress, the stubble on his face injecting a thousand needles into my cheek. For the first time I can see his face, even this close up, if I cross my eyes. He is beautiful. His hair covers his eyes, which are closed anyway, and his mouth is turned down at the sides, a kind of frown, and he looks angry, beautifully sad in his sleep, dreaming troubles. The sun isn't quite up, but the darkness seems to spotlight him anyway. I am a little in awe. I lie like this for hours, and he doesn't stir again.

Eventually his eyes flicker, and then open, and I am looking right into them.

He smiles, his mouth moves at least, and in a second it is all over. He bolts upright, and sends me flying off to the side. My hips slam against a crook lock, and my head thumps the back of the driver's seat.

He is leaping from the car, and I am scrambling to get up, but none of my limbs appear able to go in the direction they would like. I am painfully aware that I am hanging out of my bra, covering myself up in front of him, mortified that he has caught me looking at him, with crossed eyes and a gaping mouth. Mortified that he has seen me fall, that I obviously had not been driven by the same desire to get the hell out of that car the minute I had woken, with the same reflex to escape. In that moment I look like a love-struck bunny-boiling psycho refusing to leave, about to say that I can already feel his unborn child growing inside me. The truth of course, is that I do not even know him, and he doesn't know me. All I do know for certain is that he is breathtaking, and I am not, so why in hell am I still here? He obviously didn't envisage waking up with me.

In the silence between us, the absolute deafening fucking silence with neither of us saying a word, I hear the radio playing, softly, for the first time. It has been on all along, and I only hear it now. It is Tony Bennett singing "The Way You Look Tonight", and I remember where I am. I am in Vegas.

He is searching for his mobile phone in his jeans pockets, patting his chest when he can't find it, despite the fact that he is naked from the waist up. He has a fantastic chest, carved and sun kissed and skin pulled tight over the perfect bumps and twists of his muscles, while I have a roll of fat hanging over my jeans. He looks . . . ruggedly good. I just look rough. I manoeuvre myself out of the car, and see that we are in a half full McDonalds car park, and he is leaning on a truck parked next to this car, his car? He has found his phone on the third attempt into the back of his jeans, and is talking quietly, holding his head in one huge hand, rubbing his chest. I scramble into my top, which gets caught and twisted around my breasts for what seems like hours, and rub my eyes, anticipating a clearer view of this situation when I re-focus. Should I just walk off? Should I say goodbye? He is showing no signs of hanging up his mobile phone, and I don't even know him for God's sake! We don't owe each other anything. At least I hope I don't owe him anything – please don't let me have actually paid for sex! Although it would certainly explain things a little better.

By some miracle my purse is on the front seat, and I reach in and grab it, check I haven't handed over a credit card, because by the look of him he would cost a few thousand at least. But my cards are still there, and my room key, and a couple of dollar bills, but mostly pound coins that I have neglected to remove at Heathrow. I lean on the front of the car, which is already heating up, and I realize the sun has almost reached the middle of the sky. I am uncomfortably warm and sticky, and my head is pounding, and I could quite easily vomit right here and now. I have no idea where in hell I am.

He is still talking, laughing quietly, twisting his neck from side to side, flexing his shoulders. I have to leave. He doesn't want to talk to me and is praying I will just walk away. I turn and try to make it clear that I am looking at him properly, that I want his attention, and after an age he notices. I instantly react with a kind of spasm, which was meant to be a nonchalant wave, and turn to go, but he grabs my arm and spins me round. He gestures with his fingers at his lips – what is he doing, is he blowing me a kiss? No of course not, he is making the international sign for a cigarette, and I shrug 'no' without even checking, mouth 'sorry', and leave.

Walking slowly is the best I can manage, and with my head down so as not to acknowledge the bastard sun trying to combust my head by being brighter and hotter than it has ever, ever been before. I realize my feet are filthy in my sandals. I have cuts slashed along the toes of my right foot. It is not a great intellectual leap to deduce that at some point last night I must have fallen over.

Something is digging into my hips, in my pocket, and I retrieve the offending ring pull from a Coke can. God I'd love a Diet Coke. I always and without fail need a Diet Coke to get me through a hangover, and I am in a McDonalds car park after all. But it will be even brighter inside the restaurant than it is out here, and the air conditioning will be freezing, and I will end up having a burger, no matter how sick I feel. I think all of the above would send my body into medical shock, and it is probably best just to get a cab with the few dollars that I have, and get back to the hotel.

I hear running behind me and I turn to see him jogging towards me, all taut limbs and tan. I shield my eyes, the sun is right behind him. He starts speaking before he comes to a stop.

'God, I'm so sorry, that was my boss. I'm kinda' late for work, and he's going shithouse. I had to calm him down. I shouldn't be here.'

'Oh God no, that's fine. I had to go anyway. It's fine.'

He smiles and I hate him. I hate him for making it so

bloody obvious how bloody all-American bloody gorgeous he is, and how completely out of his sober league I am. Not 'good for me'. Not 'look what I managed to get because we were both so blind hammered drunk'. No I do not feel fine at all. I feel the same way any one-night stand makes you feel, because if you really liked that person you would not have done what we did. You would have chatted, got a number and a goodnight kiss, and got excited. Not had a drunken shag in the back of a car because you were both so drunk you didn't give a shit who it was you were sucking and kissing and moaning with.

Seeing him now, looking so good, it doesn't make me want to grab him and start doing whatever it was we had done the night before all over again. It actually makes me want to smack him, for making it so glaringly obvious that I am not the leggy blonde he wanted to wake up next to unexpectedly. Of course I know that these are my judgements and not his, but I am hungover, and I'm tired, and men think like that anyway, I don't care what you say.

'Look, I really do have to go, and I'm sure you have to get to work.'

'But do you know where you're heading? I mean, I could give you a ride.'

I want to say 'you already did' but that would be embarrassing and inappropriate, so I just say,

'No I'll be fine, I can see that Sphinx thing, so it can't be far.'

'Sure? I feel really bad about this.'

'Yes of course, now go to work. And have a good holiday. You are on holiday, no you're working, on a working holiday . . . is that right?'

'Yeah' – a muted, head down, embarrassed you've made us both look like sluts for not being sure kind of reply. Well done me. Two very enthusiastic thumbs up for me please everybody.

'So thanks, but I'm going to walk. Clear my head. See the Vegas sights.'

'OK, sure, well thanks as well. I think we had a good night. You know, if you can't remember you've usually had a good night.'

What I want to say is when you are sixteen it means you've had a good night. When you're our age it just means your kidneys are going to start hurting soon, and you can't handle your liquor, and you're spectacularly immature not to know when to stop drinking. Instead I say,

'Unforgettable.'

Not with sarcasm, which would have made it only a slightly less stupid remark, but with eager sincerity, resulting in us both just standing, looking a little confused and embarrassed for a moment. I am officially crap. Stamp me with it: I'm crap.

He pats me on the arm, in sympathy I think – there will be no real physical contact here and I smile and walk away. I hear him jogging back and starting his car. But instead of speeding off, he pulls alongside me slowly, and I walk my most casual walk, as he winds down the window. Now I really wish he would just fuck off, I cannot make any more small talk this morning. I pretend not to see him, while obviously not being able to miss him, and the car keeps moving beside me, until inevitably I have to turn around and feign surprise.

'Christ, I didn't see you there.' I am so crap.

He shouts through the window, over his radio which has been cranked up,

'Look I don't care what you say, I can't leave you here, I feel like a real shit. What if you got mugged? We can find your hotel. I've been here for over a month, I know the town better. I can't leave you in a parking lot for fuck's sake!'

He has a nice accent, sort of half American, half English – not that god awful twang that every other American in this town seems to have. He is, I suppose, being sweet. I am just going to look like a bitch if I say no again.

'You know what? You're right. That would be great.'

I climb in, conceding to myself that I am actually lost. Besides which just walking away makes me look and feel a little like a prostitute to us both. He swings out of the car park, and takes a right.

'So, what's the name of your hotel?'

'Sorry?'

'What's the name of your hotel?' He doesn't turn the music down, just shouts louder.

'The Sunset – opposite Jacks Casino Palace or whatever. That big palace place.'

'Shit that's a block away – you could have walked!'

With that he screeches up outside my hotel, and I'm out of the door before the engine stops running, tripping over the pavement, falling over myself to get away.

'Bye then, thanks for that . . . Mark.'

'Matt, yeah see ya, I remembered your name at least!'

We both laugh and cringe at the same time.

'OK bye then, Eve.' I smile at the sound of him saying my name. It doesn't sound quite right in that accent. I'm used to a deeper British voice. I close the door of the car, and he says goodbye again, and uses my name, again, to make the point – how the hell did he remember that? When did I even tell him for Christ's sake? Has he stolen my passport? I knew I shouldn't have carried it with me everywhere. I don't want him to say it again. God damn travellers cheques!

'Oh well done. Matt, that's called 'showing off' in England, and it's not attractive.' But he is already changing his music, he stopped listening to me seconds ago.

I walk into reception, as I hear him drive off behind me.

Bollocks. About everything.

No

The hotel is immaculate, the lifts are pristine, the carpets spotless. My room however is a bloody mess, as I left it. My moisturizer has become a nasty deposit on the floor where I trod on the tube before going out last night. Green eye glitter is all over the sheets, where I neglected to make the bed from the night before that. I catch my leg on my tongs, and after a couple of seconds realize they are burning me. Scarily, they are still turned on, and have somehow not torched the whole place down. Could they have traced that back to me? I'm not sure.

Do I clean up and then sleep, or just sleep, or have a shower . . . and then sleep? The shower option is the least disgusting, so I take my clothes off and wrap last night's still wet towel around me. I don't know why I need to cover up, I'm alone after all, but there is a certain kind of body confidence to walking around naked that I just don't have. In the absence of a hair band, although I know I packed at least ten, I manage to split a few ends by putting a pencil in hair that would honestly stay up on its own, it's that dirty. I decide to run a bath instead, which is much less effort despite the fact that I always feel I'm lying in my own dirt.

I walk into the bathroom, rubbing the mascara out of my eyes, but leaning over to turn the taps on, I hear a strange noise behind me. I didn't register it at first, in my tired, much weakened state, but now I realize it is not the plumbing. It is a noise that should not be coming from my bathroom, it is not an appliance. It is something foreign, something that should not be in here with me. Someone is breathing heavily, behind the bathroom door.

As fear spreads in less than a moment to every nerve ending in my body, widening my eyes, tightening my throat, sucking in my chest and stiffening my already shaking fingers, I hear this person move, and the door slam shut behind me. I am completely frozen with one hand on the hot tap as the water gushes out into the bath, but still above this noise, I can hear his excitable rasps behind my back, no more than a foot away. I do not turn around, because somehow I can't. I feel my neck and back turn to rock as I wait for the knife between my shoulders, or the arm to shoot around to cover my mouth, or the hands to circle my neck. All I can hear is the breathing getting harder and harder, and I am waiting for whatever it is to come. This stranger is a foot away, and there is no room for me to defend myself with one well-aimed kick. There is no way to turn and bolt from the room: the door is shut, this person in front of it, just enjoying these few seconds of my fear.

I am still frozen waiting for something to happen, but as nothing does, I begin to scan in front of me for anything I can grab for defence. Shampoo bottles and a loofah are the only objects on the side of the bath. But still I don't budge, and neither does he. I can't lean to pick anything up without firing him into action, sparking whatever atrocity awaits me. The sheer terror between my shoulders is paralyzing me. If I don't move maybe he won't either.

I flinch as I hear a sudden movement behind me, instinctively grasp for the first thing, and swing around, terrified, eyes closed, gasping, lashing out with my loofah, not so much cutting the air as removing the dead skin cells from it. But I am making contact with nothing. My eyes flash open involuntarily, and as I focus I let out my one scream, stopping almost as soon as I start, and begin to shake and sob . . . with relief.

The waiter, room service, is crouching behind the door with his arms over his head, trying somehow to crawl into the wall and disappear. He is frankly too small to do me any real damage, and he begins belatedly screaming enough for the both of us. He looks like a Mexican Munchkin.

I fall backwards and sit on the side of the bath, breathing in deeply, closing my eyes, resting my hands on the sides to support my back and stop me falling into the rising, scalding water. Within seconds my body has been transformed from granite to jelly. I gain some sort of composure, and realize that the waiter has stopped screaming. I open my eyes to look at him properly, and he takes this as his cue to take a deep breath, refill his lungs, and start squealing all over again. I stare at him, and he stops his screaming, self-consciously. He is not wearing the ski mask I had envisaged, just his little bow tie and uniform. My shoulders collapse, as my body finally registers I am completely out of danger and, moreover, I am too tired for this. I feel like there should be a pool of terror at my feet, feel every emotion rush down my body to the floor, grounding me.

'Oh my God! What in Christ's name do you think you are doing? You terrified me! I was fucking terrified! I thought you were a . . . I thought you were going to . . . well it doesn't matter, but what the hell do you think you are doing? And what is that on your head – is that . . . my bra? Is that my bra on your head? What in God's name is my bra doing on your head?'

I reach around to turn off the tap. I appear to be the one in control here. Unlike me, he still appears to believe himself in mortal danger, and is trembling like a child. I have just been scared half to death, petrified by this doorstop of a man, and it seems that I am going to have to be the nice one. This is insane.

'I think you must . . . you must have slipped? Or something. Anyway you've got my bra fastened around your head.' Jesus wept, give me strength. Why I am trying to console him I don't know. Why is he more scared than me? I don't look that bad, surely. Frankly, that's just rude.

'Look, it's not even clean, but I suppose that's the point is it? Take it off. I need to have a bath now so can you come back later and clean up, or whatever it is you were supposed to actually be doing. Please?'

'Yes, madame, I much sorry. I do that. I slip on the soap,' (unopened, on the soap dish) 'and this ladies' garment,' he gestures to the Mickey Mouse ears on his head 'it get caught, it stuck see? I think it is caught, as it cannot come off see?' He is tugging at the thing, but it's not moving, and I think it might be cutting off the circulation to his head somehow. He is turning purple. He is starting to cry, talking in little breaths between sobs.

'I go now,' sob 'but I empty your bin later,' sob, 'and I bring you a complimentary light snack for the convenience.'.

'Inconvenience, you mean.'

'*Que?*'

'Whatever.'

Unable to remove the bra, coughing and crying, and on the point of choking, he still appears to want to leave with it on. Frankly I'd let him, but it's one of the only ones that gives me any real support. It is too tight to be pulled off over his chin, and he'll pass out in the corridor if he leaves it on.

'Come here and I'll take it off. You can't have it, it's mine. *Comprende?* Stand bloody still.'

It takes a couple of seconds because he has hooked it wrong: this is not a man with extensive bra experience. Seen this close, his eyes are very red, and his face is kind of crumbling, disintegrating in front of me, framed ridiculously by my best black bra. I begin to feel terrible for the poor little bastard, and I wish I could just give him the damn thing, but then I would have errant nipples for the rest of my holiday.

'Please don't get upset, it's a complicated one to unfasten. You HAVE to stand still though. For God's sake stop backing away!'

He is still sobbing and now I am starting to get upset, because let's face it, wearing women's underwear on your head, in this town at least, does not make you a pervert. In any town for that matter. It is only a little strange.

The bra finally pops off, and he flies out of the bathroom door.

'Wait a minute,' I yell after him, and he turns and looks petrified, covering his head with his arms as if I'm going to hit him. But I have no intention of hitting him; I tip him the few dollars from my purse. He looks confused as hell, waving his hands in front of him to say no, he doesn't want it, and then snatching it anyway, bursting into fresh tears. I have no idea why I have given him this money, maybe so he can buy a bra of his own to play with, and good bras like this are expensive! Or maybe because I am in a guilty state of mind, and trying to prove to this one, very small man, that I am not a bad person, and that I understand more than anyone that we all make mistakes. And he looked so upset, so mortified, as if it was the first time he had ever indulged this little fantasy and had the worst luck in the world.

By the time I get out of the bath, a toasted cheese sandwich and a bag of peanuts are on the chest of drawers just inside the door, and I'm glad I tipped him. He understands, he feels the guilt too, and has done all in his power to make it right. Of course that only amounts to a sandwich he didn't even make himself, but nonetheless. It's the thought, of course, that counts. He was good to his word.

For the first time since Matt's car I think about last night. It's a terrible thing to have blackouts from drink, whole chunks of your life that go missing, never to be seen again. It always makes me feel seedy, and a little pathetic, and even scared. There are bits I remember, like the restaurant and then sitting in the bar afterwards. I remember the argument with Henry, and him storming out. Where is he anyway?

His clothes are all still here, so he hasn't left me thank God. Oh Jesus, now I remember – I asked Henry to marry me . . . and he said no.

Why We Do It

A brief tangent; bear with me. There's a point.

According to Greek mythology, Pandora was the first woman. She was created by Hephaestus the Smith, in his luxury Greek forge, with a view of the sea and easy access to all transport links (those being his feet, or possibly a donkey).

Initially she was a mere metal statue, don't ask me what kind, let's say tin, although it's bound to be wrong. But she was so breathtakingly beautiful even with her metallic sheen, like a shiny new jeep if you will, that Zeus decided, just this once mind, to give her life, the way most male Gods get around a new four wheel drive. Now I know it all sounds a little implausible, but then none of the Greek myths hold an awful lot of water. Let's go with this one for the moment though, if you don't mind being a little less 'twenty-first century' for a few pages. Science is only the new Bible after all, and the Bible was the new Greek myths for a while, before our ancestors tried to make water out of wine themselves and failed. After that they were just bitter and sober, having effectively been promised booze on tap, and decided they needed something new. And hey presto, we have 'science'! Protons and neurons, oxygen and evolution blah blah blah. We'll believe any old rubbish if the time is right.

Hephaestus had not even meant to create Pandora, and it hadn't been on his mind to grant the male world a mate. Earlier in that fateful day he had strolled along to see his friend Troy of the Sheep (a lesser known Greek character, who doesn't really figure in many of the other myths if he is sounding unfamiliar, apart from the ones specifically about sheep, and there aren't many of those.) Hephaestus hadn't relayed his personal loneliness to Troy or his sheep that morning, or his increasing depression at the solitude of it all. He'd been quite chipper actually, talked about some new tools, and then watched his favourite sheep, Lightening, eat grass for a while, while he himself lay back in the sunshine with a clear head and a smile.

Troy too had enjoyed the afternoon, as he did every afternoon, sitting in the sun, tending to sheep who are quite self-sufficient anyway. Dipping his feet in the stream, Troy slept without thoughts, or dreams, or nightmares to wake him.

Imagine it for a second. Imagine not knowing about love. Or sex. What would you do with your time? Would you worry about your appearance, would you assess the stage that you are at in life, how successful you are? Would you even go out? Would you do half, a quarter of the things you do now? And what would your future hold? No marriages, no children, no home, no money really – who needs it? Who are you impressing? Imagine the time you would have on your hands to do nothing but relax, lie back and enjoy the sun like Hephaestus on that fateful morning.

Eventually he wanders back to his forge to make something or other, for the fun of it, for the beauty of the creation, for its own sake. Poor Hephaestus has no idea of the nightmare that awaits him. He works, and smiles, thinks of food perhaps, thinks of sunshine, and the way it makes his body feel warm.

From nowhere, while his thoughts idle and he 'creates', there appears a form in front of him. A head and a body but not at all like his own. A softer, rounder creation. A figure that hypnotizes him, and bewitches him from that first moment. Zeus, too, looks down from Olympus, sees this chrome beauty, and gives her life. He feels he must; he finds her so enchanting, wants to talk to her, feel her, get close to her, be in her. All the other gods, similarly transfixed but also upon the orders of Zeus who could be a little dictatorial at times, bestow upon her their gifts as well: grace, intelligence, skill and persuasiveness. But Hermes gives her cunning and falsehood, and Hera, a female God (she doesn't qualify as a woman), gives her curiosity that will never let poor Pandora rest. This bit is a little misogynistic, but if you have ever encountered a Greek waiter you will understand.

Zeus sent Pandora to one of his football mates, Epimethus, as a gift. Epimethus for his part was so delighted by her beauty that he took her as his wife there and then. Strange that he knew what a wife was, considering Pandora was the first woman after all, but maybe he had seen it on one of the daytime soaps. As a wedding present the particularly generous Zeus gave them a beautiful box (and we all see the metaphor so let's leave the jokes at home shall we?) covered in jewels and gold. The box was locked, although Zeus gave the couple the key with a warning to Pandora that if she wanted to live happily with her husband, she should never unlock it. Now call me perverse, but I think he was telling her to never masturbate, because from then on she would realize how crap Epimethus was in bed, and be miserable.

The curiosity that Hera had given Pandora proved to be more powerful than her will however, and one day, probably after another particularly unsatisfying sexual encounter with her husband, she opened the box. Out flew all the miseries and misfortunes that have afflicted us since – despair and pain and jealousy. Typical, blame a woman as usual. But last of all came hope, which depending on how you see it, was either a bloody great consolation prize, or the worst misery of all.

Thus from this first taste of love, came the horrors of our souls, the insecurities that plague us daily, the doubting miseries of our lives. The need to find a love, and be worthy of a love, a need that could have completely bypassed us if Hephaestus had slipped and chipped off a breast by accident.

Zeus hadn't got to where he was by being stupid, and knew that his peculiar elation at the sight of Pandora's beauty would have to be paid for in the end. You make a trade with the soul, and such highs must be tempered with the deepest lows. It's a sadness that moments before Pandora's first breath did not even exist. As soon as you feel that high, you need to feel it again, and the hope that you will feel it again carries you through today and on to tomorrow. Without this hope wouldn't we just ring the bell and call 'time' on our lives? But the hope misleads us into thinking that we'll get that high again.

Hope is a bastard, at the end of the day. I think hope is a man, and he is a nasty fucker, with a twisted sense of humour, and he's sitting somewhere having a right bloody laugh at our expense. Hope has got a smirk on his face, and long black greasy hair, and fingernails that need cutting. It goes without saying that his clothes aren't clean.

For Zeus life will be different now, for Hephaestus too. For all of us, Pandora as well. To keep a grasp on love, we must entertain and impress, look good and seem good, and present ourselves to the world in a way we have never had to before. Now what another thinks of us is as important as what we think of ourselves. Relaxation is a thing of the past, and we have traded this in for one moment of joy, to be followed quickly by doubt, and the fear that will stop us sleeping calmly in the sun.

Hephaestus actually created a nightmare for us all, but now that it exists he cannot go back. Should he just have destroyed Pandora then, strangled her new life from her, left her broken and dead on the rocks and patted himself on the back for having the unlikely wisdom to do it? If he had stopped this before it started, would he have saved the world heartache and sadness, jealousy and despair? Would you make the trade?

I ask you now to give up love. Give up the search. Give up that disappointment when you don't find it, or it goes wrong. Give up the hope and resign yourself to never looking again. Live your life on your own. Take pleasure in a day of simple things, and forget about everyone else.

Would you be happy? Maybe not, but would you be happy if you had never known in the first place? Go and live on an island and forget every film you ever saw, every love song you ever heard. They are not your words anyway, they don't say what you're thinking. Give up everything anybody ever told you about love. Even if you only manage it for seconds, it's soothing. It's calming, it eases your pains. But yes, you are right, it won't bring you that elusive moment of joy. We are our own worst enemy.

So the search begins again, while listening to Frank Sinatra and watching *Casablanca*. It's the hope we can't get rid of, the hope that sets us up for a thousand new falls. It may be the hope that keeps us going, but it's hope that will kill us in the end, with his long greasy hair, somewhere, smirking, and not smelling quite right.

The Sprinklers are Obviously Broken

I hadn't planned to ask, I hadn't even meant to ask. We had had a decent enough meal, and moved to the bar. We hadn't wandered into a deep conversation, and Henry didn't look unusually handsome – he wasn't wearing any socks for God's sake!

But there was a kind of lull, not uncomfortable or awkward, and we could have just sat there and said nothing. There was a singer, singing, but not a bad one at all. I had come to realize that Vegas singers were never bad, and the songs were lovely, not cheesy as everybody implied. "The Way We Were", "Feelings", "Making Whoopee", all with lyrics you want to sing, to belt out, and feel. A sequinned explosion of a woman was in fact belting out "The Look of Love". Henry had his gin and tonic, and a lopsided content look on his face, and I had a whiskey and ginger and freshly curled hair. Everything was going fine, as it should have been, because so far the holiday had been great.

We had talked over dinner about the heat being bearable, the people being friendly, and the wedding we had seen earlier in the day outside one of the hotels. We hadn't laughed at it. I thought it was sweet but strange to come all this way and wear a big white wedding dress, especially as that was just the groom! Seriously I had said, if I was going to get married in Vegas, I'd wear a large white cowboy hat with rhinestones around the edge, and white cowboy boots. I would want Elvis to be the minister, and sing "I Just Can't Help Believing". I don't think I mentioned the groom. Maybe I said I'd want him to be wearing a black cowboy hat, but I don't think I did.

Henry said getting married in Vegas appealed to him because it would be cheap, which is true, but also that the two of you could just spend the day together, not having to think about anyone but yourselves. It could just be a fun day for you both. It didn't have to be spiritual or soul-searching, you just had to have a great time that you would both enjoy more than most other days in your life. I loved that he had said that without any prompting.

But that was not why I asked him to marry me. I wasn't thinking of that when I asked him. It just happened: me saying 'would you like to marry me?' more of an enquiry than an actual request. Almost out of curiosity or at least that's how it might have sounded.

He had looked at me strangely, not shocked, or scared, or freaked . . . more bemused.

'Eve, why are you asking me? Are you asking me to marry you?'

'Sorry, Hen, yes, not would you like to, well of course would you like to, but I mean will you . . . marry me . . .' I trailed off. But I knew what I was doing, what I was asking. I wanted him to say yes as well. I have to make it clear that I wasn't asking on a whim, or as a test, or because I was caught up in the whole Las Vegas married thing. Or even because I was desperate to get married, that doesn't come until you are at least thirty-three. I am not making excuses for asking because I got turned down. I really wanted it, but he just said,

'No.'

It wasn't malicious or cold, it just sounded like the most honest answer anybody had ever given.

'Do you mind if I ask why not?' I wasn't being aggressive, I was just curious I suppose, and a little surprised if I'm honest. I was of the subconscious belief that Henry would love us to get married. I thought he would ask me eventually, so why not ask him first? I thought the reason he hadn't already asked me was not because he didn't want to get married, but because he thought I might say no. But by my asking him I had eradicated that problem, so why was he declining?

'Because it would be something to do, not because we thought it was the right thing to do. Because it hasn't really occurred to me.'

Hadn't occurred to him? What an arse!

'But Hen, don't you think we are at an age now when you realize that you have found somebody that you love, and that's enough.' That was not a good answer, not a convincing argument. It sounded weak. It sounded like we were . . . settling for each other. As if I had slammed a cynicism cocktail, and I was drunk on pessimism. That was not what I had intended. I had intended to say that we really loved each other, which was a rarity, and that we knew each other inside out, and that we wanted to make a commitment. But it had come out all wrong.

'You do love me, Hen?'

'Yes, Eve, I love you.'

'So, don't you marry the person that you love?'

'I think that's the mistake that people make.'

'Oh Henry, that's bollocks, I mean it's word play. It's insulting! You've told me that you love me, OK, so give me a proper reason, a proper fucking reason, Henry. No actually don't. Actually I don't want to know. You've said no, it's fine. Case closed.'

'Well you haven't given me a reason have you, so don't get all nasty with me. You haven't said, Hen, I want to marry you because you have transformed my life, and things will never be the same again, or even you're the best fucking sex I've ever had! You've asked me to marry you, and you have no fucking idea why, Eve! Would you really want to say in ten years' time when our kids ask how did Daddy propose, oh Mummy asked Daddy because she'd had too much wine, and Daddy said no, but then Mummy convinced Daddy by making him feel bad for hurting her feelings, despite the fact that Mummy woke up the next day with a raging hangover and couldn't remember a damn thing and made Daddy look like a tosser for wanting to get married! And then little fucking Tommy or Jenny or whatever their fucking names will be will say, is that why you got divorced before I was five? Is that why I'm from a fucking broken home?'

'Well I hope our kids won't be saying fuck before the age of ten.'

'You know what I fucking mean!' Henry had started to raise his voice. He got angry, banging his drink down on the table and swearing under his breath. Other people in the bar had turned towards our commotion. He was looking at me, and with contempt, because I'd forced him to spell it out. Of course during this whole little speech he had going I had necked my whiskey, and was feeling indignant about the refusal.

'Oh Jesus, Henry, is this your whole parents issue again? Just because your parents are divorced does not mean that everybody's parents get divorced, and you were fourteen for God's sake, not five . . .'

There was absolute disgust in his eyes now and I thought that he might hit me. If I was a man he would have hit me. Nice people don't say things like that, they don't mock events that have shattered a person, they don't seem incredulous that a person hasn't got over them. I don't think a man should ever hit a woman, I didn't believe there was ever a decent excuse, but I pretty much offered him my chin to take his best shot. Because there is no worse a statement I could have made, apart from possibly bringing up the fact that his dad had tried to kill himself, unsuccessfully, when his mother had walked out on him.

All credit to him, it didn't even occur to Henry to hit me. He just stood up, doused me in his gin and tonic, and walked off. On his way out of the bar, as I sat and watched him go, he went and paid for our drinks. I realized for the first time, and not out of anger, or pride, how sorry I was that he had said no. But he was right about one thing. I had no idea why I had asked.

The waiter that he'd paid looked over at the table, saw

me dripping in gin and tonic, and rushed over with a towel, and another drink.

'Thanks, I think your sprinklers must be broken because I'm a bit wet. Thanks for the drink, did he pay for this one as well?'

'No ma'am, that one will have to paid for.'

'Shit.'

I necked half; it could have been a double I have no idea, but it would explain my becoming so very drunk so very quickly. I wiped myself off. I passed him back the towel, and noticed how good-looking he was, but then all the waiters were good-looking. Probably a 'budding actor' isn't everyone doing a bar job in America a budding actor? He mopped up the table, and I asked for another drink. Then it all starts to get hazy. I remember that he brought it over.

'Can't you have one with me? I feel fucking conspicuous sitting in a bar, soaking wet, on my own. Please. I'll even pay for it. Please?'

'Ma'am, if you're wet maybe you should go and get changed. Get out of your wet clothes.'

'Well yes I could do that but I don't particularly want to go to my room right now, so good suggestion, and I like your thinking, but there will be no tip for you this evening.'

Being nasty to waiters is never a good idea, but the thought of going back to the hotel, and the room, and a silent sulking Henry was the least appealing prospect facing me. Besides, I felt like shit for saying what I had about his parents, and I didn't trust myself to apologize properly, without getting indignant again. I felt like a fool. So I stayed on my own and drank my next gin, probably a double, stumbled to the bar, and ordered a whiskey. The waiter somehow became the barman, I don't remember how. After this everything is a snapshot, an image of a point in the evening, with massive chunks missing.

I remember being outside, staggering, holding on to the waiter's arm.

I remember having a thumb war, and me ending up on the floor.

I remember being in a club, and dancing to terrible eighties pop, and everyone making a 'wooh wooh' noise.

I remember going to the toilet.

I remember both of us leaving together.

But that's it.

What I know, is that I woke up with Mark, no Matt, my waiter cum barman, and we were in his car. We might have had sex, but we both still had our jeans on, although they were unbuttoned. He was on holiday from New York, a three-month working vacation, and had come out here to try and get an agent, or a show, and see his friend Scott who was also a budding actor. He was having a good time, that bit I remember – he liked Las Vegas, and the different people that he met.

I don't remember him saying he liked me.

Henry's Back

I hear the key go in the door, and I panic, literally jump out of my skin. I fluster. It's Henry, and he is going to be . . . unimpressed, to say the least. He opens the door and stops in his tracks as he sees me by the bed. Henry is glaring, fuming. Something is rising in my throat, but it's not an explanation, and I'm not going to be sick, although I do feel a little off. No, it's a feeling of dread, but it's definitely not the truth racing to get out. What do I say?

'Hey Hen, where did you get to then?'

'Are you joking?'

'No, where have you been, breakfast? You could have waited!'

'Well I didn't know how long you'd be, did I? I didn't know where the bloody hell you were did I? Eve, where the bloody hell have you been all night? I was worried sick, fucking sick. I've just been at the reception asking them for the number of the hospital. Where the fuck have you been?'

'Oh baby, I know this is going to sound terrible, but I'm

not sure. I drank a lot, *a lot*, after you stormed out, and left me on my own by the way. And I can't remember much, but I'm ok. Just got a bit of a hangover. I've taken some pills though, and they should kick in soon. I've had a bath, let me dry my hair, and I'll be ready to go in about half an hour. So what's on the agenda?'

'You don't know? You don't know where you've been all night in a town where every other psycho carries a gun! Are you stupid? Are you completely fucking stupid, or mad, or both? You can't just stay out all night, on your own.'

'Well apparently I can, because I did. Oh Henry, I don't feel up to an argument. My head hurts more than I thought, can we talk about this later? Jesus, it's not as if I'm dead.'

'Were you with someone?'

'What now?'

'Eve, were you with someone last night?'

'Well there must have been people there if that's what you mean. I had to order all those drinks from someone, after you left me on my own.'

I don't know how long I can play the abandoned card before he remembers why he walked out in the first place. I'm on thin ice, in the middle of the desert.

'What I mean, as you rightly know, is were you with a man?'

'Oh Henry, for God's sake, right now I feel like shit, and you're asking pathetic questions. Actually, yes, I shagged the entire squad of the Denver Broncos. So not much walking today, OK, I'm not up to it. Jesus, Henry.'

'We're not in Denver, we're in Nevada, you silly cow.'

'Oh whatever, the Nevada Broncos then, and don't call me a cow, you know I hate that.'

'Cow.'

'Henry, grow up.'

'Where did you sleep then?'

'In reception.'

'Classy girl.'

'Whatever.'

'Why didn't you come up to the room?'

'I think I passed out.'

'Oh Jesus.'

But at least he's smiling – half-smiling. That doesn't mean I get any more conversation though. He strops about on his side of the room for a while, then just throws himself on the bed to read tourist guides.

As I do my make-up I start to relax. This gives me more time to decide what to do. To tell him or not. I still might. A knock at the door interrupts my chain of thought. I bet it's bloody Pedro again, with another bloody snack. Jesus, how many times can one man apologize over a bra? He should really let it go. But I could always distract Henry by telling him about that whole incident, and whip up a little jealousy. All of a sudden I have a plan.

I whisper to Hen as he's about to open the door.

'Hey, if that's the waiter, the Mexican one, I found him in here when I got back. Shush, I'll tell you when he's gone, but he was wearing my underwear.'

Henry looks confused, but opens the door anyway.

But it's not Pedro with a sandwich.

It's Matt.

Oh sweet Jesus, my heart is in my mouth, literally. I feel it rush up my throat, and every pulse in my body starts to pound at once. Oh shit, oh shit.

I'm off my chair in a second and at the door. Henry thinks it's room service and walks off, over to his side of the room. Matt speaks first,

'Eve, I need to speak to you.'

'I'm sorry I didn't order anything you must have the wrong room.' I try to close the door on him but he sticks his arm and foot in the way.

'Look, I'm sorry but I'm freaking here and I haven't got time for this shit. Look what I found, look what I fucking found in my pocket! We got married for Christ's sake. We got married! Oh this is a pain in the ass!'

Matt throws his hands in the air, with a certificate in one of them. I turn round crazily to face Henry, who is staring at us from the other side of the room.

'Look,' back to Matt, and through gritted teeth 'can you wait downstairs with that.'

'Yeah, but what are we going to do? We're going to have to get an annulment thing. Oh shit, this is the last thing I need. It happened to Scott about six months ago. It's a pain in the ass. Oh Jesus.'

'Please can you wait downstairs, I'll be down in seconds. I need to talk to my boyfriend.'

I'm glaring at Matt, desperately imploring him, my new husband, to go away. Oh my God, now I really do feel sick.

'Yeah, sure, whatever, but come down in a minute because the quicker we get to the court, and moving on this, the quicker we get out of it. OK?'

I slam the door on Matt.

Now what do I say?

Saying Sorry

Henry and I are alone in the room which all of a sudden seems like the most terrible and tragic place to be in the world. Pictures that aren't ours on the walls. Dirty clothes on the floor. A television quietly reporting the weather in places I have never been, and would never go. Adverts for things I don't recognize. It's hot, but not sunny outside the window. The sky above this sea of neon is more grey than blue, more cloudy than clear. All the buildings below it, this spectacular view that we have of the town, are the most depressing sight of all. Everything looks so new. There is no character in the buildings, they are made from the same brick, they are all glorified warehouses with sparkly fronts, and filled with people I don't know. I am standing on the crumbs of a half-eaten toasted cheese sandwich. I've just had a bath, but need a shower now more than I ever have. I need to be somewhere else, but not in this town. There is nowhere within a thousand mile radius where I can have the conversation I am about to have with Henry. I need to be at home, in the office, in the Swan by his flat. There is nowhere for me to get some confidence, some reinforcement. I need my massive jumper, need to hide my hands in its oversized arms, but of course it's at home. Why would you ever pack that jumper for a trip to Vegas? I am wearing a towel.

I stand by the door facing Henry at the window, and even now at midday, the glare from the neon shines from behind him. I don't even want to talk to him, I want to run from the room and never see him again. Or see him in two years time, by accident in Soho in a bar I never go to. I want him to be so surprised to see me, so off-guard that he would forget what I had done to him on that holiday in Vegas a couple of years back, and hug me hello, smiling his Henry smile. I want to leave, but how can I? The only thing I can do is stand here and wait.

For minutes Henry stands in the same position and says nothing. I look at his steel-rimmed glasses, that suit him so well and that he wears more than he needs, because he knows they look good. I look at the hair that only in the last year or so has grown into its own; it seems thicker and darker than it has ever been and is slightly longer than he thinks he should have it. With his tan coming and his dark hair, he looks like someone I should be scared of, someone living a sinister life. He looks like a Goodfella.

His shirt pulls slightly at his stomach – we've eaten a lot since the day we got here. His hands are on his hips. The button on his trousers is undone, the trousers I bought him just before we left. He is barefoot, head down, and all I can hear is the occasional breath, a few gasps at a time.

I want to cry. I want to stand there and exhaust myself with crying, for myself, for Henry, for what will happen now. I know that I can't. It would be the worst thing I could do. The most self-indulgent. I think it's the only thing that could paint me in a worse light, if that is possible. Feeling this sorry for myself, even more so now than before, I whimper slightly, but keep control. But the whimper is enough. It is like a starting pistol firing in Henry's ear, shocking him back to life.

'Don't you cry, don't you dare fucking cry! What the fuck have you done? What have you . . . Don't fucking cry for yourself now. You lying bitch!'

'I'm not crying!', and then floods of tears. Nothing I can do to stop them. I am a pathetic sight clutching at my towel, my hair drying on its own, fuzzy and limp. I'm not wiping my eyes or my nose, I'm just crying. Henry picks up his shoe and throws it at me, hard. It hits me on the shoulder and I fall backwards onto the door. Still crying, but softly now. Looking up, daring to look at him, I feel like I shouldn't even do that, like I've lost the right. His face is down again. He sits on the bed, and looks out of the window with his back to me.

I don't know why but I walk round and kneel in front of him, and yet still he won't look in my eyes. I try and pull his face down to see me, and with both my hands I'm clutching at the sides of his face, dragging his eyes to look into mine. If I can see his eyes, I'll know whether I can make this right. But he won't. He gets up, and pushes me off with enough force to land me down on the floor, but not hurt me. He walks out of the room and slams the door. I don't hear any movement for a second, another second, and maybe he's going to come back in, hug me, tell me we'll sort this whole mess out together.

I hear the sound of footsteps padding off down the hall, Henry walking away barefoot.

Barefoot in Vegas

Henry doesn't even realize he is barefoot as he walks through reception and out on to the street. He feels for his wallet in his trouser pocket and it is there. He takes a right, and walks a block to McDonalds, and still doesn't realize he is barefoot, until he notices people giving him odd looks. He stops and looks down at his feet, and sees there's already a cut on the side of his little toe, but he can't feel it. He registers that he must look strange, and it's not as if he is dressed like a tramp, in which case it would be ordinary. But he's dressed normally, sensibly, aside from the lack of footwear. He walks into a gift shop next to the drive-in and absent-mindedly buys a pair of sandals, one size too big. He shoves them on and leaves. A good-looking woman walks past him, and a car beeps across the road. He puts his head down and walks on. He heads into the nearest casino, and walks in a trance, still head down, to the nearest roulette table. Getting out his wallet, he goes straight for the traveller's cheques.

'Will you cash these, I have my passport.'

'That will be fine, sir, if you could just sign for me.'

'Fine.' Henry hands over the cheques and collects his money – a thousand dollars. He puts down a hundred on black 25. There are two other people at the table, both men, both wearing suits. They put their money on red, and the dealer spins the table. It spins forever. Henry has never been so angry. In his entire life he has never felt this out of control, this frustrated. He left before he hit her. The table starts to slow, but he wants to keep spinning it. He doesn't want to look away, wants the table to keep turning and turning, and the colours to keep merging. He doesn't want to be able to make it out. The table stops spinning but he can't visualize the number, or the colour, his eyes blurring. The dealer pushes more chips his way. The table has come up black 25. Henry is up three thousand five hundred bucks. He pushes the chips together, and puts a thousand, with a determined shove, on black 14. The table spins again. The other two men at the table are smiling at him, they think he has balls. He does have balls.

As she stood there crying he wanted to just shut her up, stop her crying for herself. He cannot even think.

The table is slowing down in front of his eyes again, and he looks away, at the slot machines, and the rows of people sitting in front of them in the middle of the day. Back home everybody would be at work at this hour. What are these people doing nudging their way through their time, instead of doing something productive? Are they all on holiday like him? What are they doing in this place?

The dealer is pushing thirty-five thousand dollars worth of chips towards him. The table has come up black 14. The other two guys at the table are patting him on the back, laughing, asking him to pick their numbers for them. They are both American. Henry can't even bear to hear their voices, that terrible twang. He wants to hear an English accent. He takes his chips and walks away from the table. Dejected, he makes his way to the dice; there are more people at these tables, more tourists, he might hear a familiar accent. He forces himself to the table, and just stands for the first two rounds staring at the hands putting chips down, picking chips up, throwing dice. He had picked her age and her birthday, and they had both won. He had picked black and it had won. He had bet on her, and wanted to lose, and he had won.

Henry feels like his mind is draining of everything he has ever known except Eve. But to think of her makes his stomach turn, and the anger rises up inside him, literally swells into his lungs, until he feels every breath that he is taking is red-hot, and he is exhaling smoke. He picks up a handful of chips and puts them down on a square. He doesn't pick a number, a hard eight, an easy eight, and he doesn't know how much he is putting down. He doesn't give a damn.

He wants to go back and scream, but just throwing his shoe had been out of control, and he can't trust himself. He wants to cry, and he feels his eyes starting to glaze over, getting wet. But Henry has no idea how to cry, he only knows how to stop himself crying, and this is what he does, subconsciously. She has done this to him.

The dealer is talking to him,

'You can't put that much money down on this table, sir. This is a hundred dollar-limit table'.

Henry shrugs. And?

'Sir, you've put three thousand dollars down. You can't

put that much money down. You should move to another table if you wish to bet that much.'

Henry picks up his chips and pushes past the people standing around the table chattering and laughing at him. He finds another table, and slumps down. He is the only person at this one, apart from the dealer, who is shuffling the cards.

'Blackjack, sir.'

'What?'

'Blackjack . . . twenty-one?'

'How much can I bet?'

'This is a five hundred-minimum table, sir.'

'I have to bet at least five hundred dollars per hand?'

'I'm afraid so, sir.'

'No that's fine. That's what I want.'

Henry puts down a thousand, and the dealer asks him to split the pack.

And all he wants is to forget it. Pretend it didn't happen. He wants to go back to the room, and say yes of course I'll marry you, I was testing you. I was waiting for you to prove to me that you wanted me the way that I want you. But that is impossible now. How can he look at her without seeing her weakness, the stupidity of what she has done? And he wants to kill that guy. Who the fuck was he? He looked gay, he probably is gay! She's probably married a queer and she doesn't even know it. She's had sex with him too, that's if he could get it up for a woman. Just one look at him and Henry could tell he had fucked her. It would be Eve's wet dream to get someone that pretty as well, and not all big and clumsy. But Henry is a real man, not some queer, and he doesn't need this shit.

He twists on 17, and gets a 4. The dealer busts, and he

wins another grand. The dealer goes again, but this time Henry puts down five grand. He just pushes it all out. He has lost count of how much he had, but this looks like about half. He sticks on 19. Dealer shows two faces, and takes his five grand from the table. Henry exhales. This is what he wants, this is more like it. He needs to lose all this. Who is he going to share his winnings with anyway? She's not getting it.

He needs to be with his lads, in the Swan after rugby. He can't deal with these emotions that are racing around his body, the sick feeling, the need to scream and shout, and burst and trash a room. How could she want to make him feel this bad, so far from home, and on his own?

Henry bets another five and a half grand, and loses it on 20. He bets three grand and loses it on 18. He wins back a grand and a half on a black jack. He loses five again straight away on another 18. He needs to talk to someone familiar, but he's not going to talk to his brother – how can he, after what he put Mikey through?

Henry loses another five grand. And another ten. He gathers up his chips and walks away. He cashes in seven thousand, five hundred dollars. He has won a lot of money, but it doesn't even register. Walking out of the casino, the sunlight hurts his eyes, but he can see a phone box on the other side of the road, and suddenly he is right by it. He looks back across the road he has just crossed, and the cars whiz past. Did he cross that?

He has huge amounts of American change in his pockets, and puts all of it in the payphone, dialling Tim's number, subconsciously hitting the two fours for Britain. After five rings, Tim picks up, sounding half asleep.

'Hello?'

'Tim man, it's Henry.'

'Henry? It's the middle of the fucking night? What the hell are you phoning me for?'

'I'm in Las Vegas.'

'Oh Christ yeah, I forgot. You and the little missus.'

'Yeah, me and Eve.'

'How is it?'

'Yeah it's cool.'

'You don't sound too impressed.'

'Yeah well . . .' Henry can't tell him. He can't tell Tim what Eve's done. He was the wrong person to call.

'Is she getting on your nerves mate?'

'Yeah a bit. You know what she's like.' He feels strangely disloyal.

'Yeah mate, couldn't handle it myself. A bit too much of a handful, and I'm not talking about her tits.'

'Yeah alright, Tim, take it easy.'

'Sorry mate, yeah, she is your girlfriend. Is she being that bad? What a nightmare, all that way as well. Sorry mate.'

'Yeah all this way.'

'Look mate, I'm knackered so I'm going to go.'

'Yeah OK. Just wanted to know who won the rugby at the weekend'.

'Oh, good man! Yeah we did. I scored two tries. Bloody good game. Phil's brother stepped in for you and he's a bloody good hooker actually.'

'Yeah? Good news. Well anyway I'll speak to you when I get back.'

'Yeah mate, hope you manage to enjoy yourself. Just ignore her if you have to, enjoy yourself. I'm sure there's plenty of talent over there, all those birds with fake tits. Do they look weird?'

'Yeah, I'll see you later.'

'Oh alright mate, yeah. See you later, Henry.'

Henry feels worse. Sitting on a bench by the phone box, head back, staring at the sky. Tim was the worst person to talk to. He had never particularly approved of her and Henry. Thought she was a bit of a tart. But Henry wasn't stupid; Tim would have shagged Eve eventually if it hadn't been for Henry and Eve going out.

It doesn't matter what Tim said though. He knows he only feels this bad because she wasn't a tart. She was the woman he loved, and he loved her more than anyone he had ever been with. If only she hadn't done it. He wishes that she hadn't, and then he wouldn't have to hate her. He doesn't want to, but she has forced his hand. How can he forgive this? It is the ultimate. It's a no going back situation.

If only she hadn't done it. Now he has to feel this way.

A Proper Argument

I can see Henry sitting on a bench on the other side of the road, outside that bloody McDonalds. He isn't moving much. I came out to get some fresh air, thinking possibly that I might see him, but not really believing it. But there he is, just sitting there, and this is my chance. This is what I want, surely, to go and talk to him, or at least try to. The sun is incredibly bright, this must be the hottest day so far, but I'm all covered up. I won't be getting a tan. I'm wearing a baseball cap, and sunglasses, and trousers and a long-sleeved top. I feel like I'm in disguise, like a star walking around Vegas hoping nobody will notice them.

Henry doesn't know I can see him. I can't stand here forever, but I desperately don't want to cross this road. I have no idea what I am going to say, and it strikes me that I should go and rehearse somewhere, get my words sorted in my head. I've got nothing else to do now today.

Matt made some telephone calls from reception, drove us both to the Vegas town hall, and we filled out some forms.

Because I'm British, and on holiday, they appeared to have bumped us up to the top of the queue, and they all liked my accent. I think they felt sorry for Matt as well, as he seems to have taken this very hard. He looks crazy, and did little but swear in the car. I gleaned that he has a girlfriend in New York, who he felt obliged to tell all about this. He kept mumbling about it all being 'fucking sinful', which seemed like a strange two words to pair. I wasn't really listening, I was thinking about Henry. I don't like the thought of him being on his own somewhere in this town, getting drunk or worse, and slagging me off to some anonymous waitress.

I have to be in court tomorrow morning, with Matt, where we both declare we were of unsound mind, and the annulment is granted on that basis. After that it should take a day or so to get the paperwork sorted, but then it's done. I thank God it is so straightforward. Matt nearly cried when they said we would have to go into a courtroom. I tried to explain that it's not as if we had done anything illegal or even wrong, it was just to make it official and legally binding. He lost it.

'Well you might think this is all some fucking joke, but I ain't finding it funny. This is not the way it is supposed to be! It makes the whole thing look like a laugh, it makes the sanctity of marriage look like a drunken joke for Christ's sake! Well I am sorry but I was not brought up that way. I'm sure it's much more fucking cosmopolitan in London, but that's not how we do things out here. I am in love with my girlfriend! She won't find this funny! That's why I love her, she has respect!'

'Matt, I do not think this is funny at all. In case you

haven't noticed my boyfriend has gone AWOL because I had the misfortune to meet some randy barman who knew where the nearest chapel was! All I'm saying is that going into a courtroom is the least of my worries, if it gets this thing sorted out.'

'Typical Brit, they say you guys have got some kinda sick sense of humour.'

'What? Did you hear a word I said? I don't think it's funny!'

'Yeah laugh it up, whatever. Jesus Christ!'

'You are insane. They could get you on temporary insanity right now. Matt, will you calm down.'

'You're like one of those Spice Girls. You think everything's a joke, and you kid about, and you ruin peoples lives!'

'I am NOT like a Spice Girl. I am nothing like any of them, although, which one are you thinking of, Posh?'

'You come over here and you sing and dance and ruin peoples lives!'

'Matt, what are you fucking talking about? I haven't done any singing or dancing, I am nothing like a Spice Girl. You are going insane. What have you got against the Spice Girls anyway? Are you some kind of misogynist? Or an Anglophobe? Matt, what harm have the Spice Girls ever done you? What has this got to do with anything anyway?'

Matt stopped talking after that, apart from the swearing under his breath. Apparently my new husband isn't in to Girl Power. I also think he might not be that bright. But Matt isn't even a concern, I couldn't care less how he is feeling. I'm not being cold, I just don't know him, and I definitely don't love him. The only person I can think about is Henry.

And now I'm staring straight at him, sitting on his bench – it seems like his bench already – looking at the sky, and I can't think what to say to him. I have no idea. I have no excuses, I am all apologies, but that is just not going to cut it. A guy walks past me and nudges me off the kerb, and I cross the road.

I sit down on the bench, but Henry doesn't even notice.

'Hen.' I clear my throat, hardly any noise is coming out.

'Henry.'

He rolls his head round to the side and looks at me blankly. His eyes are red, from staring at the sun I suppose.

'Henry, are you . . . have you . . . where have you been?' no answer. He looks away, but now he is clenching his teeth, I think maybe it took this long for him to realize that it was me sitting next to him. He looks pent up.

'Henry, I've been down to the town hall, and this really is an easy procedure.' I'm speaking matter of factly, trying to be business-like. I think maybe it will make him see it as a clerical error, and not a marriage, or a betrayal.

'So I can go down to the courthouse tomorrow and then that's it. They get this quite a lot apparently, and it's common, you know, so they know how to sort it out, you know, really quickly, because it's like a nothing, a non-event. They see it for what it is, you know? A drunken stupid joke that goes wrong. You know? Henry? This doesn't have to be huge. Does it, Henry? Hen?'

'Will you fuck off now?'

'Henry? Can't we talk?'

'If I look at you again, I'm going to do something I regret, I swear, so please just fuck off.'

'Henry, please, I just want to talk to you, you don't have to look at me . . .'

'JUST FUCK OFF! HOW MANY TIMES DO I HAVE TO SAY IT? I can't bear to look at you – I don't want to see your pathetic whinging miserable fucking face! I don't want to be anywhere near you. You have no idea what you have done. You have no idea how bad you look in my eyes, because, Eve, if you knew, you wouldn't be here grovelling now.'

Henry turns and walks off, and some masochistic urge makes me follow,

'Henry, I know that you're angry now, but you have to think about this at some point, because, well you have to, and . . .'

'I swear, I swear to you now, leave me alone, or I will not be responsible for what I do to you. Please just leave me the hell alone.'

Henry sprints off down the road, and I don't even think about following. I am left on the pavement, with people staring as they walk past, as I look coldly ahead of me, my jaw set to stop me from crying again. This is just starting to hit home. I think this could be . . . really . . . bad.

I need a drink. Another drink. It was drink that got me in this bloody mess in the first place, but I still need another one. I can't sit about feeling like this for the next two days, waiting for some olive branch from Henry that may never come. I refuse to feel this bad for any longer today. I need that drink.

Walking back to the hotel, to camp in the bar for the rest of the day, trying to think about somebody other than Henry, I try to picture the wedding. I try to picture Matt and me, standing at an altar together, saying 'I do'. I have no recollection of it whatsoever, which I suppose is a good thing. What I cannot get over is how I did it. How I said 'I do' to a complete stranger, and let him say it to me, without the enormity of the situation dragging my sober self back from the brink, and stopping the whole damn thing. Given how much weight I put on marriage, or at least the initial commitment, the saying 'yes' of it all, I cannot comprehend saying it to anyone and not realizing what I was doing. I can't make the picture of me and Matt hand in hand at the altar work for me. I can't picture us at all.

Did I do it out of spite? Did I do it to spite Henry for saying no? Or did I do it to prove to myself that Henry and I aren't meant to be? Did I do it to prove that marriage and me weren't meant to be?

Or was I just drunk? Ladies and gentleman, I think we have a winner.

No Shame Left

Without my knowledge, without my prior and written consent, I appear to be on a stage in our hotel, with a group of 'FunSeekers' from Derby dressed in togas, singing "Mamma Mia" at the top of my voice. I've foolishly taken the lead, shushing the others down if they try to join in with the verses. I'm belting it out now. The Derby crowd took pity on my miserable plight, and asked me to join them at their table. I had been sitting quietly having a self-indulgent drinking session, thinking about the day, about what the hell I was going to do. I had to get up early to go to court tomorrow with Matt, who hates me, to get our annulment. This random man that I barely even know sees me as the root of all evil. I wonder if the annulment will have an Elvis look-a-like as well. I wonder if they'll try and keep it light-hearted, as opposed to making us feel like criminals. I doubt it. I wonder if Henry will come and throw eggs from the gallery, and pelt me with his abuse.

Back to the present, and I have a finger in one ear, diva

style, trying to hear my voice above the clapping Derby sheet wearers. The tablecloth I unashamedly fashioned into my outfit for the evening as I started to get into the spirit, rum being the particular spirit I had got into, is somehow staying up. It's been knotted lovingly by Ken and Stella, a 'smashing couple', who are missing their pub quiz final to be here. They didn't think their team would get through the quarters, and now Frank and Sylvie at home aren't talking to them for dropping out. They are both putting on an incredibly brave face I say. I want to cry for them, for the questions they could have answered, for the cooker and washer-dryer they could have won. Life is such a shit I say, while Stella rubs my back and asks if I'm going to be sick.

There is a bit of a commotion at one end of the stage. It's David, the accountant who lives next door to Ken and Stella and whose wife left him for a much younger woman three months ago – shocking business, I've cried for David already this evening. David, while smiling at a comely waitress who had been serving us most of the night, has unfortunately slipped out of his toga, which has even more unfortunately come loose in the pelvic department. David has apparently gone 'native' this evening, and is also rather excited to be on the stage. Stella is doing a bloody good job of trying to cover up his quite considerable erection by just forcing it down with her hand. Poor David, tears in his eyes from the embarrassment, and the pain of Stella's faux diamond ring punching down his penis. Ken has lost it, and is crying with laughter, frankly drawing more attention to it than David needs. True professional that I am, I refuse to be distracted by David's wandering third eye, and I sing louder than ever. It actually hurts my throat to sing this loud. It seems to hurt my stomach as well, for some reason. I'm in pain. I stop singing, which is good, because the karaoke tape stopped about thirty seconds ago. Looking up, tears in my eyes, stomach spinning, face red from singing, wearing an ill-fitting tablecloth covered in coffee stains and ash, I think I glimpse Henry walk into the bar, and stop in his tracks when he sees me on the stage.

Lunging forward, I realize my foot is caught in the microphone wire, and I feel myself falling for an age before I smack my chin on the side of the stage. I taste blood on my lip just before I throw up.

You can't buy class you know.

Meeting Henry – The False Start

I was in a bar for the leaving drinks of this guy from work. We were not quite hammered, but well on the way. It was nothing out of the ordinary – we got blitzed every time we went out with work. We all got on well, and I wouldn't have classed us necessarily as just workmates. It wasn't one dodgy accountant here, one crappy receptionist there. There were only about ten of us, out of a building of about two hundred, and we were mostly friends. Henry was actually a friend of Tim, the guy who was leaving. I was mainly there because I was besotted with Tim, and I knew his bloody girlfriend wasn't going to show up. They lived together but he did not seem like a man in love at all. He was constantly out on the piss, and Druids worshipped stones smaller than her nose, so I thought there was hope.

Anyway, I had spent most of the night with Tim, having a laugh, taking the piss, being a little too tactile, but having it all reciprocated. I thought that maybe, if we carried on rocking until 3am, the least I would get was a little taxi action.

Who else was there? Henry, as I said. I had met him twice before, but I didn't know much about him, other than he lived in his own flat in Ealing. I had tried to convince him to let me move in with him, for very cheap rent and occasional cooking duties. My rent was so high living on my own; I was going to have to move eventually. He was having none of it I remember. Kept saying he would seriously consider it, which in my book is a fuck right off. If he could not see what a wonderful flatmate I would make, and how much more exciting his life would be with me in it, then he could piss off.

He also said that we could have a problem – two young attractive people living together, there could be sexual tension. I remember I told him that as far as I was concerned we had no sexual tension whatsoever, which was rare, and therefore the situation would be perfect. Of course, all of this had been conducted in a kind of flirty crappy way, but no different to the way you talk to any new member of the opposite sex. I hadn't even considered that he might be attractive, as I was distracted by how attractive I found Tim.

Jimmy was there as well, drinking too much for someone who frankly cannot handle half a shandy. Karen was there, lovely Karen, and we did our whole double act entertaining thing, which consisted mostly of me calling her plain, and her saying how dull I was. I don't know why, but it seemed to work and everybody found us . . . mildly amusing. We laughed at least. There were other people there but I can't remember who.

So we are getting steadily more lashed, music comes on, and I'm feeling very relaxed and being very social, but in a directed at Tim kind of way, which is great.

Until his bloody girlfriend, the walking Stonehenge turned up. Of course she wasn't jealous in the slightest, she couldn't have given less of a shit, as Tim was so very in love with her. She was completely one of the lads. She didn't wear any make-up, was always smiling and cracking crude jokes, and was one of those girls that blokes love. I mean they all absolutely adored her, not because she looked like Marilyn Monroe, but because she looked like she wouldn't be any trouble. She was a girl who would never take an hour to get ready, or complain about staying in a tent, or ever, ever, get jealous. She was a very lucky girl. I wish in a way I was more like that, but she had obviously led a charmed and completely secure life, and wasn't worried how she looked without mascara.

As soon as she turned up I have to say my mood altered slightly. I don't think the taxi action would have been quite so appropriate with her sitting next to Tim, rubbing his thigh, and laughing at the taxi driver's jokes, while Tim and I got it on.

Karen slumped over, and in a very pissed way mumbled something like 'oh dear, she's here', and then opened her mouth as wide as she could to ensure some of her drink went into it. She had acquired a big-suited New Zealander who she had met at the bar, and who was quite happy just to stand there while she swayed.

Jimmy staggered over – Karen thought he was good-looking, and I'd thought they might get it on that night. I couldn't see it I'd told her, largely due to his very silly, very long curly hair, that had plainly been shoplifted from a member of Bon Jovi in the eighties.

Furthermore, he appeared to have the EEC gel mountain

on his head, which looked like it would hurt to touch. But she thought he was good-looking so I encouraged it. Jimmy tried to form a sentence about needing help, about missing his train, could he crash at mine if necessary? I had the same 'absolutely no sexual tension joke' running with him too, and I actually believed it, so I said fine.

I needed to do something to distract me from just staring at Tim and his godforsaken girlfriend, when I heard Stevie Wonder circa 1970 come on. I grabbed Karen, moved towards the middle of the floor and demanded she dance with me. Karen and I both had rhythm, so it didn't take much persuading. Unfortunately she was in a bad way, and couldn't manage an awful lot more than a little Lionel Blair arm-swaying, making her resemble a small retarded girl I had brought out with me for the night. I however felt like I had sobered up quite nastily since the arrival of Tim's girlfriend, and wanted to have a good dance, a fun dance, to take my mind off everything.

I looked around to see what other people were doing, and realized that I was in one of those places where everybody dances exactly the same. It's not that they didn't have rhythm, which we should all be thankful for, but they were all too cool to actually have fun. They did the same dance to every song no matter what the tune, which consisted of casual in time clapping, putting one leg in front of the other, and swaying their shoulders. It was boring. It was a fun song, and I wanted to have fun, and forget about everything the way you can when you are having a really good laugh on the dance floor. The way I always could when I was out with my friend Watson and Stevie Wonder came on.

The only contenders were the big Kiwi, who just wanted

to prop Karen up, Jimmy, who was doing some sort of break boy moves from the Run DMC era, and Henry. Henry was standing at the side of the floor, bobbing his head a bit, still drinking his bottle of lager, but with a smile on his face that implied that not only would he like to dance, but that he might even be good at it. I did the whole dance over to him in a body shaking kind of way , grabbed his hand and dragged him over to dance with me. What a bloody revelation! He propped his drink on the ledge, clapped his hands, and was off! We shimmied, we did the whole robotics shoulder thing, we dragged one leg across the floor to meet the other Sammy Davis Junior style. There was no terrible 'let me try and jive with you' nonsense – who can actually do the jive and be in a club at three in the morning? The whole time we kept laughing, and spinning around, dancing off in one direction and coming back.

Not only did he have rhythm, he looked really cool, not taking himself too seriously, smiling a lot, and grabbing my hand.

I think we must have danced like this for about twenty minutes, before I realized I was gagging for a drink, and wearing myself out. I grabbed his beer from the side, and he walked over, stood a little too close to me while I had a sip, and took it out of my hands to have some himself. It occurred to me then that he was actually quite lovely-looking, not stunning, or even my type particularly in the way that Tim was – tall and blond – but he was nice-looking. He was solid, he had a strong face. He had MASSIVE hands.

We had a conversation in each other's ears, over the music, me on my toes, about how absolutely terrible Jimmy looked, and how absolutely fucked he was. I suddenly realized that

I could look just as bad, given that I had been drinking since 5 p.m., and sweating for a good quarter of an hour. I'd be back in two minutes, I said, I had to go the ladies'. I grabbed my bag and dashed for the toilets.

Why is it you only ever realize how pissed you actually are when you are alone in the toilets, slamming about against the walls, trying to undo your trousers, laughing to yourself, holding your head and opening your eyes too quickly to make the world stop spinning. It's a cliché, but it's damn true, the world literally does spin, and it feels bloody awful. But a pissed inspection in the mirror resulted in me, rightly or wrongly but very drunkenly believing I looked OK. I reapplied lipstick, somehow straight, and powder to my top lip which I'd removed the hair from that morning, and which was still a little sensitive and red.

Fluffing up my hair, sorting out my top, I dashed from the toilets and threw my bag down, and saw Henry talking to some girl from Sales. Her name was Karia, and she was Asian, very pretty, but dull, and she had come because she too loved Tim a little too much. Karen had drunkenly, and very loudly commented on how very boring she was earlier in the evening, and so Henry couldn't possibly be enjoying it. She was a hanger-on. He had obviously got trapped, and would thank me for the escape. I stumbled over, and he smiled, but didn't mouth 'thank you' as he should have done. They carried on chatting. Where did she come from? Near Reading apparently. He was obviously being nice, so I surveyed the room while he finished up his pleasantries. It had emptied out a lot – Jimmy was propped against the bar, head down, looking wrecked. Karen was sitting on one of the sofas grinning at the City Kiwi. Tim and his girlfriend were chatting to some bloke from her work that she had brought with her. No jealousy of course, no doubt that it was strictly platonic. How stable they were. How mature, and obviously not in love. Or maybe completely and utterly in love in a way that I had never experienced, but that was too depressing to think about. The barman looked tired, and was clearing up his counter, preparing to shut up shop. But he knew that he had to keep serving for as long as we refused to go home. It was that kind of place.

Only a few people were still dancing, one of whom was a man in a wedding dress with his wallet stuffed down one of his socks. We *were* in Soho.

The twig tree things with the lights hanging from them looked good, and I entertained the thought that I could steal one for my bedroom. Obviously it would be easier just to buy one, and some fairy lights and do it myself. The song was some seventies tune which I didn't know exactly but which had been sampled a thousand times, making you feel like you knew it. Turning to talk to Henry, I realized I was standing on my own in the middle of the dance floor, and that Henry was actually getting his coat, as was dull Sales woman. They were leaving together. After ten minutes they were leaving together! I felt my stomach go. It could have been the drink, but it wasn't. It was the rejection feeling. It was the 'I don't actually fancy you,' feeling. It was the 'I find her more attractive,' feeling. It hurts like hell, as you may know. It really kicks you so hard that your eyes well up for no reason, and all of a sudden you just want to be in bed at home in tears. I hate it when it happens, it's very sobering. I wanted to leave right then. I wanted to go home and not be reminded that I was on my own, and that tonight nobody wanted to spend any more time with me. Nobody wanted to wake up with me, or kiss me. I was taking it quite hard, but it felt like I'd been rejected twice in one night, and I'd had enough.

I grabbed my coat, and Jimmy was beside me, mumbling about crashing on my sofa. Whatever, I didn't care, I just wanted to go straight away. I kissed Karen goodbye making the Kiwi promise to walk her home to Covent Garden. He could have been a psycho himself, but I had to take my chances because I had to leave.

Jimmy, in the cab, stroking my hair and calling me Karen. Bloody wonderful. But I don't care because I have no feelings for him, and he's sleeping on the sofa anyway. He's trying to hold my hand, and I let him. It's some sort of cold comfort I suppose, some misguided affection, not even meant for me. But it helps because no matter how sober I feel, deep down I know I'm drunk. I pay the cab driver with Jimmy's money, and stumble into my flat. Jimmy falls asleep straight away on my bed, which is fine I say, as long as he doesn't grope me. I take off my make-up, mascara now half way down my face, and climb into bed.

Of course he gropes me. I'm still drunk, otherwise I wouldn't be having unprotected sex with a pissed guy from work who I don't even fancy, and who doesn't fancy me.

I spent the next day off work, sick as a dog on the morning-after pill, cursing bloody Jimmy for being so fucking randy, and completely depressed at the thought that this pill could bring on a stroke at any second because I smoke, according to my bitch of a doctor. She is a Catholic, so what did I expect.

So that was the time I fell for Henry. Went well I think.

Henry's Story

Henry got home from school and slung his bag by the door. It was soaking wet, and left a puddle straight away, but teenage boys don't think about that kind of thing. They aren't house-proud as such. The weather had deteriorated in the afternoon from cold and overcast, to black and pouring with rain. Henry was soaked; he didn't have an umbrella, not because they were poor, which they weren't, but because fourteen-year-old boys don't mind the rain. They don't care about the clothes they wear, or the accidental haircuts on their heads.

Lights were on, somebody was in, but it didn't affect him. He kicked off his shoes in the laundry room, and peeled off his socks. His feet were still wet, and he did a skid into the kitchen. He did another one to the cupboard, on tiles that were wet themselves – somebody must have just come in, but it didn't occur to him. All he thought was that the tiles were wet enough to do skids. Teenage boys don't need a cause, just the effect that helps them skid.

A packet of crisps, a carton of Ribena and television were the order of the day. Homework wasn't even entertained. He chucked some magazines on the floor, and shifted the jacket – his dad's, it didn't register – and slumped onto the sofa. The cartoons were on the other channel and then *Marmalade Atkins*, not bloody *Blue Peter*, thank God. He got up and changed sides.

For the first time, he heard somebody moving around upstairs. They were banging about, and he couldn't hear the TV properly. He got up again to turn up the volume. The rain was still hammering on the windows, and he was very damp, but it would dry. He didn't want to have to move again.

Someone came thundering down the stairs at lightening speed, but he wasn't sure who. You can recognize a person's walk up and down the stairs, he had noticed. If he was still awake at night he could guess who it was coming up, his mum or his dad, by the way they walked.

He couldn't be bothered to move; it was probably one of his brother's friends. He didn't care. The person was heading for the front room anyway, and then a woman came crashing through the door, buttoning up her coat. He didn't recognize her at all. She stopped and looked at him for a second, then they both turned to face the thundering footsteps on the stairs again, his dad this time, he could tell.

His dad came flying in to the room seconds later, as the theme tune to *Marmalade Atkins* began to play. He was fully dressed but he wasn't wearing any shoes.

'Alright, Dad.' Henry was fourteen but he knew exactly what was going on. He didn't know the woman, but she and his dad were both red and sweating. His dad was having an affair.

'Henry, get changed before you make the sofa soaking bloody wet.' That was all his dad said, and Henry left, while the pair of them started mumbling in the living room. He was cold, and felt really wet now, wetter now than he had been in the rain. Now, he noticed his dad's shoes lying by the stairs as he went past. Walking up the stairs, he could see through the kitchen door a scarf that wasn't his mum's lying on the counter. He realized that the car parked outside the house wasn't theirs. Walking past his parents' room he noticed that the door was closed, it was never closed. Henry told me afterwards that it felt like the first time he had ever really seen anything. Not only that, but that he'd been forced to see. He had wanted to watch *Marmalade Atkins* but instead he'd seen the aftermath of his dad's adultery with what turned out to be the lady from the council offices.

The woman had left before Henry came back downstairs or his mum got back from work. He said nothing to his father, and in return wasn't spoken to about the incident. But in the days and weeks that followed Henry couldn't avoid the glaring signs that pointed to his dad's continuing adultery.

When the phone rang after eight, his dad was only on there for seconds before hanging up. When his mum complained that his dad was half an hour late again, Henry knew what was going on. When Henry ran home from school in the rain, which now seemed to thump him like stones, he would sometimes see the red Fiesta with the rust, pulling off from outside his house. But he did not say anything. They were an average family, he wasn't closer to his mum or his dad particularly, and his brother was rarely there, even if he had wanted to say something. Tracey at school was always going on about how her parents were divorced, and it was boring as hell. He didn't want to talk about it. Besides which, nothing seemed very different at home. His parents didn't argue any more than usual, they seemed OK. He didn't sit in the front room any more though. He stopped watching the TV. Mostly he went to his room.

At school he noticed that his teacher, Mrs Campbell, spent a lot of time with the caretaker, even though she was married, and had a son in the class below him. He noticed that the Vice Principal, Mr Armstrong, spent a lot of time with the P.E teacher, Mr Mathews. He noticed them walking off at lunch times, round the back of the field where he played football with his mates. He noticed that he noticed that now.

It must have been months later – the weather was warming up, he didn't need his coat every day – when it happened.

He was early coming home from school, because they had games last lesson, and Mr Mathews had cut it short. Henry hadn't bothered to get changed, but ran home in his kit, with his clothes in his bag. When he came in he noticed that his dad's keys were on the side, there was unpacked shopping by the stairs, and his mum's driving shoes were on the floor in the kitchen. He heard voices in the living room, but he didn't go in. He wanted to go upstairs, but he knew he would make a noise as the stairs creaked, and nobody seemed to have noticed that he was there. He stood stock still in his gym kit, and heard his mum slap his dad. He heard the clap as her hand hit his cheek, and he knew it hadn't hurt, and he wished she'd hit him harder.

His mum was shouting but not crying. His dad was crying; he was sorry, so sorry he said, and so stupid. He loved her, he was so sorry for what he had done. He hadn't even been thinking. He loved her so much.

But it had happened before she said, twice before. Was she an idiot? Is that what he thought? A stupid old idiot who would have to stay for the boys, who couldn't get someone else herself? Was she that stupid? Had he enjoyed making her look a fool again? Was he happy that she'd found out from Susan next door? Was she just old, and ugly and stupid?

Henry found the will to move upstairs, and he went as fast as he could. He didn't care about the noise now, they were making too much noise of their own to notice.

His mum walked out that night, taken a bag and gone to stay at Aunt Laura's. She phoned him the next night, to explain that she was going to be staying away for a while, but she would pick him up at the weekend and they could go shopping for his new trainers.

When she arrived that weekend to pick him and his brother Mikey up, his dad fell apart, dragging her into the living room, and slamming the door. Mikey waited in the car, he was sixteen. He said that things like this happen all the time in a kind of world-weary farcical way. He was trying to be mature, and he said it like it was happening to him, like he was the one getting the divorce. Mikey had just got a girlfriend, and decided he was all grown up.

His mum came out of the living room minutes later, with tears in her eyes, and his dad shouting at her from behind, that he was sorry, he would never do it again. Henry looked at his father and saw the weakest man he had ever known. A coward of a man falling apart and not knowing what to do about it, or how to make it right.

When they came back from shopping, his mum dropped them off at the house and Mikey headed straight off to his girlfriend's house. Henry let himself in, and found his dad on the kitchen floor curled up in a ball sucking on a Ribena carton – one of Henry's Ribena cartons. His dad grabbed Henry's legs and pulled him down, and sobbed strangely for what seemed like ages. Henry kept struggling to get away but his dad held him tighter, making strange gurgling noises that meant he was crying, and saying he was sorry over and over again. Eventually Henry got free, and bolted up to his room. He heard his dad come up a little later, and shut the door.

The next day Henry's dad woke him and Mikey up at eight in the morning, saying he was going to take them to a rugby match. He already had his coat on and was going to get them breakfast on the way. Henry and his brother with sleep in their eyes stumbled into yesterday's clothes, and into the car. Both of them fell asleep and didn't wake up until they heard their dad shouting outside the car. They were parked in front of Aunt Laura's house, on the flowerbeds, and their dad was screaming and chucking stones at the windows. This was her family he said, sitting out in the car, waiting for her to come home now. How many times did he have to apologize? They were all there and waiting for her to come home. Uncle John came out and told him to leave, asked if he'd been drinking, and then shoved him back into the car. He told him to, 'Fuck off, you stupid prick, you've done this to yourself. We could all do it, but we don't.' Uncle John looked disgusted. That was three years before he left Aunt Laura for his cousin Julie.

Henry's dad drove them home, and left the front door

wide open, going into the house, marching straight up the stairs and into the bathroom, slamming the door.

Henry and Mikey watched TV for a while, but it was Mikey who heard the thump, and found their dad in the bathroom, slumped on the floor, and the pill bottle on his chest. They were his mum's sleeping pills, the ones she had asked Henry to get for her, and he had forgotten. Mikey phoned the ambulance while Henry sat in the kitchen. His dad had been out cold for a while, but had been mumbling and dribbling for five minutes by the time the ambulance turned up. Mikey went with him to the hospital, and Henry phoned Aunt Laura's to tell his mum what had happened.

Uncle John came round that afternoon, packed a bag for Henry and Mikey, and took Henry back to his. His mother was at the hospital, and Aunt Laura fussed over him all afternoon, until finally his mum came back, looking exhausted, but saying it would be OK. He hadn't taken enough she said. She had said 'enough' which Henry thought was strange. He hadn't taken 'too many' would have meant she still wanted him, but hadn't taken 'enough' meant she wished he had. He knew then that they would not be getting back together.

His father checked out a few days later, and moved into a flat, eventually, months later, moving in with the woman from the council offices. Henry and Mikey and their mum moved back to the house, and carried on living there until Henry went to university, when his mum sold up and bought a flat nearer town.

Henry still saw his dad all the time. They weren't close, but closer he thought than they would have been if his parents had stayed together. At least they took time out to talk to each other, didn't take each other for granted this way. His dad had married Jean, the woman from the council offices, but they had split up a few years later, when Henry was at college. His mum didn't remarry. She moved in years later with a man who became known as 'Uncle Jerry', but she refused to make it 'official'.

At Mikey's engagement party, she and Henry's dad sat and talked for ages, and they seemed comfortable, but they watched the rest of us with a knowing smile. Sitting there together they saw themselves as a lesson learnt, an example not to be followed. They had done their suffering for us, and if we were wise, we wouldn't follow their lead.

Not Moving In

Henry had agreed to meet me in the travel agents at 1 p.m. He was dashing out for twenty minutes max he had said, and we could decide where to go and then I could do the rest. Of course it was 1.15 p.m. already, and I was only just stepping out of the lift. I'd met Tim in reception – he'd started back a couple of weeks ago, after his former boss had been done for e-mail porn or something, and they'd headhunted him back. He hadn't seen Henry for a while and I hadn't seen Tim, so we got chatting. Of course I found him attractive, in the way that you always will find someone attractive, if nothing happens between you, and at some point you wanted it to. You don't get a chance to kill the feelings off, ruin them with an unimpressive reality. Spending time with someone will do that, but I had started seeing Henry a couple of days after Tim had left. I had never really put Tim to rest, though, and each time I'd seen him since I'd been with Henry, and they were really good friends.

Tim was a little bemused at first that Henry and I had

got it together. Actually, I think Henry had been warned off.

Tim was more than aware of our existing flirtation, and was under the impression that I was using his friend for the same purpose, until something better came along. I admit I didn't go into it with the highest hopes, partly because of the dull sales woman fiasco, and the fact that I had to question Henry's judgement if he was into very pretty but very dull. Any man that follows that route is always worthy of suspicion, like a man who electric shaves, or wears driving gloves, or walks on tiptoes. I don't know why because I've been down that road myself once or twice – going for the handsome but dull, I mean, not the driving gloves. Or, for that matter, the electric shaving, unless one failed attempt at an Epilady that left me with rashes all over my legs, and crying out in agony counts.

But Henry had called me a few days after Tim's leaving drinks at work, on the pretext of getting me to see his flat. He said that if I was actually interested in moving in I should come and see it. I was curious of course, about the flat, but more curious to find out whether he had slept with Karia. (Obviously nobody had any idea about the whole Jimmy thing which was tantamount to a national security secret.)

I had met Henry in the Bathhouse on the corner where we had started out for Tim's leaving drinks. It was bloody freezing outside and my nose could not have been redder, my eyes streaming with tears from the wind when I ran in ten minutes late.

Henry had looked so concerned,

'Oh my God, Eve, what the hell is wrong? Have you been mugged? Has somebody . . . died?'

He had given me a hug right there and then, although I barely knew him, like the big brother I never had. Or rather, the boyfriend I didn't have. I pulled away and laughed,

'No, God no, I'm fine. The wind always makes my eyes water, and my mother's, and both my sisters'. It's a family thing. No, there's nothing wrong apart from this bloody weather, and of course, Henry, the fact that I haven't seen you for so long, nearly a week is it?'

Flirt, flirt, blah, blah, blah.

He had bought me a drink, and we settled in a corner. I had kicked the whole thing off, gently,

'So Henry, how are you? Did you sleep with Karia?'

He had looked a little shocked. I don't know why, because leaving the pub with her was the last thing I had seen him do. But then he started laughing.

'No I did not! I just put her in a cab! For goodness' sake, do I look like that kind of bloke?'

'I don't know, maybe, in a certain light. You had the look of love in your eyes that night. And maybe dull turns you on. I would like to make the point that she wears that scarf all the time though, the one she was wearing. The one that looked like she had wrapped road kill around her neck. It wasn't a quirky thing, she always wears it. Apparently she really feels the cold – she'd cost you a fortune in central heating bills if you married her.'

'Thank God you told me in time.'

'I know! I just thought you should know. You could have been considering it.'

'Hadn't crossed my mind to be honest.'

'Oh that is a shame, you'd make a nice couple. Apart from the fact that you'd have to wear Bermuda shorts a lot, you know, to cope with the tropical heat in your flat when she moved in and turned the boiler up to breaking point.'

'What are you talking about?'

'I don't know, I don't know! Buy me another drink.'

And that was how the evening progressed. I felt like a slut for the whole Jimmy thing of course, but I liked Henry a lot for not shagging Karia. Of course he could have been lying, but if he was, I liked that he lied.

We chatted about Tim leaving,

'So, Eve, are you going to miss Tim then? Miss *not* working with him?'

He asked this a little too pointedly for my liking, but the man had eyes, and he had obviously seen what I had been planning that night up until the point that Tim's girlfriend had showed up.

'No, I don't even know him that well really. And besides, he's only going down the road, so no, I don't believe I shall miss him at all. So how long have you two been friends?'

'What me and Tim? God forever, primary school. Yeah he's a really good mate – can be a bit of an arse with the women, but we go way back.'

'OK, so I have to tell you about this woman on the train this morning, sorry to butt in, but I just remembered it. I got on the train, and then she got on behind me, and then accused me of pushing her! How can I push her if she's behind me? I didn't understand it, anyway, she called me a stupid cow! Can you believe it? How rude is that? She doesn't know me, my dog could have died just that morning, and she's hurling insults around like some train Nazi! That is just rude, really, isn't it? Henry, agree with me now.'

'I'm not being funny, and don't take this the wrong way, but she did only call you a stupid cow. It's not that harsh. It's not like she called you a c— really bad word.'

'Yes but Henry, what you don't understand is that her calling me a cow *implied* to the whole carriage, a packed Northern line carriage, that I was fat, and that isn't nice. I had to stand the whole way to Tottenham Court Road with the whole carriage thinking the reason they were so squashed, was because I was fat, and on their train.'

'I'm sorry I don't understand, did she call you a stupid cow, or a stupid fat cow?'

'Are you trying to make things worse?'

'No, I just don't understand how cow equals fat.'

'Oh Henry, it just does, in woman speak. It just means fat.'

'So what did you do about it?'

'I called her a fucking bitch.'

'You did what?'

'I called her a fucking bitch. Oh Henry, I'm not a morning person OK, and she called me fat, and I got annoyed.'

'But even so, bloody hell. How old was she?'

'I don't know, about sixty, seventy? It's hard to tell when they get that old.'

'You called my grandmother a fucking bitch?'

'Does your grandmother live on the Northern line?'

'No.'

'So how could that have been her?'

'I'm making a comparison. She was old enough to be my grandmother.'

'Does your grandmother call people she doesn't know "stupid cow"?'

'No, I don't think so, no. I hope not'

'Well there you go. Completely different. I have never sworn at your grandmother, and I shall try not to, if I ever meet her.'

'I'm going to get her to call you a stupid cow.'

'Well then she'll get a mouthful of abuse, which won't put either of us at ease. That would be a bad thing to do.'

We got on really well.

'So my brother is going to ask his girlfriend to marry him.'

'Oh Henry, good for him. Will you be best man?'

'I suppose.'

'Don't sound too excited.'

'He shouldn't be marrying her.'

'Why not?'

'They are the most boring couple, they don't even particularly like each other. Whatever, it's a mistake.'

'His mistake to make though, Henry.'

'I know, but she is so blatantly not his 'one' you know? She's not even that fit, at least then I could understand it.'

'Nice.'

'You know what I mean. She's nothing, and he's nothing with her.'

'Do you still believe in that whole 'the one' thing anyway? I don't think I do, any more.'

'No, I do, and she's not it.'

'Well as I said, his decision, not yours. Don't say any of this in the speech at the wedding.'

'No it's fine, I'll just tell dick and sheep jokes.'

We were really, really getting on. We stayed in the pub for hours, and got steadily more pissed on red wine. I couldn't bear the thought of leaving. I had wanted to just keep talking to him all night. I had wanted him to hug me again, the way you so desperately want to touch someone when you know you really like them. Really.

When the bell finally went for last orders, we had necked our drinks, put our coats on, and moved outside, me with the firm intention of seeing the inside of his flat. But when we got outside he hadn't walked towards the main road to get a cab. He had just stood there, looking a little bashful, a little apologetic.

'I don't think it's such a good idea that you move in after all.'

And once again, I had the wind knocked out of my sails. It seemed he was just on a mission to make me feel shit about myself. Was he meeting Karia later?

'Oh right, OK. Well thanks anyway.'

'No, what I mean is I don't think you should move in, because I'd like to see you again, and I think it would be a little too early to move in together. That is of course if you think we have sexual tension yet?'

'Do you think we do?'

'Yes, I think there's a little something there.'

'A little something, I suppose. Either that or you have too much static in your suit.'

'What are you talking about?'

'I don't know.'

I kissed him, or rather we kissed each other, outside the pub, in a way that you don't get to kiss many people. In an innocent way, which was something that hadn't happened to me for a while. To kiss someone you really want to kiss, the first time, and have it feel great and feel your stomach go, is the rarest feeling. It makes some of the rejections seem worth it, for the next couple of days at least.

'I'll phone you in a couple of days, we could go for dinner. Will you get a cab home? I'd feel better knowing you got a cab.'

'Sure.'

He had put me in a cab, paid the cab driver, and kissed me goodbye.

Henry had phoned the next day, and laughed a lot when I told him I had seen his grandmother again on the tube that morning, and how I had to pretend I didn't recognize her, and hadn't actually called her a bitch the day before. From nowhere, I was smitten.

Of course it wasn't laughing Henry, flirty Henry, waiting for me in the travel agents when I was twenty-five minutes late.

'Your mobile rang and you deliberately didn't answer it, knowing full well it was me, because you are so bloody late.' Henry was not pleased.

'I ran in to Tim it's not my fault, he's your friend. He said that you hadn't called him to confirm this whole Center Parcs thing, which I thought we had confirmed last month, and which I gave you the money for last month actually. I couldn't very well just walk off without saying anything. I said we were going, by the way, and that you would phone him to sort it out.'

'Fine. Looked good did he?'

'Oh Henry, for Christ's sake. Don't be so fucking juvenile.' Me thinks the lady doth protest too much.

'Come on then, let's book this bloody holiday so I can get back to the office.'

'Bloody holiday? Nobody has a gun to your head. Don't come if you don't want to, I'll go on my own, probably have more fun. Arsehole.'

Henry grinned and hugged me, and smacked my arse. Romantic.

'Shut up, you know I want to come. And on holiday!'

'Will you pipe down. Did my arse feel big when you slapped it? Did it reverberate against your hand?'

He ignored me, and we asked to see the brochures for Hawaii. The brochure that we actually got was for North America, so I flicked through it while the woman tried to find a more specific one. Henry saw Las Vegas, though, and his eyes lit up. I could tell it was where he really wanted to go. He didn't relish the idea of just sitting on the beach all day, while I read books, and he kicked sand and wanted to play football. No, Vegas was more his kind of thing. It was a man's Mecca. Honestly, I wasn't that keen, but he so wanted to go.

He didn't even say it, he just snatched the brochure off me and stared at the neon and the casinos. And I suddenly got the urge to be the best girlfriend in the world, and to prove that Tim was well and truly out of my system, and that I was sorry for being late.

'Look Hen, go back to the office, we've already decided on Hawaii anyway. I'll end up picking the hotel no matter what, so you may as well go.' He looked so dejected, but he didn't protest. I wanted to hug him and say only kidding! I'm going to book us a holiday to Vegas! And not the Hawaiian paradise I had planned. But I was going to keep it a secret until that night at least, and then it would be a glorious surprise, and he would fall in love with me all over again. Or be really pleased, at least.

'Hen, I'll come round tonight and cook us dinner, and show you the pictures of where we're going. I'll even put it on my credit card . . . for now.'

He went back to work all business-like, pretending he didn't care, and I booked our Vegas trip.

And although I wasn't particularly thrilled with the prospect, I felt bloody good about myself, and the Sunset Hotel where we were going to stay, and the casino opposite the hotel. Of course I felt pretty good about the five days in San Francisco at the end of the trip, but then fair's fair. I didn't feel great about how much the whole damn thing cost, but it wasn't that much more than we had planned to spend on Hawaii.

But mostly I felt great, that night, when I showed him where we were going, and the bloody fantastic sex that followed.

The Sex Thing

Sex is a strange one. I always seem to have blackouts and not just when I'm tired and/or drunk. I never remember the foreplay wholly, although I know that most of the time I insist on it. I think modern man is, from my experience at least, quite into foreplay. I remember him opening my legs from behind, sliding a finger in, another finger, sucking on my neck while he does it, squeezing as much of both of my breasts as he can at one time. I always feel the rush, always fight the impulse to just get well and truly shagged in two minutes, because I know it won't feel as good if I don't wait. Mostly now I wait.

Now I'm grinding my hips back into his fingers, as they work their way in further, and I've pulled his other hand into my mouth while I suck on his other fingers, and lick and bite them. But then there will be the lapse, for about a minute I think, and God knows what happens. All of sudden, and I swear this it true, I remember that I'm having sex, and I start up all over again. It's the strangest thing.

I turn myself around, keep his fingers working inside me, kiss him hard and wide on the mouth, lick his tongue, pull back, lick again. I'm astride him now, of course this is what usually happens, I'm astride him, my hair falling all over the place, resting on his chest, getting in my mouth, in his mouth. I sit up, and take both his hands and make them squeeze my breasts really hard, which actually isn't that hard I suppose, my hands over his, then one hand down, guiding his dick into me, squeezing his balls. I'm rotating, and both his hands are on my arse now, pulling me further on to him, him fucking me slower and harder.

And again, I'll lose it for a while. I don't fall asleep or anything, I don't know where I go. I just go. I hear myself, making noises, him saying my name, and me just groaning, because I hate to actually form sentences during sex. I hate it when he does. I hate that he has the presence of mind to tell me that he has wanted me since he first saw me, whether it's bullshit or not. I just want to be completely lost in it.

Generally he'll get a blow job. I love them, love to give them, and not just so that I'll get a little southern action myself. I like to lick and nibble at his dick, feel it getting really hard, then squeeze it, squeeze it, and suck his balls, and fondle them when I move back up the underside of his dick, run a line with my tongue, stop at the tip, play for a while. I really love it. I wonder why so many women don't. I don't find it degrading at all, but maybe I'm just naïve. You could bite, hard, at any time, grind your teeth. He knows it. You know it. Surely that's what makes it more fun?

I'm ashamed to say that size really does matter to me, girth being of particular importance. Maybe I'm just incredibly shallow, or particularly roomy.

I think about sex a lot. I've never really discussed it with anyone, though, so maybe not more than you. Men are supposed to think about it, is it every seven seconds? Is that right? I don't think about it that much, especially if I'm really concentrating on something else. But whether I'm having twice a night and once in the morning, or once every six months, it occurs to me a lot. At work, I think about how men would be. Certain men. Not just the good-looking ones, not even the good-looking ones. But if I'm talking to a man, if we are laughing and getting on, I'll generally get a flash of what they'd be like. If I'm on the tube in the mornings, and not falling asleep, I'll scan around the carriage, thinking did they have it last night? This morning? What would they do if I just went over to them now, undid a few buttons and climbed on top, asked the person sitting next to us to move their leg a bit.

Not even sex. Have you ever wanted to go up to a complete stranger on the tube and just really give them a good kiss? A ten-second tongue-tingling kiss. Grab the back of his neck, pull him into you, and really kiss him. The doors would open and you could get out at Warren Street instead of Goodge Street, because of course it wouldn't work if you had to stand there afterwards for a couple of minutes, with nothing to say.

Are they thinking the same thing? That would be strange, but we will never know, because no-one is ever going to do it – who would do it? but it could kick-start your day. It shouldn't change your life. Maybe we should all do it once. Have a National Kissing Day. Only one person mind, no hedging your bets and tonguing everyone in sight. And it shouldn't be classed as adulterous behaviour. Let's have a day, a 'National Kissing a Stranger on the Tube Day'. You are obliged to get off the train at the next stop. You are obliged not to talk. You MUST have just brushed your teeth. Let's make it November the 14th of every year. That's my birthday.

Rolling Away

Henry returned to the hotel hours later, after wandering around Las Vegas for the rest of the day. Las Vegas, this fake jewel in America's crown. It reflected everyone it saw in the worst light. They looked like normal, average, run-of-the-mill people at a glance. But if he looked back, even only for a second, at the face of one of the many who passed him that afternoon, all he could see was the yellowing teeth, or the beer belly, or the baldness. This was not the worst of it. You could see the arguments and tensions that would generally go unnoticed. You could see who was to blame, everybody wearing their problems, and insecurities, and guilt, on their T-shirt sleeves. To Henry, on this whistle stop tour on foot, the faces were distorted, tears masquerading as sweat, emotional exhaustion disguised as heat exhaustion.

Henry had walked and walked, and seen nothing of the scenery, nothing of the town. Only random faces passing him. He had stopped and sat for periods, and then got up again and carried on walking. His newly-bought sandals had flapped behind him, a size too big, as he strolled through the streets. It was a resigned walk. Henry walked waiting for an answer. He thought that he would go mad just asking the same questions over and over in his head; he didn't want to entertain thoughts about why she had done it, or how she had done it, any more. He figured he could stop asking the question, but it would still be up there, in his head, unanswered. If he walked for long enough, concentrated on nothing, and didn't allow himself to be distracted by any other pursuit, the answer would come on its own. He just had to walk and wait.

He didn't want to drink, which was the other option. He was fighting the urge to just get completely blitzed. That wouldn't make things clear. He was fighting the drink for as long as he could.

He was also fighting the urge to go and pack his bags and just get the hell out. He had already made enquiries at reception, but all the planes flying to Heathrow had been fully booked for the next day and a half. He wasn't going to go and sit at an airport on his own, waiting for a reserve, not get it, and have to come back into this town. When he left he was going to leave for good.

He had walked until it was very dark, got lost but not really known it, and somehow found himself back on a familiar street, and made his way back to the hotel. He had thought about that drink then, faced with the prospect of going upstairs where she was no doubt waiting for him. He could down a few shots and strengthen his nerve. He could block her out.

Henry walked into the bar without thinking, without really registering the god awful noise coming from the stage.

It was packed, and he stopped and scanned for a table before deciding whether to get that drink or not. It was then he recognized the voice belting out some twisted evil version of Abba from the stage. Henry looked in the direction of the noise, and clocked about seven middle-aged tourists all wearing sheets. But one in the middle wasn't middle-aged. She was red-faced, straining to hit a note she was never going to get anywhere near, wearing some filthy white tablecloth, with mascara all over her face. The music stopped and she carried on singing, so badly, so flat, while at one end of the stage a woman and a man seemed to be having some sort of fight. The man next to them was collapsing in hysterics. People at the tables all around Henry were tutting and remarking, and even shouting, 'get off'.

She stopped singing suddenly, looking like she was going to be sick, and gazed drunkenly over, concentrating, realizing it was him. He couldn't even hold that gaze for a second, and walked out. There was an almighty crash behind him, but Henry didn't look back. What the fuck was she doing? Pissing it up, doing karaoke? He, Henry, was trying to think, trying to sort this thing out in his head, trying to come to terms with what to do now, what to do next. Eve on the other hand, was pissed and singing Abba. Was she taking the piss? It had been one day, not even twenty-four hours, and she was having the time of her life.

Henry stormed to reception and phoned the airline again. Was there absolutely no way he could leave tonight? No, unfortunately it would be a day and a half, sir, before he could get a flight, on the ticket that he had. Then how much was a single to London? Manchester, anywhere? Any ticket on any plane to get him out of here and back to England. That would not be until tomorrow evening, sir, and he would have to stop over in New York for five hours. He would arrive in Manchester the following day, and it would cost six hundred dollars. The airline, surprisingly, suggested he wait. Henry slammed the phone down, and stormed upstairs to the room.

He went straight to bed, hoping she would have the good sense to stay out all night again, commit bigamy or whatever. But he was stirred a couple of hours later by her familiar-smelling body trying to give him a hug. He was disgusted with her for even daring to touch him. If he wanted them to touch, it was his decision to make, not hers. She couldn't railroad him into relenting for the sake of some much needed affection. Henry, in truth was more disgusted with himself for wanting to hug her back, even now. He kicked her, and she withdrew and rolled over to her side of the bed. Henry had lain awake for hours, picturing her lying next to him, but not turning to look. Wanting to roll over and hug her, picturing it in his head, feeling the distance between them, and the tension.

It reminded him of the first time they had slept together, that first night when she had fallen asleep so easily, and rolled away from his arms. Henry had just laid still, wanting desperately to pull her back in, but wondering if he should, or if she didn't like to be hugged in her sleep. He had debated the issue, wide-eyed and desperate to touch her, until she had lazily rolled over and nestled back under his arm without a thought.

But not tonight. Something in her sleep stopped her tonight. He wanted her to roll back to him, but she stayed away, on her side of the bed. Eventually he fell into an uncomfortable sleep.

Henry woke early the next morning, when the room service guy knocked on the door, and brought in an unordered bowl of pretzels. He was trying to quietly slip them on the top of the chest of drawers by the door, but Henry jumped up out of bed. The little Mexican jumped out of his skin, at the sight of Henry in his boxer shorts looming over him, and fled from the room. Henry opened the door and threw the pretzels after him, while he ran and screamed, 'I so sorry, I never do it again, I never do it again,' and disappeared into the lift at the end of the hall.

Even this noise had not woken her: a nuclear siren couldn't wake her in the mornings. Henry had a shower, and opened the cabinet to get his shaving foam. The painkillers and the foam were the only things in there. He had had the foresight to bring the painkillers, she hadn't even thought about it, and yet she was the only one who had used them thus far. Well they were his, not hers, and she wouldn't be using them this morning. She could suffer with her hangover for as long as it took to get to a chemist's. Henry crept back into the room and pushed the pills, in their box, under the chest of drawers. He tried not to feel petty. Actually it was making him laugh, and he had to hold it in until he got back into the bathroom and he knew he was far away enough not to wake her. The funniest thing was that it was exactly the kind of thing she would do, and she'd know he'd done it. Henry smiled as he pictured her smiling, head pounding, when she couldn't find them, knowing full well he'd hidden them. She would respect him for that, in her twisted way. Shit.

Henry crept out of the room with his wallet, some suntan spray, and shoes that actually fitted him. He had no plan other than not to see Eve all day. Going downstairs in the lift so early, it was eerily quiet. Reception was deserted. He checked his watch, 7.10 a.m. He walked out on to the street, which was scattered with last night's hangers-on, refusing to put a great night to bed. It was too early for the suntan lotion. Today he was going to lose himself in something else, forget about everything, and concentrate on not feeling lonely. Henry walked off in an unfamiliar direction.

Trying to Get it in Heidi

Henry is playing crazy golf. He is trying to hit a golf ball through a big slice of Edam. After that, it needs to bounce off a row of plastic tulips and up a bridge into a windmill. It needs to pick up pace as it speeds down a spiral inside the windmill, and then fly out into the open mouth of what appears to be Heidi. Well, a plastic head with pigtails.

Henry is on his sixth go, and he hasn't got it yet. It's the third hole on the course, if you can call it a course, and it's the first one he hasn't holed in one. He is determined to get it in one. He has thoroughly studied hole three, and he thinks he can do it. It's a hard hole, this early on in the course, which is bloody unfair he thinks. But he will get it. He reaches into his back pocket and retrieves the bottle of vodka, and takes a swig. The bottle is already half empty.

Henry lines up, takes a practice swing, but hits it by mistake. The ball takes flight, and smacks the head of a smallish boy standing at the fifth hole, who promptly screams. Henry spins round and looks in the other direction, pretending to gaze at the skyline. A couple of seconds later he turns back, and sees the boy standing with his father, who is looking partly concerned but mostly angry. The father stares over at Henry, who is the only other person playing on the course. Henry smiles and waves his club in the air,

'Morning!'

The father ignores him and rubs the back of the boy's head, feeling for a lump, while the boy cries. Henry sniggers to himself, and gets another ball out of his pocket. He has bought a pack, but only has three left after this one. He shouldn't lose any more. He drops the ball down, and gets it in place. He stumbles up to the hole again, and studies the tulips. It's all in the tulips he has realized. He crouches down to survey the angle that the ball needs to take out of the cheese, starts to fall, steadies himself, and then falls over. Getting to his feet, he sees the father and son looking over at him again.

'Morning! Tricky hole this number three.'

They both ignore him, and he stumbles back to the start. He takes another swig of his vodka, and eyes his ball. He lines up his club. Henry does his practice swing, a little too vigorously, but high enough not to hit the ball this time. However the weight of the swing spins him round, as his arm doesn't seem to want to stop going, and he flies off, led by his club, into the Eiffel Tower. France was hole two. Henry lands flat on the floor, the French landmark a broken heap under his body weight. He gets up on his second attempt, and surveys the damage. They deserve it, bloody frogs, for World War Two. Bloody wimps, even their most famous monument can't stand up to the weight of one grown man. Sniggering, Henry stumbles back to the third hole.

Henry whacks the ball again, and it shoots off through the Edam at speed. He follows it unsteadily with his eyes, as it smacks the tulips at the correct angle and hurtles off and into the windmill. It comes flying out at the bottom, and . . . smacks the legs of the smallish boy who has taken a seat on Heidi's head, bored, and rubbing his new bump. His dad has moved further up the course, to hole eight. The boy looks up as the ball hits his leg and stops by his feet, and sees Henry approaching at speed. He pushes the ball into Heidi's mouth quickly, and looks up again to see Henry standing over him. Henry, swaying, holding his club in one hand, puts his other hand over his eyes to survey the boy. He looks at least ten years old, which is old enough to know better. Henry smacks him round the back of the head.

The boy starts to cry and Henry drops his club and legs it in the other direction, as the boy's father comes running over.

Henry is peeking out from behind the Taj Mahal, and witnesses the boy pointing over in his direction, explaining to his dad that that man has just hit him. The father starts to run over and Henry, realizing that Gandhi is about the only bloke small enough to hide behind this pride of India, pegs it in the other direction, and hurdles the gate. The father is still coming after him, and Henry grabs his three remaining golf balls from his pockets, and hurls them behind him as he runs down the grass to the pavement. He hears a cry from behind him, and turns around to see the father bent over and rubbing his eye. Henry keeps on running, but slows to a jog.

What to do now? Henry had planned on the crazy golf taking up another hour at least. He checks his watch and realizes it is actually half past three in the afternoon. He must have looked a fool, saying good morning to that bloke, but never mind. He takes another swig of vodka and looks around.

Henry has had an active day. He started out with breakfast at a diner across the road from the hotel, where he only just avoided that bloody couple from the karaoke last night who were having breakfast as well. What were they doing up at that hour for God's sake? It was half past seven in the morning and they were on holiday! He was there because he had to get out of the room before she woke up, but they were just up for no good reason. He saw them straight away, ducked towards a table in the corner, and hid behind a menu.

They were both wearing what looked like white sarongs, but which Henry realized were actually their sheets from the night before. Bloody hell, they hadn't been to bed! They both sat there like butter wouldn't melt in their mouths, filling their mouths with pancakes smothered in melted butter. She was doing sums on a napkin, and he was counting money. They must have been out at a casino all night. Henry laughed to himself. It was probably the most excitement they had had in years! He couldn't bear the thought of getting to their age and watching everything he ate, not smoking, not drinking – he could tell they were the type. Just being as boring and sensible as possible on a day to day basis, for no reason other than that they were middle-aged. Good for them, Henry thought, they're letting their hair down for once. He still didn't want to talk to them though, so he got the waitress to skate over a paper and hid behind it for the entire meal.

Sober and just a little depressed, Henry decided that the

casinos were not the place for him today. He had no idea how much money he had made and lost yesterday, but in a more steady state of mind he didn't want to repeat the performance. What else was there to do in Vegas? He walked for a while, looking for somewhere he could spend some time without risking huge amounts of cash, and eventually he came to a cinema. Looking at his watch he realized he was in time for the 10 a.m. showing of either *Honeymoon in Vegas*, *Leaving Las Vegas*, or *Casino*. It was obviously a very self-indulgent cinema. He had no intention of seeing the first one, all things considered, and didn't want to get the bug for gambling from the third one, which he had seen anyway. *Leaving Las Vegas* it was.

He emerged a couple of hours later, thoroughly depressed. What a bloody awful town this was. It seemed that people came here to die. Why had she brought him to this terrible place? He would have been happy with Hawaii. He felt guilty for this thought, which he knew was a blatant lie, but he was in the mood for shifting the blame, and Jesus did she deserve blame.

Strangely, the film had actually made him want a drink, which he guessed was not its intention. Henry walked into the first supermarket he saw and bought himself a bottle of vodka. He didn't feel like Nicolas Cage though, singing and tossing bottles into a shopping trolley. He felt like a loser buying hard liquor at lunchtime. This feeling was enough to propel him to open the bottle there and then, on the 'sidewalk,' and take a massive swig. He hasn't looked back since.

Henry ate lunch in a pizza restaurant that looked like an industrial complex on the outside. However, on being seated, he realized he actually was in Italy, or a bloody good impression of it. What a complete fake this whole town was. It was made of lies. He drank a bottle of red wine with his lunch, and tried to think about the rugby season, work, his brother. She only managed to creep in there a few times. By the time he left the restaurant, the sun was blazing. He realized he was pissed when he tried to spray himself with the suntan lotion. It was supposed to be less messy than the normal cream stuff. But Henry kept missing his arm, and then when he tried to spray his face, he concentrated so hard on keeping his eyes closed that he forgot to close his mouth. He swigged the vodka to take the taste away, and decided upon some outdoor pursuits, but nothing too strenuous in this heat. That was when he spied the crazy golf course on the hill. At first he thought it was closed; from a distance it looked deserted. But on closer inspection he could see a father and son presumably about to 'tee off'. Why was it so empty? Because nobody in this town was healthy! They spent all their time indoors chasing after money to bring them happiness, when all they needed was a little air in their lungs to remind them they were alive. Henry was disgusted, and swigged more of his bottle as he climbed up to the crazy golf course.

But here he is now, with nothing to do. He'll go to a show. The first place he sees is advertising Tom Jones, but not until later. That would have been great. He saw Barry Manilow with her a while ago, because she so wanted to go. He had expected to hate it, but actually quite enjoyed himself. That was a funny night. Maybe Tom isn't such a good idea. He doesn't want to think about Eve.

A few blocks down, Henry realizes his bottle of vodka is

empty, and he is in a bad way. He can't see straight, and has vague recollections of hitting a small child. Smallish anyway. He staggers into the first door he sees, which he realizes is a coffee shop. Henry orders a large black filter coffee, slumps on a sofa in the corner and falls asleep with a paper over his face. By the time he wakes up it is dark outside. Sitting up, he waits for the hangover to kick in, but realizes gratefully that he is in fact still very drunk. The coffee is cold, and looks disgusting with a film on top of it. What Henry needs is another vodka.

Anniversary

On our nine-month anniversary Henry booked a table at the Oxo Tower, because he likes views, and I like cocktails. London is a strange sight at night, a mess of history and smoke, old and historic, tattered and ravaged and at the same time new. It's like they find an inch of the town that isn't used and fill it with either a revelation in technology and architecture, or a homeless person. This of course is the view from the Oxo Tower, not Finsbury Park tube station.

As much as it hums and buzzes, and pulls you along at its own pace, London doesn't mesh any more. It has become a flashback to an age that has already gone, a time that was. Everything seems to sum up yesterday. When you look at London from a height, in the dark, you never see its future, just the sums of its past. It doesn't seem to have a tomorrow.

But Henry loves views. He was drawn to smoke from a building miles away, a building that we would never know, or enter, and a boat on the Thames that he could see had just two passengers. A tiny little boat making its way up a route of kings. He could stare for minutes at a spot I couldn't see, but then he would turn his head from left to right, and span the whole scene, to sweep London with the slightest movement of his eyes.

He noticed everything now. The good and the bad, he saw it all. I don't think I had ever known someone so aware of their surroundings, or ever been so aware myself that the person I was with was so very aware. It opens your own eyes too. In the time I had spent with Henry I had noticed a change in me. Spending time with someone new, a great deal of time with someone you like, changes the person that you are.

You realize as you get older that you are either a combination of, or a reaction to, all the people you have ever been close to. There is the self: the what you are just because, the bit that makes your core. But the layers of your personality are not really your own, and you would never have come across them by yourself. You are what you see in other people's eyes when they look at you, what you hear when they talk to you. You are built of all your rejections, your praises, who you have loved and how you've been loved in return. You are only in small part responsible for you.

It is worth noting, however, that anybody who changes too much depending on who they are with, is a person not worth having around. These are the people too scared to be the mishap that has become themselves. If all you do is reflect, and not emanate, what can anyone learn from you? It is only when you give and take that you become the person you should be.

What I had learned from Henry was to stop and look

around. The time that it takes you to inhale your surroundings gives you a knowledge that would otherwise pass you by. It made him incisive. It made him wiser. You cannot witness that much, breathe it all in, and have nothing to give back. It made his world and mine more interesting.

So Henry liked views and I liked cocktails. Henry liked to take it all in and deal with it. I liked to take it all in and then blot it all out with a Margarita. A large part of the person Henry had become had been fashioned that day in his living room, at the age of fourteen, in his soaking wet clothes, staring at the woman from the council offices. This premature opening of his eyes had taught him that if he knew what was happening, if he observed his father having his affair, his world would not come tumbling down when the truth eventually did out. His backbone was built on being able to prepare for the inevitable, because he had seen it coming. This is why Henry did not like surprises. I on the other hand had led a very different kind of existence. Although the threat had often hung in the air, nothing really bad had ever happened to me. I had never seen the ones I loved torn apart, I had never lost them to death, or another. I had led, if not a charmed, a safe existence.

My answer, unlike Henry, was not to be prepared for the worst by making sure I knew it was coming, but to look away and hope that it wouldn't happen in the first place. Or ensuring I was numb enough to take the first blow when it eventually came. Because some day it would come. People don't live forever, and my parents, my sisters, even Henry, were not the immortals I could convince myself they were, while nothing bad happened to any of us. The threat was constantly there, that some day soon, and for the first time something would happen that would bring my world crashing in around me, and I had no idea if I could stand it or not. Henry was scared of not knowing. I was scared to know.

Of course these weren't the thoughts dancing around our heads as we sat in the Oxo Tower on the occasion of our nine-month anniversary. Things were in fact going very well. I had fallen for him, for our differences, for his laugh. For the way he stood behind me in pubs, right behind me, that made me feel safe. I had fallen for his eyes in the morning when he was waking up, and he registered that I was there. I had fallen for the way that he had progressively stood up to me more and more, and would stamp out my attempts at an argument, with a 'stop that before you even bloody start because I won't be listening.' He had put his foot down on my jealousies, saying that it just wasn't necessary. But I had also fallen for the little streak of jealousy that reared up in him occasionally, and that he was so ashamed of.

I liked that his shirts were big enough to cover my breasts in the morning when I needed something to throw on and still feel sexy in. I liked that he liked that my breasts were that big in the first place.

He liked rugby, he liked my parents and they liked him. He and my sister's husband had hit it off almost immediately, and I liked that they liked it if the other one was there to talk to. I liked that he would flirt with 'safe' girls, and not women I would actually be very jealous of; I liked that he had that radar. I liked all these things, and I was the first to admit that I had fallen in love, but this was the problem. I had fallen.

It had taken over six months but now I was in love. If you have to fall, if it isn't instant, then at some point you are waiting to hit the ground. I had fallen for someone who I believed was not my soulmate – not that I was any closer to defining what that was. But I had let myself be in love with someone, knowing full well that at any moment I could fall out of that love. This was my predicament. It's glaringly obvious of course, what was happening. It's the fear thing again. I was scared. I was thinking of stopping something wonderful that made me happy, because it might not last . . . because it might fall apart.

Not that I should have bothered, because it transpired that Henry had his own thoughts on the matter, and they didn't necessarily include me.

'This is great, Eve, this is really nice, but I don't know how appropriate it is considering.'

I didn't know what he was talking about, but I had a bad feeling in my stomach, that needed to be quashed, quickly. I poured myself a huge glass of wine.

'Henry, what are you talking about? Sorry did you want some of this wine as well? Should I order another bottle?'

'No it's fine, I'm fine without it. Do you think it's working out? I mean, do you think we're doing OK, Eve?'

'Well obviously, *you* don't, otherwise you wouldn't be asking.'

Silence.

'It's not that I think it's going badly, it's just that I think I could be feeling something more than possibly I do. I'm just trying to be honest.'

Henry had been quiet all night. Now I knew why.

'Well don't try too hard' – I was trying desperately to keep something light-hearted that had no intention of staying that way. I looked like a wimp. 'So, Henry, are you saying you don't feel anything for me? Are you trying to tell me that you aren't in love with me?'

'I'm not saying that, I'm just saying . . . I don't know if I am or not.'

'Then you shouldn't say "I love you" all the time. You shouldn't keep saying that you love me if you don't because it's not fair. In fact it's lying.'

'When I say it, I mean it. I don't lie.'

'Quite obviously you do, otherwise we wouldn't be having this conversation.'

'Oh here we go, straight away. You can't have a conversation without getting defensive and frosty. I'm trying to talk about this. I want to sort it out.'

'Oh fuck off, Hen. Any chance of you dismounting from the maturity horse at any point this evening? Jesus.'

'Fine, you know what, I'll tell you, if you're going to be like that. I thought I was in love with you, but in the week when I went out for a drink with work I met Sarah in the pub. And although I was very drunk, I am not going to make excuses for the fact that I ended up snogging her, and only just made it back to my own flat and not hers. Is that immature enough for you? I cheated on you and I feel like shit, but I have to think about why I did it, because you know I hate fucking cheating. If you ever did it to me that would be it. So can I have double standards like that? That is what I am actually trying to say.'

'Sarah?'

Sarah was his ex-girlfriend. He had broken up with her a couple of months before I had started seeing him. He had met her in that pub. They had only seen each other for about two months. What was the word he had used? Vacuous. His word, not mine. So then I had a choice – to drink more wine, or throw it up? It was in the balance. This lovely guy that I had been scared of hurting, this all round Mr Fucking Nice who was so good for me, had managed in the space of two minutes to make me feel physically sick with emotion. Who was the idiot here?

'Why didn't you sleep with her?'

'Because it was wrong, because I thought of you.'

'In what order?'

'The other way around,'

'Oh great. Did you not sleep with her because you thought of me, or because your bloody morals kicked in?'

'It's the same thing!'

'No it is not. You didn't fuck her because you love me, or because cheating isn't something you do, because you didn't want to be a cheating arsehole like your dad. Do you see the difference now? I do.'

'I deserve that. This is what I'm saying, I don't want to behave like my dad.'

'Well then don't, Henry! It's your bloody choice. Nobody has got a gun to your head, saying 'sleep around, Henry, be an arse!' You make your own decisions. What is killing you right now might be that you have hurt me, but that's not all of it at all. It's that the thing you hate most, is actually you. What your dad did, what you have judged him for, for all of these years, is you. You hate how this makes you look. And you think that by admitting it, it somehow makes you better than him.'

'Maybe you're right.'

'Oh fucking bully for me! For being so bloody wise.'

Silence.

'Is there anything else? Any more bombshells you want to drop?'

'No that's it, but I want to talk about it.'

'Well I'm going to be a better person than I can sometimes be, and say that we shouldn't talk about it right now. I will be spiteful, and that is not necessarily how I want to react to this. Necessarily.'

'So what do you want to do?'

'What I would have liked, what I wanted, was to sit here and have an anniversary meal with my lovely boyfriend, but seeing as he's not quite so lovely as I thought, I think I'll go home. I'm not being spiteful now, I'm not doing this to make a point, or make you feel worse. I want to decide what I think about this.'

'Do you want to go back to yours?'

'I think that would be wise, I don't want to see your bloody face at the moment.'

'I'll go and get you a cab.'

'They get one for you at the bar.'

'Then I'll get that,'

'Fine. You fucking shit.'

Henry went to the bar to get a cab ticket and I just sat there. Strangely, I'd calmed down which was surprising for me because I have my father's temper and usually I just blow up, and then calm down the next day. But I knew that if I had talked to him then I would have said things I couldn't take back, and I also knew that if he didn't want it to end then neither did I, necessarily. However I wasn't about to say that right then, as he needed time as well. He needed to think what he wanted.

At least he didn't sleep with her, although I don't know

why that makes such a difference. Sex and snogging are hardly miles apart but it seems that way. I think the thing is that you get taken by a moment and can kiss someone without really making a choice as to whether to do it or not. But sex? Sex is supposed to be a choice that you make. It's a line that you cross, drunk or not. You know you aren't supposed to do it. It's not even the act, it's the decision to act. At least Henry didn't do that.

We got our coats in near silence, we went down eight floors in actual silence, and we stood and waited for the cab that would take ten minutes to arrive. The fresh air did me good. I felt really mature. I felt in the right. Henry looked as though he was in the wrong, which was something. He wasn't trying to brazen it out any more.

'I know you don't want to talk, but all I'm going to say is that I was wrong: I do know whether I love you or not. I love you, I just can't understand why I did it. I'm not saying that to make you think any better of me.'

'Yes you are.'

'No I'm not. I feel like shit. I really want to sort this out.'

'You know what, Henry, think about what you want, before you call me. Think if you actually want to call me, I won't call you. But at least, at least you didn't sleep with her.'

I hadn't meant to say that, but I was being honest. I hadn't meant to give him a sign that it might be OK. But I think I wanted it to be OK.

The cab arrived, I got in, and Henry leaned in to kiss me on the cheek, but I turned quickly enough to miss it, and he got a mouthful of hair.

As the cab pulled off I was choked up, more at the whole

tragedy of the scene, the fated romance of it all, than because I wanted to cry. But later on, in my flat in my bed on my own I did just want to cry, and I did.

Talking it Through

'Conversation enriches the understanding, but solitude is the school of genius.' Edward Gibson said that. Fair enough I suppose you can only really think things through on any subject if you are left alone to do it. If you're out with your friends having fun, having some drinks, it doesn't generally occur to you to go and sit and muse on something you've never mused on before. What I resent is the suggestion that being a genius is automatically a good thing, and that spending time with your thoughts makes you a better person in some way. I think it's the opposite. Spending time on your own, just thinking, will in fact make you a much more complicated person to deal with in the long run, and a much less social one in the meantime. I mean if you're sitting at home dwelling on life's puzzles, you're not getting in your round at the bar. But then I suppose it depends on what you are thinking about. For example, solving a mathematical equation does you no harm, unless you are particularly clumsy and take the bit of protective rubber off the end of your compass.

If you are thinking of shopping that's fine. You need eggs, you remember to buy them by thinking that you need them, you have an omelette, everybody's happy. But I always assumed that it wasn't that kind of solitary thought Gibson was referring to. If he is talking about thoughts on life itself, what we are doing, why we are here, then it doesn't take a so-called genius to work out that the outcome of all this pondering is going to be a hefty dose of depression. The real genius is out and about, on the town, whoring and laughing and drinking them self into a blissful oblivion. In short, spending no time on their own to mull it all over. To answer questions like,

Why am I here?

Don't know, to procreate? Are you happy?

Not really. I'm not in love, and I don't have any money.

What has money got to do with anything? What the hell is money?

It's the paper that lets you have two holidays a year.

Why do you need two holidays a year?

Because my life is dull, and a constant battle to make ends meet. I'm not satisfied.

So the money provides the means of escape from the life, but doesn't really change the life, so doesn't really make you happy.

If I had lots of money, loads, I could spend my time looking after the sick and righting great wrongs like homelessness and poverty.

Why can't you do this without any money?

Because I wouldn't have any shoes.

Well what do you want, really want?

I just want meaning, but my own meaning, not somebody else's.

So we're ruling out religion then.

Yes indeed. I have no desire to live my life by some set of rules in some two thousand-year-old handbook which would, quite frankly, stop me having any fun.

Well go for the fun then. Spend your time having fun. That would be good wouldn't it?

No, that doesn't work. Only pop stars get that, and even they turn to drugs for escapism.

What are they escaping?

The fact that even when they get everything you're supposed to want, the fame and fortune, and success, they have nothing that actually gives their life meaning. Make another song? Oh why not, I've got fuck all else to do.

So what about the other thing, 'love'?

Well there is the problem you see.

No, what problem?

Well you have to find someone to love you in pretty much exactly the same way you love them, otherwise you have arguments, you get jealous, or you feel unloved, or suffocated, and that doesn't make you happy. And love never seems to last for anyone. An answer should last, and this answer never seems to. You can't make somebody love you in the way you want them to, and you can't seem to love somebody effortlessly and forever. It always goes wrong, apart from maybe your children. And besides, you can't just love somebody, for a living. You have to have the other parts of your life working at the same time, for example the money thing. Yes the only people you can really love are your children, and most of them seem to fuck their parents over. But, I suppose children seem to be the answer.

So back to the procreation thing.

Yes but then you have to change nappies, blah blah blah, your life isn't your own.

You haven't tried it yet have you?

No, children are very expensive. I don't earn enough yet.

So you have to wait until you earn enough.

Well I think you should be able to feed them.

So you have to be old enough to be able to afford children?

Yes. Otherwise they'll hate you for putting them in Green Flash trainers when everybody else is wearing Nike.

So, if a child has a decent pair of Nikes, would this make them happy?

Generally, as long as they aren't being abused or anything terrible like that, if they have good trainers, then yes, they are happy.

So children can be happy, even if adults can't?

Only until they are old enough to sit and have depressing conversations with themselves.

So be a child or have a child seems to be what you are saying.

Hmmmm, so my options would appear to be getting pregnant by a man who I don't really love and who will eventually cause me pain, or spinning around in a circle until I get dizzy and fall over, and playing tag with my work-mates.

You'll get fired for the spinning thing. And running in the corridors at work.

So you're telling me to get pregnant?

Yes I think I am.

Well find me somebody I'd want to have a kid with, and I will.

Oh for goodness sake, just shag anyone!

That's my point, that's what I'm going to have to do. I can't have my happy life can I?

Not if you insist on thinking like this. Get poor, get caught up in mortgage repayments, and the size of your arse, and jealousy because that man you don't really like but intend to spend the rest of your life with might be shagging someone else.

Is the key then, to as happy a life as I am going to get, to not actually think at all? Get so distracted by essentially meaningless shit, that it doesn't occur to me that it's meaningless?

I think that's what I'm saying.

You're a genius.

I spend a lot of time on my own you know. It can get a little lonely. I wouldn't say I'm happy.

Who the hell am I talking to?

On the Train

In the days that we spent apart, thinking, the days directly after Henry's declaration of adultery with Sarah, I felt terrible. I realized that what Henry had actually done was pull back from temptation. He had been roaringly drunk, and he had not slept with her. I was sitting on the tube when it really hit me.

At first I had been so upset I had just cried myself out, not exercised any self control over the streams of tears that came every five minutes. I had been pushing for the point when you just cannot cry any more, when you are so exhausted with the effort, and your eyes are just dry. But I wasn't crying at the magnitude of Henry's indiscretion, which in truth was not that great. He hadn't been having an affair, or done anything that would crumple my small world to a point where I would never forget. He wasn't leaving me for someone else, emptying my life of its main player. Henry was still in the wings, waiting for his cue. He didn't like anybody more. He had simply got drunk, and kissed somebody he had kissed before and stopped it there. Nothing really bad, or unforgivable had happened.

Even if he had stopped because of this code that he was desperately trying to live by, and not solely because of me, well that was something. How many men carry that much guilt around with them in their briefcase every day, a guilt not even their own. Henry felt the pressure of another man's failures, and brandished his morality in front of him as he walked in the dark, to fend off the same fate. How many men feel that bad over something so small? That was surely a sign that he would never go too far on me, never break my heart with someone else. For in truth, my heart wasn't broken, or even cracked. Mildly scratched perhaps, but nothing terminal. He loved me, and my tears were at the prospect of not being with him, a decision that was mine to make.

He had phoned four times already, in twelve hours: yes he still wanted to be with me. I was crying, why was I crying? At the prospect that I could let this go. Think of standing on a tube station while the train comes in, and the urge you sometimes get to just throw yourself under. Not even the urge, but the possibility that you could just jump. Or at the side of a cliff, with nothing but 100 feet of rocks and waves waiting for you, and you could just fling yourself over, and find out what's next. You won't, but you could. It's what flashes through your mind straight after the urge that scares you most. The thought of what you would be leaving behind. It was this thought, and the fear of losing Henry, that had made me cry so very hard, because I knew, as you know on the side of the cliff, that nothing is going to end. You will walk uncertainly away, having scared yourself with the possibilities of your own actions, as I was walking back to Henry.

So I was sitting on the tube, trying desperately to wake up, trying to remember whether I had just had a shower. I am incredulous every morning on the train, that I have managed to get myself to that spot somehow, without actually waking up. I let myself sleep for as long as possible. I sleep in the shower, which is why I find water even slightly too cold to be so offensive. I am not a 'morning' person, as clichéd as that sounds.

I had turned my mobile on just before we went underground, and there was a message from Henry.

'It's me. Hope you're OK. I'll phone you later.'

I had debated whether to call straight away, and let him know it was all going to be fine, and that I was fine. My mind was made up, but this was payment time, make him sweat time. If he hadn't kept phoning I would have succumbed and called a lot sooner, but thankfully he was there afresh on the answer-phone, reassuring me that he hadn't found somebody else yet. How the hell would he have done it so quickly anyway, although it would have been typical, just my luck, like falling over at graduation, or throwing up on my boss, both of which I had done.

I had got a seat on the tube, thank goodness. I can't bear it when you have to stand for the whole journey, or worse, if you get a seat, possibly the last seat, and then at the very next station, with over half an hour of the journey to go, some old bastard gets on and you have to give them your seat. Or some pregnant bastard! They always look so bloody smug, while they thank you in a patronizing voice. They know you have to give it to them, because some bugger has to stand up for them, and nobody else ever does! It is always me! On the rare occasion that someone offers their seat first, it is always, and without exception, a woman. I swear that not once have I seen a man offer up his seat on the train. The sods look down at their newspapers, and pretend not to notice. I suppose they are all feeling defensive, given the millennial assault on their masculinity, or maybe they are just selfish bastards. I have never been in a situation with Henry where he would have to offer up his seat, which would be a test. I think he would give it up though, straightaway, but then I love him, so it's not objective. It would be part of his 'what makes a real man' code, I think.

It struck me, sitting there, that if I saw him sitting opposite me on the train, and of course I didn't know him, whether I would fancy him? I don't like the idea of some woman sitting opposite him, or next to him on the train, or leaning into him if they are both standing up, finding him attractive. A girl with blonde hair no doubt, they always have blonde hair, it is the bane of my life. Sarah had blonde hair. She would smile at him if they accidentally knocked into each other when the train jolted. She would stand closer to him than any stranger ever should, but that is what taking the tube in London now dictates, surrendering any notion of personal body space. By then I had made myself jealous, unhappy even, and resolved to call him as soon as I got off the train. There was a blonde girl sitting opposite me, and I stared at her until she caught my eye, and I met it with a scowl. Do not ever, ever flirt with my boyfriend, bitch.

Then I did my usual scan of the carriage for any attractive men. This is not flirting you understand, just something to do in the morning if you can't be bothered to read. A problem that I have is that I refuse to let myself read anything 'light' on the train, anything easy to pick up and put down. There was a period a couple of years ago when a certain book was published about some neurotic nineties woman, and everybody on the train was reading it. Everybody! I read it out of curiosity, and because everybody else had raved about it, and it was terrible. I mean it was throwaway, it was nothing. It didn't make me think about anything new, or offer anything new, it didn't even say something old in an original way. It was trash, and it wasn't even fun trash with ponies and double-barrelled surnames. And it had just so depressed me that everybody had read it, or would read it, because of its marketing campaign, and not the tens of hundreds of thousands of other books worth reading. They wouldn't read Tolstoy, or Graham Greene, or Tennessee Williams. No, I like books with irony.

I was looking around the carriage anyway, to see the morning's talent, which was zero! That was standard. There was a boy in a suit with trousers that were too short, and he was reading a science fiction novel and listening to his Walkman at the same time. Walkmans have come a long way however, previously the scourge of every train traveller, now replaced by mobile phones of course. I couldn't hear a thing, couldn't make out what he was listening to, but something must have been playing because he was nodding his head to a beat. Unless he insisted on silence and had a twitch.

Apart from that it was mostly women, and I have never really had a bisexual urge, so I didn't eye them up. Just think how it must open up your options though. But I go back to the men. Some people say one in four of us is gay, and some say we are all a little bit gay. But those people are always gay themselves. Maybe it happens in later life, or needs to be triggered.

There was a guy sitting on one of those high seats, the ones where you can't really sit if your legs aren't long enough to reach the floor. I suppose he was good-looking in a very average way. I think if he had a good personality it would sway it for him, and he would be one of those men for whom it would be a real decider. He could either be really attractive, or really nothing, depending on how funny he was. I wonder which one it was.

It occurred to me then that what I was doing was no better than what Henry had done. I was seeing what was on offer, but in my case, doing it soberly. Of course I would never do anything about it. I never have. There have been on occasions some very good-looking men on the train but, single or not, I would never have gone up to them, winked, and given them my card. Yet still, I was being unfaithful in a way. If Henry was sitting on his tube doing the same thing, I would have hit him. There are different degrees of betrayal and this one only sits a little lower down the scale than Henry's.

It counts when they like them more. It's not a physical thing at all. It's who they like. Unless you are one of those people who only goes on the physical aspect. It's when they say, 'I want to spend time with this person, more than I want to spend time with you.' That's the hard one to swallow, the choker in the throat.

I got out my book and decided to read. It was the Bible, I kid you not. Some of the stories in it are really good, the Old Testament at least. I did get some strange looks, as if I was wearing a badge with the words 'I know God loves me' on it. People do assume you are weird. Not that I would ever wear a badge like that, it's just a comparison. God doesn't even know me.

I waited until I got to work to phone Henry, as I couldn't risk the mobile cutting out.

'Marketing, Henry speaking.'

'Hen, it's me.'

'Hey how are you? Did you get my messages?'

'Yes, but I was on the train this morning when I got the latest one. On the tube. How was your journey into work? OK? Squashed? The Northern line was a nightmare, I was squeezed into people, into this blonde girl wearing too much hairspray, like they always do, and I got a mouthful.' I was lying, I had had a seat for the whole journey. It was a test.

'What? No it was fine. A bit stop-start.'

'Did you fall asleep?'

'What? No not really, look, how are you? Have you thought it all through, does this phoning me mean we are OK?'

'Yes I think so. I'm bored of being miserable. If you haven't changed your mind that is, if you do want to be with me and not Sarah.' Another test.

'Of course I bloody do, you know that. So are you serious? Can you come over tonight?'

'Shit, Henry, my other line is going, hold on.' No it wasn't. Just for fun.

'I'm back, were you singing?'

'Yeah you've still got The Rolling Stones as your hold music.'

'How depressing. OK, so I'll come over tonight then. But you can bloody cook.'

'Fine. Do you think we should talk about it, or do you want to not mention it, just so I know.'

'I think we should probably forget about it, don't you?'

'Fine. Fantastic. I just thought you might want to talk about it.'

'Nope.'

'Fine. Whatever you want to do.'

'We're not having sex though. Not tonight.'

'Fine.'

'Well we might, but I don't know.' I had expected more of a fight than that.

'Fine, whatever you feel like.'

'Well I don't know what I feel like yet. We'll see tonight.'

Car Chases or Conversation

We had conversation in common, but not opinions. I talked to Henry about everything, and invariably I couldn't help but smile. If I looked at him while I was speaking, I was often overcome with embarrassment, and the sensation that my eyes were giving me away, and completely exposing my every feeling for him.

But we did disagree on many things, looked at things through very different eyes, and from standpoints miles apart. Politically we were at different ends of the spectrum. We only mutually bestowed greatness on one film: *Goodfellas*, of course.

I liked music that I could sing to, that lifted my spirits, made me happy, just while singing it. Henry liked miserable maudlin 'deep' numbers, with 'meaningful lyrics', where you could literally slit your wrists to the beat.

We would argue our corners blue, which is what we had in common. We enjoyed the discussion in itself, we enjoyed the intellectual play fight of it all.

I began to feel, as we lay in bed talking at 3 a.m. instead of having sex again, or sleeping even, that what I said was important to him. It wasn't just that I was important, I already knew that. I genuinely began to feel, no, more than that, I actually believed that he enjoyed my thoughts.

Henry wouldn't grow tired of some dubious mental tangent I spun off on without warning, and in fact began to do the same thing himself. Talking with Henry very quickly became one of my favourite things. It was . . . atypical. It was something new for me.

We shared all our stories, and I flinched if they involved him being sexual with any old flame. We talked about one-night stands featuring coffee on body parts, about passing out cold after too much illegal Jamaican rum. About competitions won, holidays taken, parental embarrassments, running away from the manager of Kentucky Fried Chicken, throwing wings back over one shoulder to try to slow him up. That was Henry, by the way.

And we talked about what we wanted to do, where we wanted to go, how we wanted to be. Of course we talked about jobs and trains and weather, and all the day to day things as well. Not every conversation was some bizarre exploration of our subconscious. We weren't exhausted from theorizing the world every second of the day. But sometimes, and before even realizing it, we would be so deep in conversation that it would take a knock at the door, or a phone ringing, or a waiter giving us our bill, to alert us to the rest of the world.

But yes, we did think differently. I was the dreaming realist, and he was the down-to-earth optimist. I dreamt Elvis might still be alive, even if by now he was clinically obese.

Henry knew he was dead, but that hopefully it would have reduced his cholesterol.

Don't get me wrong, I don't mean to suggest that we had suddenly, with the help of each other, awoken to the fact that we were the most interesting people around. No, it was just that we fitted, somehow. We disagreed, we thought differently, but we enjoyed it nonetheless. Even when we argued, we threw everything into it.

Perhaps because we were so dissimilar, we didn't seem to lose interest. There were times when we would agree to meet after work, for a drink, to see a film, to cook dinner for the other, to just go home together. I could be exhausted from another frantic day, as could he. I would stumble towards our arranged meeting point, feet aching, eyes blurring, just wanting to sleep, but when I saw him gradually my eyes would open, and the fatigue would be postponed for a couple of hours at least. Henry was my Pro-plus substitute at times.

Oh I know it's all gone a little bit *Love Story* but sod it! Do you want the truth or not?

That's how it was. How it is. Sorry.

Well while I'm here and cliché-ing, I might as well get it all over and done with. Do you want your car chase now? Do you want me and Henry speeding through lunchtime traffic against the clock, with the only known cure for cancer in the glove compartment, and very little petrol? Henry could be a brilliant yet unbelievably (!) young ecological scientist, with quirky ways but a brilliant mind, a square jaw and a six-pack. I could be the hit woman hired to take his life by the Russian/Iranian/Japanese mob, before I accidentally fell in love with him and his ideals.

Should I be able to fire a gun with alarming accuracy,

despite never having held one in my life? Should I be a stranger on a street that he knocks into, or better yet, the woman whose car he jumps into and then tells to 'step on it', as I speed off like a racing driver on acid, never getting lost despite not consulting a map once.

Or would you prefer a courtroom battle? I could be the brilliant yet remarkably young (!) lawyer, about to make partner despite only being out of law school for three weeks. Henry could be accused of a murder we all know he just did not commit, of course he had been framed! I could work with him on the case, late at night over takeaway Chinese food, and although we hate each other at first, he just can't help falling for my long blonde hair that was hidden in that nasty bun before, or my forty-inch legs, or my incredibly pert yet massive breasts, none of which we had realized were there before.

Or how about we spend twenty minutes preparing a case with all the odds stacked against us, and then three months in a courtroom making ridiculous emotive speeches that would be thrown out of every court in the land, except we luckily have a kindly judge who is about to retire, and I restore his faith in the vigour and justice of the legal system?

Should Henry be a peace activist? Should I be Prime Minister? Should we both be models? We should be rich, at least, shouldn't we? We should have two houses each and a boat of some description. Is that what you would really prefer? Honestly?

Actually, do you mind if I don't?

Me and Henry? We mean nothing at all. We won't change the world, But this was our own small personal hell for a time, and it was enough to bear without explosions, and guns and high speed chases. Those things would just have been a distraction. We were trying to make our lives, feel our happiest, and get hurt as little as possible. These were the real distractions, and as you probably know, they are more than enough.

Feathers and Adam's Apples

Henry is sitting in a gay bar in Las Vegas, and he's started smoking again. He didn't realize it was a gay bar, he was already very drunk when he stumbled in, and he just thought that all the women on the stage were very tall. But they were all wearing feather headdresses as well, so it was a little confusing. Drunk as he was, he realized after a second bloke had offered to buy him a drink, that he was being hit on. He didn't care, he just lit another cigarette. It was amazing after all this time, he inhaled like he'd never given up. When that first lick of smoke hit the back of his throat, curled its way home to his lungs, it felt like he'd inhaled sex. If felt like an orgasm in a breath. How had he ever given up? Somewhere in the recesses of his mind he knew that tomorrow, hungover and sober, it would feel like someone had taken a penknife to his throats and slashed a thousand tiny slits. Unless he just lit another cigarette, then of course he would feel fine. Henry was officially taking up the weed again.

He was leaning over the table, not sick drunk, just sick and tired. He was worn out with ignoring her, worn out with Las Vegas. He just wanted to go somewhere, sit in a room from which he couldn't see a single flashing light. An epileptic could never come to Vegas, he thought. The hell of it was the shit they'd already been through. He'd beaten himself up about snogging Sarah, but he had admitted it at least, and they'd got through it; it was only a bloody kiss after all. He hadn't slept with her, and he knew that was what had kept them together. And he had wanted to sleep with Sarah, oh yes. Sarah, all innocent invitations back to her flat and they were kissing outside the pub, and she had her hands under his shirt. And Sarah was so lithe, not clumsy or a little heavy at times. Sarah's naked breasts wouldn't keep popping the buttons on his shirts in the morning.

But Sarah wasn't the issue, and the woman couldn't hold a conversation about anything but TV or interior decoration, or the courier that had come into work that day that had fancied her. If he was laughing, and Sarah was there, it was never with her unfortunately, which made him feel like a shit.

Yes the issue now was not Sarah, though, but Eve. Eve, his girlfriend, his funny, intelligent, supposedly lovely girlfriend, had married another man for fuck's sake! How was he supposed to forgive that? He remembered now what had attracted him to her in the first place. Apart from her tits, although they were actually the first thing, but of course he would never admit that to her. He had liked how much she made him laugh. Funny girls were usually loud, crass or vulgar, but she wasn't like that. She could be a little loud, but she was never rude. She was never embarrassing even when she got drunk, she never came over all *Birds of a Feather* and dick jokes.

No, she laughed at herself, and at him. She laughed at him all the time, but it was strangely flattering, and never nasty, and it was always followed by that look and that smile that showed she really enjoyed making him laugh. She had a sexy look just after she'd taken the piss, after she'd laughed at the trousers he was wearing, or the haircut he'd had, or something stupid he'd said. But it was always flattering, he wanted her to laugh at him and no-one else. Yet even when it started he had never meant it to last. Never thought it would. He thought they'd go out a few times, hopefully have a bit of sex, and then she'd get bored with him, or him with her, and by then he would have met somebody more his type. More normal, and that would be that. It was really just to see him through a dry patch, and get some sex. He'd always been a breast man.

But it had lasted. Jesus, they'd been together for a year and a half! She hadn't come on all strong either, which he hated. She had just kept taking the piss each time they met, which turned him on. If he was being honest, he was initially more up for it than she was. He knew she fancied Tim, and Tim had even warned him off! He had said that she was a flirt, a bit of a slut with him and some other guys at work, but that had made Henry want her even more. Henry had fancied Tim's girlfriend at first, had introduced them in fact. Tim had been on a lady spree at the time, but he was besotted with her now, and they were getting married. So it wasn't as if Henry was taking Eve off Tim, but it was a little victory. Tim had made some remark, early on, about her having a fair pair, and at least Henry could say that he'd had a hold!

Yes she had grown on him unexpectedly. Before he knew it he had met her family, who were refreshingly normal. Given his own disastrous bloody mess of a home life it was something that had always carried a certain cachet with him. It had been another point in her favour. She was more intelligent than him too, which she never ceased reminding him. Every time she beat him at Trivial Pursuit, or even bloody Scrabble. He'd never played Scrabble with a girlfriend before, he'd always thought it was sad to admit that you liked it. But he was bloody good at it, and had always thrashed everybody at university. She had suggested they play one night, seeing it in his flat, and he'd been surprised she didn't think it was crap. Secretly he was loving the idea of kicking her arse – she brought out the competitive side in him, made him want to win. She was like one ongoing really bloody good game of rugby, she was Bath and he was Leicester, he was England and she was Australia. It had become addictive.

They had played and the game had taken hours, with both of them refusing to give in. It had gone on until 3 a.m., and she had got both blank squares! Luck! This was the reason she had won, and the fact that she'd been able to make LYNX on her last go, with just a Y and an X, and those two bloody blanks. On a triple word score.

And would she let him forget it? Like hell. She was whispering it in his ear before he'd even woken up the next morning, and had emailed him the word LYNX about twenty times that day. That evening in the pub, Tim had cried with laughter at the fact that Henry had tried to tip the board up before they could do the final score. In fact his leg had gone dead and he was just trying to move it and wake it up.

But the whole time she was only teasing him, and kissing

him to make him feel better about not being 'that bright', calling him her 'Lenny', saying she'd buy him some dungarees and a puppy. Thinking about it now, it was just bloody annoying, but at the time it had meant even better sex, when he finally got her home and stopped her talking.

Yes she had grown on him, but he had held something back. Even after the Sarah incident had been resolved, even when he had realized and told her how in love he was. Because Eve was holding back too. Something in his subconscious alerted him to the fact that she had no intention of this lasting. She was having an inward dilemma, claiming not to believe in a 'one', but worrying that he, Henry, was not hers. They weren't particularly alike he knew. He was quieter, but more confident. She spent half her time burying her head in the sand, with arguments, with money. Letters would come from the bank, and go straight in the bin. If she knew she didn't have the money to pay the bills, then she couldn't bear to look at the statement. At the end of each month, when she got paid, she would desperately try and pay off as many debts as she could, as much as she could, and then straight away she was broke again. But somehow she managed to keep going through the month, to keep going out to dinner, and the pub, and parties. Sometimes, because of him lending her the money, but he always got it back, with some stupid little present as 'interest'. The last one had been a pair of pants with her face screened on to the front.

He could tell however, that in the back of her mind, she thought there was something missing. That they didn't have the right chemistry, or that he wasn't quick enough for her, or whatever the ingredient was that would make them last forever. He could sense that at some point she would let him down (his point proven!), or he would get depressed with not being able to completely give himself over to her, and he himself would do something silly. What Henry wanted was a relationship where he could completely trust himself, where he could rely on himself to be faithful, to not hurt that person, no matter what. And he didn't feel it with her.

The feathered dancers have finished "The Lady is a Tramp" and are walking through the audience with their ridiculously long, muscled legs. A cerise explosion of sequins with a huge Adam's apple comes over to his table and sits down.

'You OK, honey?'

A voice so camp you could give it a piano and call it Liberace.

'No. My girlfriend and I, we're breaking up.'

Henry doesn't think it will do any harm to let this guy know he is straight.

'A lot of men end up here, honey, when the little lady gets too much. Nobody understands a man like another man.'

The guy is massaging Henry's forearm, and he realizes that he has been coming over all repressed homosexual.

'No, I still love her. It hasn't made me, I mean, I'm not gay.'

'Not even a little curious?'

'No.'

'Fair enough.'

The voice drops about three octaves, and Henry looks up expecting to see someone else, but it's still the feathers and sequins, just with a man's face and a man's voice.

'To tell you the truth, actually let's get some more drinks in,' the feathers gestures to the bar for two drinks 'I'm having a bit of girl trouble myself.'

'You're having girl trouble? Oh I see, is that what you call each other? Like one of you is the man, and one of you is the woman?'

'No way man, I'm not queer, the boys out the back are queer. That's where they make their big money in here.'

Henry notices that all this guy's mannerisms have changed suddenly, and this bloke sitting across from him is just one of the rugby boys from back home, but in fancy dress.

'Are you Australian?'

'I'm English.'

'No way, on holiday? That sucks, if you and your girlfriend are having a bad time. Bet you always wanted to come to Vegas as well, huh? I'm on holiday too you know, just a few months. Came out here from New York to get a job, get an agent, do some stand-up or something, get signed, get some experience, get representation. It blows. I wind up waiting tables and dressing up as a girl on my nights off, playing pimp to a bar full of drunken married arseholes.'

'That is shit. But at least you look good in the sequins mate.'

'Yeah whatever.'

'So what's your girlfriend trouble? Is she out here with you?' Henry wanted to hear a story as sad as his own.

'No, New York. Oh I did a stupid thing with some girl the other night. Got hammered, confessed to my girlfriend yeah, but hey, I didn't have to tell her. Well really I did, I tell her it means nothing and I love her, and she gets pissedl! What the fuck am I supposed to do? I told her, for crying in the night! She's flying down in a couple of days, see if we can sort it out.'

Henry gets an attack of morality.

'The thing is, man, you don't admit it for her sake, you do it for you. Believe me I know, I did it too. But the thing is, if you tell her, and you don't have to tell her, a lot of blokes wouldn't even tell her and do fifty times worse. But if you tell her, you know she'll feel bad, but you'll feel better. If she hits you, you'll still feel better. Because you got it off your chest. And you tell her you were drunk, and somehow it works out.'

'Well I hope so.'

'Shouldn't have done it in the first place though. Shouldn't have to be easing your conscience. I don't want to do it again. How do I not do it again? You get drunk, look at me now, I'm drunk, and it gets to a point where you don't know what you're doing, and if you're that drunk then you know, any hole's a goal.'

'What's that?'

'You know, any hole's a goal, you never heard that one before?'

'No man, it's kind of disgusting. Ha ha, any hole's a goal. I'll be telling the boys that one. And the chorus girls up there, they could use it too. So is that it? You've been unfaithful and now you're feeling bad?'

'No actually not this time. This time it was her.'

'Well boy, all I can say is if you're both doing it with other people, then you know, maybe you've got to take the hint and call it quits.'

'I know that.'

'Then do it.'

'Thing is, I don't want to. She was drunk she says. Can't even remember it properly. Doesn't even know what she did.'

'Well then how in hell do you know she did anything?

What's your problem? That she might have done something? Jesus, give her a break.'

'It's not that.'

'I Will Survive' has come on in the background and Henry looks round to see the place filling up. The barman brings over two more beers. He looks straight too. Does anybody gay even work here?

'I have proof. Well not really proof.'

'Is she pregnant?'

'Jesus, God knows. No, she's on the pill anyway.'

'Well what's this proof?'

'She – a marriage – she got married to some guy, some fucking waiter, they got blitzed and went to a fucking chapel and got fucking married! I mean, Jesus now do you see? I can't even believe I'm saying this. I can't believe she would do it! They're getting it sorted, broken off or whatever, and she hasn't even seen this guy since, I think, but for fuck's sake.'

Matt, in his feathers and sequins and with horrified realization sweeping over his face, recognizes Henry from the morning before. He hardly saw him then, he was just a big angry guy on the other side of a hotel bedroom when Matt showed her the marriage certificate at the door. She told him to wait downstairs and he gladly went. Henry didn't recognize him. Matt is now, thankfully, wearing a face full of make-up, false eyelashes, false breasts, and a Cleopatra wig. Thank God! But Henry is on a roll.

'I mean I know it's my pride that's hurt, or whatever, but it's like we can't go back now. I did it, she's done it. It's always going to be a part of our history, to bring up, to throw back at each other, to use as an excuse. If we stay together and a year down the line I find myself in a bar with a bird that I fancy, I have an excuse sitting right there. I have a get out of jail free card. Well you married that guy in Vegas, honey, do you remember? I hardly think this is in the same league do you?'

Matt is frozen to his seat. This is unbelievable bad luck. What is happening to him?

'And do you know the worst thing? Do you know why she was drunk with somebody else and not me? Because I had turned her down. That's right, she asked me to marry her that night, and I turned her down. But do you know why I turned her down? No, of course you bloody don't. I said no because I didn't think she meant it. I don't think she would have woken up the next day and still have wanted it. She would have regretted asking, and I would have looked like a twat for accepting. Because I do want to do it. I did, anyway. I know about divorce, you see. My parents are divorced. Are your parents divorced?'

'Yes they are, nine years.'

Matt is running on auto-pilot. His mind is whirring. He needs to get away.

'So you know what I mean, mate. I don't want to go through that. I don't want to put kids through that. That's why we have to be sure you know. And I tried to make her see that, that she needed a good reason to ask me, that she had to have thought it through. But she's got a fucking temper, and she just got angry, and that was that.'

Henry slumps back in his chair, as Matt looks absolutely horrified. This guy in this bar, that he has just started working in, this random guy that he assumed was gay, and he could get some commission off by sending him out the back to one of the leather and moustache gang. This random guy turns out to be the boyfriend of his new wife! His soon to be ex-wife! Matt is not sure, but he could have fucked her. He thinks he might have. He'd be surprised at himself if he hadn't. But of course he won't tell her that. She was blitzed. He'll look like an arsehole.

'Man, I've got to go and do my thing on stage now. But look have another drink on me, yeah? Will you do that? Look, God bless alright. Hope it works out. I think you should work it out. I think you should try, man. It sounds like you love her. Go back and work it out. I bet she feels as bad as you! I gotta go.'

Matt gestures to the bar, and the barman brings over two more beers. He puts them both in front of Henry. Henry doesn't even acknowledge it. He picks up a beer and downs it in two gulps. He puts the bottle down, picks up the next. He has never felt so fucking confused, but he wants to see her, to be near her, to make her pay for how he is feeling, or hug her, or something. He leaves a wad of cash on the table and walks out. He gets his arse pinched three times before he reaches the door. It makes up his mind. He's not gay, but he does want sex.

The Damage is Done

The room is as bleak as before, but now I have my annulment. Well, tomorrow I will have my annulment proper, but for now I just have to settle for the judge's approval. Matt is having the papers sent to the apartment that he is renting for the summer, and is going to phone me when it comes through.

We spent all morning hanging around the court for what turned out to be a five minute hearing. It was very informal, the judge, a woman, asked the circumstances, asked if we both wanted it terminated, and that was it. Matt asked to swear on the Bible for his bit, which I found a little insulting, but if it made him feel better I didn't care. It took all afternoon, filling out the forms, and then Matt had to rush off to his job. He seems pretty sure that we didn't have sex, which is fine by me. His only reasoning for this however, is that he doesn't think he would have been up to it, he was in such a state. Not exactly watertight , but I'll use it as gospel truth with Henry. If he ever talks to me again. Or he at least stays in one place long enough to listen.

Henry is still AWOL. He was in bed last night when I crawled into the room, with a bandage on my chin from my karaoke accident. I tried to hug him, but got a kick in the shins for my trouble. He had disappeared by the time I got up this morning with another raging hangover, and all the painkillers had gone from the bathroom, a mildly amusing revenge that I will let him have.

He had tided his side of the room, which looks eerie in the light that is coming through the window. His toiletries are all in a bag, the cap is on his aftershave. His dirty clothes are in the suitcase under the bed, and his clean clothes are all in the wardrobe. Even his bloody flip-flops are neat, by the side of the bed. Where in hell did he get those? He has done his best to remove any trace of his personality when he is not here, leaving nothing that I can cling onto as him, during his absence. In comparison my side of the room looks like a tornado has got lost on its way through the Midwest, and just ripped through my clothes instead. There is shit everywhere. Personal shit, not actual shit, I haven't sunk that far yet.

I'm lying in bed, it's dark, and the lights from outside are still dazzling. I realize nobody sleeps in this town. I shouldn't be in bed, they want me downstairs, spending dimes, throwing away quarters, or dollar bills or ten dollar bills. That must be where Henry is. He hasn't spoken to me since. He hasn't spoken to me for nearly thirty hours, and I miss him.

There is a jangling at the door, and it's bound to be bloody room service again. Another bloody free snack from Pedro, or whatever his name is with the penchant for ladies' underwear. But he would normally knock at least, '*Señor*, *Señorita*?' in his tiny voice.

It isn't Pedro, it's Henry, and he's drunk. Thank God, he stinks of beer, as he stumbles in. Saint Henry is drunk – now who's sorry he hid the bloody painkillers? Serves him bloody right. Well, not really.

He stumbles in from the bathroom, mumbling swear words at not finding his pills, and collapses on the floor by the chest of drawers. I sit up to check what he is doing, and see him flailing around on the carpet, before he gives up. He drags himself up, and collapses on the bed, half on top of me. I cry out as his complete dead weight smacks my lower body with drunken force.

'Ahhh, Henry, get off!'

'Sorry, hon.' The first two words from him in what seems like an eternity. He is so drunk he has forgotten. Forgotten everything, probably doesn't even know who I am. Great. I'll wake up tomorrow with the man that I love, who now hates me, and who will also have a raging hangover. I cuddle up in the bedclothes, roll away from him, and try to sleep. I'm exhausted. I've been running on nervous energy for the last two days, and only now I realize how much I need some rest.

But Henry is crawling in behind me. Somehow he's managed to pull off his shirt and trousers, and shockingly he is nestling up behind me, arm around my waist, chin on my shoulder, and what would appear to be an erection in my back. Surely he hasn't forgotten everything! Tentatively I try to bridge the silence.

'Baby, I'm sorry, I'm so sorry, you do know that don't you?'

'Shut up, you sound like my bloody dad. And I won't be my mum. I am not my mum.'

I know what he is talking about and I shut up. But he's kissing my neck, and the neck always gets it. He's doing it softly, he's licking just behind my ear, so gently, and he smells musky, like beer and cigarettes. He doesn't even want angry sex, he wants affection. He wants a sign of love. I try to turn around but he won't let me. He just keeps kissing my neck, my shoulders, stroking my thigh, opening my legs, sweeping his hands down the inside. He stokes my stomach, moving up towards my breasts, lightly pinching. I try to reach around with my hand to his dick, but he won't let me, keeps me on my side, facing away from him, pins my hands above my head, holds them gently on the pillow. This is not angry sex, this is loving sex, but then I realize. This is loving sex without having to look at my face.

The tears roll down my cheeks annoyingly, trickling so slowly as he enters me from behind and we start to rock gently to and fro. I know now I've ruined everything. He can't even look at me.

Vegas – Single and Loving it

Las Vegas, this bizarre Mecca for young lovers. Come and get married in minutes. Come and seal your love, without the pomp, or expense, or unnecessary waiting times. Come and do it now because you are both besotted by love, and you want to be together.

But Vegas is not what is seems. Vegas doesn't really want you married. It wants you single. It wants you on your own, and it proves its point in the nastiest way. It invites you to your own impromptu wedding, to prove more than anything, that you should never be doing 'matrimony' in the first place. It makes a mockery of it, because Vegas doesn't need a partner, or want a partner. It takes your most magical day, and dresses it in plastic flowers, and dirty crushed velvet. It does everything in its power to make it the most meaningless day of your life. It denies you the luxury of friends or family, it seeks not to cushion the blow, but spotlight the mistake. Vegas is a town twinned with nowhere, and with no desire to remind you of anywhere else. Think Los Angeles, think

Miami. Think New York, think Chicago, think Boston. But think Vegas? Vegas has no future, and no past. It doesn't want kids. Like some murderous mother who eats her young, Vegas will do anything to stamp out its offshoots. It wants merely to be worshipped on its own, in the middle of nowhere, and held up for its splendid originality, and the unabashed materialism at its core. It is America. It is at the heart, and it is the heart. It is a twisted absurd vision of the United States in close-up. It's a jumble of people, none of whom really call it home. And what are they all doing there? The pursuit of the almighty dollar. It's the get-rich-quick capital of the world. Once, not so long ago, some drug fuelled crazy put Vegas under the microscope and saw swarms of people 'humping the American Dream', and how right he was. This isn't love: Vegas doesn't want to be party to anything so existentially meaningful as love. It's a town screwing itself. It's the ultimate narcissism. Las Vegas is America the great, America the Free, America the bold, having an almighty wank. Just don't get caught in the rain.

Fraying Seams

We have woken up on opposite sides of the bed. We couldn't be further away from each other on the same mattress. Henry fell asleep as soon as the sex was over, as soon as I had orgasmed. He had kept on until I had. It was some small victory for him. I lie here now, in the early light and the already rising heat, just staring at the walls. It didn't rain last night as it should have to clear the air, and the heat is beginning to build in the room, in the atmosphere.

I walk to the window, pull out the mosquito mesh barrier, and lean out. The doorman is washing down the pavement outside Jacks across the road, and the water evaporates straight away, rises up to the Vegas heavens. The McDonalds down the road is open; I haven't actually seen it close since the day we got here, or since I had woken up in its car park with Matt. Fast food, drive-thru, everything at speed. The palm trees below me, surrounding the front of our hotel are all covered in dust. The temperature is rising. It is 8 a.m.

I feel the prickles in my hair, sweat mixed with hairspray,

mixed with dirt, but I don't feel like showering. I feel the damp at the back of my knees, in the small of my back. Henry stirs behind me, edging closer to his side of the bed, as near to it as he can get without falling out. But he doesn't wake up. Refuses to wake up.

I look in the opposite direction, down the strip. People are in last night's clothes, tottering drunkenly down the pavement. Women in dresses, men in tuxes, lop-sided hair and ties undone. Suddenly I am conscious of only wearing a pair of knickers, and lean down to pull on Henry's shirt, think better of it, and reach for the top I wore under my toga. It has blood on it, or red wine. It makes me hotter, depressed. Dirty clothes always make me depressed.

Henry stirs again, and looking out of the window, with my back to him, I sense that he is awake. But I don't look around, I can't face the silence, or the conversation, or whatever I'll be met with. I hear him pad from the bed into the bathroom, and the door close behind him. The water comes on straight away. Henry at least feels the need to be clean, to wash last night off him. I am hanging on to it. I hear him coughing hard in the shower.

I get back into bed, onto dirty sheets, more heat from the pillows, laying on creases that dig into my legs. I start in the middle of the bed, but roll over to his side.

On the floor are the trousers he was wearing last night when he stumbled in, hammered. The trousers I bought him before we came away. I am staring at the hem, which is coming undone already.

They weren't expensive, and I didn't even particularly like them, but they grew on me as soon as Henry put them on. The first time he wore them, on the second day we were out here, I decided he had been right, and how much I liked them. They are fraying already. I won't sew them up. He can fix them himself.

I need that shower now. I could just walk in there with him, but I can't take the result: rejection, or sex like last night – sex that actually pushes us further apart, that makes us hate each other for being so weak, and for needing contact with the other so much that we ignore the reason for not talking.

I have to go to reception today, see about cancelling the days in San Francisco. We were due to fly out there tomorrow, but we'll be going home. It occurs to me for the first time that Henry hasn't left already. He could have just packed his bags, got the next flight home. Why not? It would have painted him in a bad light I suppose, and he would hate that. Leaving me here, stranded and on my own, Henry would never be seen to do something like that, no matter what I'd done. This way we can go home and he will be the saint, and I will be the witch. He has stayed to ensure that, no matter what, he holds all the cards, he can say yes or no to us, and is completely blameless. Either that or the planes were all full up.

In a way I wish he had left. Unless I can still get him to talk to me.

This heat, this unbearable heat already, or is it me? I feel my forehead – don't let me get ill, not now.

Maybe Henry will have lunch with me today, go somewhere and talk. The truth is I don't really want to talk, I just want him to make his mind up and then tell me what we are doing, and I will do it on the condition that we never have to discuss the whole damn thing again.

Henry pads out of the shower, a towel around his waist. He looks at me, and looks away. I get up and walk to the bathroom. With my back to him,

'I'm going to sort out my ticket today, Henry. I'll cancel San Francisco and fly to Heathrow tomorrow morning instead. Do you want me to do yours as well?'

'Fine.'

'Fine. It'll be about two in the morning I think.'

'Fine.'

'Fine.'

I walk into the bathroom, and gasp at the steam, Henry has had the hottest shower in the world, in the middle of the fucking desert! Sadist. I turn on the cold water and get straight under the spray, which I can bear for about five seconds, before I turn the hot on slightly, and wash away the last few days.

Washing my hair, scrubbing my scalp, I suddenly wonder – what am I so desperate to hold on to? Shouldn't Henry and I just sit down and say fair enough, how long do we have to go on pissing each other off, hurting each other, before we realize we aren't meant to be. We fell in love with the wrong people, and when it happens you know from the start that somewhere down the line it's going to go wrong. Because there isn't a real reason making it right. I knew it from the start. This is what happens when you try desperately to be with someone you shouldn't be with. This is the divorce rate in practice. This is five years down the line if Henry had not so wisely declined my offer of marriage. I just had the drunken sense to bring it to a head early enough, and leave no question in our minds that we shouldn't be together.

I should be waiting for my 'one'. The answer is wait.

Of course it's going to make me cry. Why wouldn't I be sad? I'm crying but I feel like a weight has been lifted from my shoulders. I feel that, now I have decided what I'm going to do, I can go out there and talk to him, demand that he talk to me. Because I can't get rejected now. I can't get turned down now.

Of course I'm running away, you're no genius for working that out. I don't want to get hurt any more.

But by the time I get back into the room, Henry has gone out again. Bastard. Just as I have decided what to say. He knew it. He knew that I had decided and the bastard has buggered off before I can tell him.

I put my make-up on, which feels like it's going to slip right back off my face from the heat, and I dry my hair. I take my time getting dressed, hoping he will come back, but he doesn't.

I tidy my half of the room, put the lid on everything, chuck all the dirty underwear in the suitcase under the bed. I strip the bed, and chuck all the sheets in a pile by the door. The phone rings, and it's reception, saying Matt is downstairs to see me.

In reception Matt is sitting on a sofa by a massive cactus. It's one big still life of testosterone but I can't say it affects me. He does look good however, despite the heat, with his polo shirt and his jeans. This is a man who should definitely be on television, he looks the part. Strangely, this is sort of my ex-husband. Even more strangely, on closer inspection, he appears to be wearing mascara. OK. Whatever floats your boat.

'Hey,' he kisses me hello, like it's fine now to touch me, because we are 'annulled' after all. He hands me a piece of paper, and I feel like we should get a photo or something, but what the hell for? To prove to the girls at home how good-looking he was? It doesn't bother me. We could pose, waving our slips of paper, two very enthusiastic thumbs up. I realize now that this is going to be no more than an anecdote. This man is going to mean no more to me than a cheap laugh at a dinner table somewhere in London's suburbs. At least he'll get a mention, I doubt I'll even make an appearance in his polite conversation.

'Hey you look really good – did you sort things out with your boyfriend?'

'Aha.' I can't be arsed to go into to it.

He breathes a sigh of relief. How sweet, maybe he does have a few feelings for me after all. Only now do I notice the badge on his shirt. He is standing in front of me, and smiling like we almost know each other, in a concerned way, and he looks ridiculously handsome. He has handed me annulment papers, and really it's a big deal, but it is all I can do to stop myself laughing out loud. He is wearing a badge on his shirt that reads 'Real Men Love Jesus.' I appear to have married a man of the cloth. NO! He must be having a laugh, but it explains a lot. Maybe I am on camera somewhere being filmed from behind a palm tree. It's a comfort at least, to know that he has the Lord to turn to in this hour of need. However it does make me feel like his mother, I don't know why, I just come over all maternal.

'So Matt, what are you going to do with the rest of your holiday? Did you find a better job yet?'

'Yes and no. I mean I've kind of been distracted by this whole thing. I had to tell my girlfriend, and she went kinda psycho. She's flying in tomorrow morning. I thought maybe it might help if you met her or something, like you could help explain, you know if she sees you, and that you have sorted it all out with your boyfriend.'

'Oh Matt, I'm so sorry, but we fly out tonight, so I can't. That's such a shame because I would have loved to have helped.' I'm lying to a messenger of God. 'I'm really sorry. Anyway I have to sort a few things out at the desk, so I should probably go.'

'Oh yeah well, I'll see ya.'

'Oh OK, take care.'

A peck on the cheek.

'Bye then, I hope your boyfriend is OK.'

'He'll be fine. Bye Matt.' Why does he care about Henry so much? Typical bloke, always blame the woman, feel sorry for the man.

At the desk they give me a number to phone about flights. Apparently it shouldn't be too difficult, because of the time of week. I'll lose most of my San Francisco money, but it can't be helped. It would be pretty callous of me to go on my own.

So I'll be flying out at 2 a.m. tomorrow morning, and so will Henry.

Do You Know Lester?

Henry knows he shouldn't have got close again. He shouldn't have had sex with her. He shouldn't have instigated it. He shouldn't have got drunk, and they shouldn't have had sex. He feels pathetic. In one look this morning she managed to convey everything – if Eve wants him, she can still have him. He wanted her so much last night, and she knew it. This higher moral ground he has been taking seems like an effect now. He looks like a joke. And a fake.

Shamefully, Henry bolted from the room this morning while she was in the shower. Any control he has previously had of this situation, or over his emotions, was offered up to her nakedly last night, on a plate. His true self still wants her, and needs her, and it was plainly there, on last night's sheets, for them both to see. He stood in front of her, in just a towel this morning, and he wanted to slip his own skin. He didn't want to be wearing his face as he looked at her. Every feeling was there, in his eyes, for her to see, and what he hated most was having it all reflected back at him. He can only dream that he will have the courage to face her again, and still walk away.

This is just too fucking painful. His stomach knots at the fractured memories of last night. He has blurred visions of pouring his heart out to some really ugly woman in a gay bar, before he remembers he was actually talking to another man, in drag.

Now, aimlessly kicking along some Las Vegas street, head down, shoulders hung low, he wonders how long it will take to get her out of his system. Right now, he seems to be living some sort of hellish existence, but it is an existence with Eve at the core. How long will it take not to think of her every minute, of being with her, inside her, hating her and loving her at the same time? It feels at this moment that she will always be there. It is dawning on him that he is experiencing what a woman's magazine would term 'heartbreak'. But he's not going to call it that. He is going to call it 'a low point in his life', and that's enough. You don't dress these feelings up, and romanticize them; they are unbearable in themselves, without all the hearts and flowers, and oh the great romantic poetry of it all! Feelings like this, if they have to be put into words, should sound harsh and cruel, and to be avoided at all costs. They should sound painful as hell, like acid in the eyes. But 'heartbreak' almost sounds like something worth trying. Henry never wants to hurt like this again. No, it should be called 'fucking absolute despairing unbelievable nauseating fucking pain.' That Elvis song should actually have been called 'Fucking absolute despairing unbelievable nauseating fucking pain Hotel'. Doesn't have the same ring to it of course. And rhyming could be a problem.

Eve has said she will sort the flights out for tonight, and he has hastily phoned the airline from reception to say she will be changing them both. She will have no idea he has already changed his, and could a note please be put on the computer changing his flight back to the original details so that she will be none the wiser. Luckily he got a bloke on the phone, and he did it after little persuading. The first time he had called, a woman answered, and Henry hung up immediately. He wouldn't have had a hope in hell with a woman. Henry plays out the imaginary conversation in his head

'Excuse me, madam, but could you please not let my soon to be ex-girlfriend know I was deserting her in Las Vegas, because even though she is a cheating bastard, I still don't want to upset her. Would you mind? Oh, yes you would mind. I see. You think I'm an absolute shit? Oh right, well I won't try to change your mind then. I'm sorry? And do you kiss your mother with that mouth madam? I have never found expletives for the female genitals that endearing in a woman, but you seem to think that I fit that bill, so I'll thank you for your time nonetheless, and say goodbye.'

As it was, the bloke pretty much did it without question. Henry didn't need to explain his absolute degradation to him, which was a small mercy. Eve will be none the wiser, and will change their flights simultaneously herself.

In fourteen hours' time he will be flying back to London, thank Christ, but what to do now, for the next few hours at least, is a problem. Henry can't spend all day packing. Besides it is mostly all done already, in his effort to keep all his clothes out of her sight in case she flew into a rage and cut them all into strips. Most of his shirts seemed intact, but he noticed, getting dressed this morning, that she has unpicked the hem on his new trousers. She has hated them from the start, but that was just petty.

Yes Eve can be petty sometimes. She has a childish spoilt streak running through her that rears its head whenever she bloody feels like it. But if she wants to be childish, Henry can be childish. How would she like it if the shoe was on the other foot? Not the cutting up of clothes thing (she would slit his throat for that) but what if he, Henry, were to get married this afternoon, before they fly home? Let's see what the verdict on that one would be. If the roles were reversed, would she be quite so understanding? He thinks not! Henry is seized with the wild-eyed craziness of a man about to do something utterly stupid. Picking up his chin which had been close to grazing on the pavement, puffing up his solid rugby-playing chest, running his hand through his thick dark hair, Henry looks around, and surveys this Vegas walkway. He, Henry, is a big British hunk of a man, and an unbelievable catch for some lucky lovely about to cross his path. He's tall, he has great teeth; he is like a thoroughbred among men, a god among mortals. Furthermore he is ready to marry anyone, anyone right now, this instant, bring it on! As manly as he is looking, as good as he feels, Henry has to concede that there is nobody around fitting the bill.

A pair of octogenarians are dragging their heels towards him, and a young man in a cropped pink top showing off his midriff, is crossing the street just ahead of them. He might be in Las Vegas, and this might just be revenge against Eve, but Henry is not going to marry a man. That is his only pre-requisite – his wife must not have a penis. Apart from that, it's firmly a case of anything goes!

Henry starts jogging up the road, a man with a plan, a guy on a mission, holding his considerable torso back and up, the way you run out on to a rugby pitch to put fear into the hearts of your competitors. This run said 'don't fuck with this guy, he's big and he's handsome and he's looking for a mate!' Henry is giving it Neanderthal.

Feeling almost divinely confident he jogs around the corner and onto the main street, and there are people everywhere! How does he choose? Which lucky lady gets this winning lottery ticket? He slows his pace, stands squarely on the pavement and eyes up a blonde walking past. Good but no cigar, looks younger at a distance than she obviously is close up, and besides which, he had always pictured himself marrying a brunette . . . like Eve. Henry wakes up to himself straight away – he is getting distracted from the job in hand. The aim is not to find a woman he likes, just some passable bit about to get the best meal ticket of her life! Oh yes, he is on fire! Besides which, she has to be blonde! That would be the icing on the cake. He could just picture Eve's face now, registering Henry and his new bride, and thinking 'at least he had the sense to pick a girl with natural hair'. No, this had to be as offensive to Eve as possible and that meant one thing more than any other – BLONDE!

Actually he *can* picture Eve's face, registering what he has done. She doesn't cry excessively for a woman, but when she does, and just before she breaks down, and as her eyes well up, her chin always crumbles, and she chews her bottom lip to try and stop it moving. Henry's mother looked unspeakably awful just before crying, her face seemed to fall apart right in front of him. But Eve never looks too bad. It makes him feel incredibly possessive when she cries, it's one of the only times he feels like he can really protect her, or that she even needs his protection. He is so much bigger than she is, and he can hold her, and make her feel safe, and she relaxes into his arms and . . . distracted again. Goddammit! Why can't he concentrate?!

Henry sees something blonde walking towards him and dashes towards her, his eyes kind of blurring, a little too much speed off the blocks. He pulls up short, but not short enough, and despite attempting to throw himself out the way at the last second, manages to take her shoulder, and her bag with him.

'You fucking asshole! You're not getting this bag!'

The woman, approximately forty-five, peroxided and Californian, and shrieking in one of those voices that generally only dogs can hear, is not happy about this potential husband disguised as a bag snatcher. Henry finds himself kicked to the ground, desperately trying to fend off her tiny, muscled legs, simultaneously trying to return the bag. This woman is the product of twenty years of daily aerobics: she is carrying no fat on her skinny frame and Henry, used to some damning rugby tackles every Saturday, just feels like he is being prodded by a small stick. An annoying stick nonetheless.

'Too fucking right you're giving my bag back, huh, tough guy? Didn't expect me to be judo-trained, did ya, huh? Didn't count on me having pepper spray either, did ya?!'

The woman is screeching and reaching into her retrieved bag for Mace. Henry realizes what is about to happen and tries to jump to his feet. The woman lurches forward with another pointless kick. She aims for his Adam's apple, and makes contact, but Henry doubts it will even leave a bruise, as he pretty much picks her up by the leg, and plonks her down next to him and gets to his feet.

'Please, Miss, listen to me, don't spray me with that!'

The woman has been screaming since the moment Henry touched her, a high-pitched wail that she has obviously been taught in self defence class as the best defence against anything, including nuclear war. It is the worst noise Henry has ever heard. Nothing could ever combat it. To avoid touching her again, Henry is now bobbing and ducking to escape the generous amounts of pepper spray being squirted in his general direction. Nobody walking past seems that interested, possibly granting Henry and his attacker a bemused glance at most.

He should just grab her arms because she does mean to do him harm after all, but he doesn't feel it's the right time or place to re-display his strength.

'Please, Miss – Jesus!' Henry ducks at the last minute to avoid Mace in the face,

'Miss, I was not trying to steal your bag. On the contrary, I was going to ask you . . .' It occurs to Henry that maybe he doesn't want to project himself as some sort of fruit loop nutcase. But the woman has stopped spraying, and is standing stock still, staring at him intently.

'Miss, I am so sorry, Please I would never have dreamt of stealing your bag, I was merely running down the street . . . yes, is there something you want to say?'

The Californian is holding one leathery brown hand up in front of him, suggesting he stop speaking. Her nails shoot up inches above her fingers, and appear to have little palm trees painted on to each one, with tiny diamonds where the coconuts would be.

'Please don't spray me with your Mace, I really didn't mean to do anything, it was completely accidental. What? Say it! What do you want to say?!'

She is still just standing there, staring at him, with her hand out in front of her, palm facing him. The palm is orange. Henry just stares back, and she starts to shake her head dramatically from side to side.

'No, mister, you just wait – are you . . . are you European?' Henry winces. Oh God, that terrible Californian nasal whine.

'European? Well I'm from England if that's what you mean, yes.'

'Oh my God – this is karma. I was just thinking about my cousin, Therese, and she lives in Leicester now, (she pronounces it Lichester! Henry winces again) with her husband. A British man, like you! Oh my God, I cannot believe that, I have not thought about her for months!'

She pronounces every syllable in 'Lichester' very definitely, which instantly annoys the fuck out of Henry, as it does every Englishman who ever has to hear an American saying Leicester, or Leicester Square, or Leicestershire. But she is putting her pepper spray back in her bag, smiling and smacking her forehead.

'Thank God, you're putting that spray away. I am so sorry.'

'No honey I'm sorry. You're British! I nearly sprayed a British man with pepper spray! Like Prince Charles! I am so, so, so, so, so, so, so, sorry. Have you ever been to Lichester? My cousin, Therese, is married to a man called David Martin. He has kinda brownish hair, about the same height as me, he's kinda pale – do you know him? He works in computers, in Lichester.' Henry, although realizing he has had a lucky escape with the Mace, cannot suppress the English arrogance that has been bred in him since childhood. And he cannot bear the thought of hearing this woman say 'Lichester' one more time.

'Actually, madam, it's pronounced Leicester, like the name . . . Lester.'

'Oh my God, your voice is so, so, so cute! Say something else. I love Europeans!'

'What, all Europeans? Even the French?'

'Oh sure, I love all you guys. Say something else! This is so much fun – I just love your voice. If I came to Europe, would you all love my accent the way I love yours?'

'Europe is a pretty big place. We are not 'all', we are very separate. We are not all the same. We are nothing like the French, and we are certainly nothing like the Germans!'

'Oh sure, honey, I know that, you all speak different languages right?'

'That's right.'

'Say something in German would ya?'

'I'm sorry, I don't speak German.' Henry is sickened by this woman already. He's starting to wish he had stolen her bag, especially if it has her passport in it. He could have saved a lot of his perfectly innocent compatriots being subjected to this same inane conversation over and over again, by just chucking it in the river.

'Oh OK, well say something in French.'

'*Non.*'

'Oh go on.'

'No, you don't understand, I just did. '*Non*' is French for 'no'.

'Oh go on, just one thing. Just say one thing. I love the French.'

'But I'm not French, I'm British. I'm English.'

'Oh OK. Sure. I'm sorry. I just love your accent is all.' The Californian's feelings are hurt, and Henry almost feels bad, before reminding himself that in the short time he has spent with her, he has actually begun to hate her.

'I'm sorry about the bag. It was nice to meet you.' Henry bids a hasty retreat. He cannot marry an American. He is beginning to think Eve was actually incredibly brave to try it. She was obviously very, very drunk.

As Henry walks away, his plan gone to pot, shoulders again deflated, he decides the impromptu marriage thing was not one of his better ideas. Besides which, if he is being honest, Henry has always envisaged getting married in a morning suit, with all the lads as ushers, in a big country church, with a hell of a lot of drink, and cigars, and dirty jokes in the best man's speech. Looking around now, and as far as the eye can see, are ridiculous pink chapels and palm trees and neon signs saying 'Love Boat Church', and 'Loving You Chapel of Our Lord'. He is taken by the urge to see inside one of these nightmare testimonials to cheap love, and witness Eve's betrayal second-hand. He walks up to a particularly garish cerise door with a horseshoe as a door knob, and ducks his head into the darkness inside.

Hitting the Right Note

I daydream sometimes, but my daydreams are strange things. They are not other places, other times. I do not find myself looking up at the Pyramids, or spending money I don't have. My daydreams are peculiarly realistic. They are invariably set in this place, and this time, and the players are the players in my life already. There is no Cary Grant in the corner, sitting on a cactus, reciting dirty limericks. The furthest I get from my reality is that I imagine my hair looking great.

So what do I dream?

Probably the same as you. I dream that I had said something else, that I had ended a conversation on a triumph. I dream that whatever I am doing will work out right. I dream I can sing sometimes, or at least that I can hit some notes, but that's not often. This dream usually happens when I am actually singing, and Henry looks at me, wincing, strangely in pain. Henry carries a tune much more successfully than I do, and my God does he know it! Given the opportunity he will always start singing.

Picture us now, in the car, on the way back from his mother's, or my sister's, or bloody Sainsbury's for that matter. A song comes on the radio that we haven't heard for a while, and he starts to hum. Within seconds he is singing away, making up the lyrics he doesn't know, and happening upon that completely unselfconscious place where putting feeling into frankly ludicrous words does not matter. But then, I try to join in. I want to find that place where I can just sing along, too, and not actually register the truly awful noises I am making. And for a matter of moments I am there, even if I have had to adjust my pitch a couple of times on my way. Then I see that sideways wince from Henry at the wheel, and I realize he has stopped singing.

So then it's just me, singing a little too loudly to a song with too many notes for me to hit even half of them, and I stop, feeling like an absolute fool. He does it every time. I class it as a form of mental abuse. Henry maintains that I am lucky not to have experienced the physical kind, given my singing voice, which is harsh.

Within seconds of my shutting up, he will start singing again. Of course then I leave him to it and stare stupidly out of the car window, wondering why I can't just appreciate my boyfriend's nice singing voice, instead of feeling the need to join in.

On a couple of occasions, when I have found myself in a particularly obnoxious mood, I have sung even louder at the first sign of his customary wince, just screaming out ill-fitting lyrics. But I have also found that it's no fun proving a point if my complete degradation is involved in the process.

Yes when I daydream, it just involves my normal life, but with a bit more talent, and a little more tan thrown in. I picture my everyday conversations and behaviour, but with me, the main player, sporting ridiculously full hair, and a complexion that's brown as a berry. Of course now, I will daydream of life exactly as it was before. The hair may not look great, the tan may be non-existent, but Henry will be smiling at least.

You're the Devil in Disguise

Henry is at the back of the chapel. He is more than welcome. He thought it would be a little harder to get into an actual service. Isn't it supposed to be private, after all? Isn't a wedding supposed to be filled with a room full of family and friends, and well-wishers? Not complete strangers, smelling of pepper spray, surly, and ready to wreak havoc? Henry thinks he poses a threat, but nobody else seems to notice. This takes the wind out of his sails slightly. He was prepared for a scrap of some sort, a minor skirmish, but nothing.

The outside of the chapel was pink, which he found offensive enough in itself, but nothing could have prepared him for the colours on the inside! The door led into a tiny dark passageway, and a smaller door at the end of this, through which Henry squeezed himself, and which opened into a smallish room that looked like somebody had vomited paint on to the walls. They were speckled Hot Pink and Sunshine Yellow. Two seconds of staring at them in disbelief and Henry felt a headache coming on. A plastic potted palm tree stood next to a reception desk, behind which sat a hugely obese woman wearing a floral tent and a veil. The fat on her upper arms overhung her elbows somehow, and she was sweating buckets. She wore rings that looked like they were severing her fingers from her hand. They gave the impression that if she waved, each finger would drop off in turn and land on the desk in front of her.

The colour of the walls was only broken up by randomly placed and framed certificates. Henry assumed that these were their credentials, or at least proof that they were permitted to perform some sort of ceremony, even if only dog weddings. However on closer inspection he found they were an assortment of oddities, ranging from the fat receptionist's driving license, to an 'I rode the Back To The Future Ride and survived!' certificate from Universal Studios, LA, dated June 1995.

There were plastic flowers everywhere – hanging from the ceiling, in vases, even on the floor. Henry could hear some kind of tinny Casio organ playing a tiny two-fingered rendition of 'Here Comes the Bride' from behind a set of double doors at the back of the room. There was a fire escape door behind reception, and that was it. No other escape. Henry realized he looked conspicuous, when the floral tent coughed loudly a second time.

'Can I help ya, sir? Are you booked in for today, because we're kinda busy! A hell of a lot of people getting married today!' The receptionist burst into loud nervous laughter at this remark, looking mighty precarious on a chair built for a lot smaller woman. Henry looked from side to side to see what was funny, realized she was laughing at what she had just said, and determined to put this woman at ease. She obviously found him a little menacing. But she had already turned back to her magazine as Henry spoke, startling her,

'I was wondering, sorry, hello, I'm Henry. I was wondering if I could possibly hang around for a bit, see a ceremony. My girlfriend and I are thinking of using your delightful chapel here' Henry gestured about him 'for our wedding. I promised her I would come and have a look, because she doesn't want anything too cheap. But this is just lovely. Do you think I might be permitted to sit in on a ceremony, just to really get a feel for the place you understand.'

Whenever Henry is attempting to be charming, particularly to a foreigner, he comes over all public school English gentleman. But it worked.

'Oh sure, just slip in at the back. Through those double doors.'

'What now? But the ceremony has already started hasn't it?'

'Oh we're very laid-back here, the Reverend won't mind.'

'But what about the couple, I mean, the people getting married – won't they object?'

'Do ya' think? No, I'm sure it'll be just fine. Just slip in at the back and try not to bang inta' anything!' The woman started to laugh hysterically again, and Henry took this as his cue to go and witness a wedding.

Now, as he opens the door into the ceremony, he hears a thud, and turns around to see the fat receptionist's legs in the air; she has fallen backwards off her chair laughing. He turns to go and help her, but the commotion has caught the attention of the 'Reverend' and his human sacrifices at the front of the chapel.

'Come in or get out.'

The 'Reverend' looks a little bit fascist, a little bit sinister, a little like Mafia, a lot like Christopher Walken. He looks . . . possessed. Henry has no doubt in that first second that he is the Devil in a smart suit. He glares at Henry over his order of service. His hair is slicked back, and his bright blue eyes are as big as footballs. He speaks in a tone of measured anger, which intimates he might in fact be carrying a weapon. He is about forty-five, but carries his age incredibly well. He is long-faced and tanned. His collar is starched white, and Henry spots expensive cuff links, even from this distance. He is pristine: personified ice.

The two teenagers at the front of the church look anxious as hell, as Henry hovers at the door. The bride looks as if she has been crying. They are both wearing T-shirts and jeans. She is holding a bunch of cheap flowers, the type you get from a garage when you forget to buy a thank-you present en route to somebody's house for the weekend.

They are young, and nervous, and are holding hands tightly. Henry looks over at the bride and half smiles. She half smiles back.

'I'm so sorry.' Henry enters the chapel closing the door on the big bundle of flesh trying to find its feet at reception. These kids don't need the interruption. One of them will bolt, and it will be Henry's fault. Henry also has the feeling that if he leaves the room now, this devil in God's clothing will devour them both, or at the least cut them up into small pieces with a chainsaw.

'Please continue.'

'Thank you so much.' The Reverend holds Henry's gaze for one moment too long for his liking. Henry begins to feel a little anxious himself.

'And do you, Billy Grechi, take Annie to be your lawfully wedded wife?'

'I do . . . sir'.

'Good. Well done. Congratulations, yadda yadda yadda. Sign the book outside and you're done.'

The teenagers look at each other again. Their nerves do not appear to have eased. It dawns on Henry that it was not getting married these two young innocents feared, it was the Reverend himself.

'I'm sorry sir, we paid for the Elvis as well.'

'Is that right?' the Reverend speaks slowly and deliberately, and the room temperature seems to drop twenty degrees. Henry doesn't want to see this guy angry.

'Billy, it's fine, we're done, let's go.' Annie, the new wife, seems to experience the same fear as Henry, that the Reverend might pull out a piece and shoot them all.

'No hon, we paid for it. Sir, we paid for "Love Me Tender", the Elvis impersonator.'

'Well he's sick today. Actually he's more than sick. He died on Tuesday.'

'Billy, let's just go.' The young bride is pulling at the arm of her new husband, but Billy has got an attack of courage, and he is standing his ground. He is a husband now after all.

'I'm sorry, sir, but we paid for "Love Me Tender", an' I think we should get it.'

'Well, if you paid for it, you should get it now, shouldn't you.' The Reverend stares at young Billy evenly, without blinking. His lips have barely moved. His eyes seem to be growing as each second passes. He carries on staring, while his head cocks very slowly to the side, sizing Billy up. Billy coughs nervously under the weight of this demented stare. It snaps the Reverend into action. Henry, Billy and Annie all jump.

'Could you just hold on for one moment. I won't be long.' The Reverend turns on his heel and walks slowly, suavely behind a curtain.

'Billy, please can we just go. We're done, and this guy gives me the creeps.'

'Hon, we paid for it, and we're gonna get it! This Elvis guy didn't die, he's probably out the back having a smoke.'

With that the curtain swishes aside again, and the Reverend reappears, this time in an Elvis wig and a sparkly flared jump-suit, encrusted in fake diamonds. Music starts booming out of speakers Henry hadn't noticed, hanging from the ceiling. The Reverend walks to the middle of the makeshift altar on platform shoes, and strikes an Elvis pose. Billy and Annie eye each other nervously and edge backwards. Billy looks around at Henry, for support. Henry nods at him conspiratorially, letting him know he has his back. The last thing Henry wants is for young Billy to back down from this Nazi creep in front of his new bride. It is imperative that Billy starts as he means to go on, with backbone.

The Reverend begins to sing "Love Me Tender", or rather speak "Love Me Tender", in time to the music, while staring young Billy down. But Billy stands firm, with Annie hiding behind him, peering out over his shoulder. The music stops.

'Did you get your money's worth, Mr and Mrs Grechi, or would you like me to stuff my face with hamburgers, throw up, and pass out in front of you? I could do a little karate if you want? I mean, is there anything else that would make this a little more memorable for you?' The Reverend had the straightest, most deadpan voice Henry has ever heard. Henry has had enough. He clears his throat.

'I'll sing it – what are the words again?' Henry's mind has gone blank. 'Shit, just start me off. How does the first verse go? Just give me that and I'll carry on. How does it go?'

The Reverend glares at Henry, who glares back, as menacingly as he can, clearly looking into the eyes of Satan. A fight is going to kick off after all. Seconds lapse, as the two men stare at each other from either end of the chapel.

Henry is distracted, and looks away first, at Billy and Annie edging backwards towards the door, opening it behind them while staring straight ahead.

The door closes, but a moment later bursts open again, just long enough for Annie to shout, 'You asshole', at the good Reverend.

Shrugging his shoulders, raising an eyebrow and smiling, he moves back behind the curtain.

Henry feeling a surge of indignation on Billy and Annie's behalf, and psyched up for a fight, strides up to the curtain and throws it back. The Reverend, in underpants and his Elvis wig, is chopping cocaine on a Bible.

'What the fuck? What the fuck do you think you're doing punk, get the fuck outta here.' Despite being almost naked, the Reverend is not fazed.

'I apologize for the intrusion but I just wanted to say that I think you're a complete sadistic bastard, and you scared those kids half to death, and ruined one of the happiest days of their lives.'

'So fucking sue me, dickwad. Happiest days of their life? Have you seen this place – take a look around, it's a fucking dump. If they wanted spiritual they should have gone to a church. Now get the fuck outta here.' The Reverend turns back to his coke cutting.

'That's as maybe, but it was your responsibility, as their priest and everything, to at least be nice.'

'Fuck off.'

'Are you even a real Reverend?'

'Am I fuck – get the hint, jerk-off, that marriage will last five minutes, they were both in diapers. What the hell has it got to do with you anyway? Playing good Samaritan, huh? Nice singing by the way. But let me tell you, they don't need it here. This is the last place for religion. You seen my wife out front? On reception? Now tell me there's a God, OK. Tell me that when I married Miss former fucking Nevada out there, and I swore in sickness and in Goddamn health in front of our Lord, that he wasn't laughing his ass off at the prospect of me in ten years' time. Now will you please just fuck off.'

'That is really sad.'

'You bet your ass it is, I have to roll her out of bed every morning.'

'So get a divorce.'

'I'm a fucking Reverend, how would that look? I wouldn't work in this town again. Jesus, do you have shit for brains or what?'

'I thought you just said you weren't qualified?'

'You say tomato blah blah blah.' Henry is thrown. This is not at all what he was expecting. The Reverend strokes a line up his nose as Henry backs out. He has seen all he wants to see. What if Eve got married like this – does it even count? Bizarrely seeing this whole thing has shifted everything in his mind. He had pictured her and that guy hugging in front of a benevolent old Irish priest, in candlelight, with "Ave Maria" playing in the background. But what if her experience was even worse than this – of course it was, they were both drunk, for Christ's sake, she probably didn't even say 'I do'.

Walking out into reception, Henry's brain seems to clear slightly; a fog seems to lift. He can't forgive her for sleeping with another guy, but getting married? It doesn't even qualify – it is a joke. He will still have to end it, but he can't hate her now. There is no question in his mind, for the first time, that it meant nothing. They are over, but he doesn't hate her. He even feels sorry for her in a way, having to endure the degrading performance he has just witnessed.

The receptionist is upright again, and Henry feels immensely sorry for her, being married to that vicious bastard back there.

'Thank you so much. That was a very valuable experience. It really helped straighten me out.'

'Oh my pleasure, sir. Will we be seeing you and your young lady back here soon?'

'No I don't think so. Thanks again. Have a nice day.'

'That's what I'm supposed to say!' The receptionist collapses into hysterical laughter again, and as Henry pushes open the door, he hears a thud behind him. He looks back only once, to see her massive legs flailing in the air.

Stupid Cult

Matt is drumming his fingers on the steering wheel. He is agitated to say the least. Raquel, his girlfriend, is due to fly in early tomorrow morning, and even though she seemed calmer than when he had first told her about Eve, she is still likely to be mad. And of course, he is nervous about actually seeing her.

It has been a bizarre couple of days. The annulment has come through and it's all done and dusted. He never has to see that mad British girl again, which is a blessing. Matt found her strange, strangely cold. Nothing like his girlfriend – they share every feeling they have, every thought in their heads. But Eve? Matt thinks she had an overwhelming air of confusion about her. From where he is sitting, Eve tries to give the air of a woman who knew what she was talking about, but inside, didn't have a clue. She uses longish words. She is obviously educated, but Matt doesn't put much stock in stuff like that. Matt has attended the School of Hard Knocks. Yes, he has a diploma from the University of Life, he doesn't need an actual high school diploma. Algebra is never going to help him anyway, unless he ends up playing a mathematician at some point, and even then, they give you the lines! You just have to put on some glasses, and wear a lab coat.

Eve probably thinks *too* much. He feels really sorry for her boyfriend. Matt could see he had been really hurt. And if he stays with her, and it looks like he is going to stay with her, he has more pain on the horizon. The worst thing in the world is a woman who doesn't know what she wants. Matt shudders at the wheel, just thinking about it. A happy life is a simple life, in his book. He is bewildered that more people haven't realized. Cooking and cleaning and looking after babies – it might not be mentally taxing, but it has kept plenty of women happy for centuries. This feminism thing, burning bras and not shaving your legs, the goddamn Spice Girls – Matt grimaces at the thought – has ruined more marriages than any amount of Playboy clubs. Matt doesn't need a high school diploma to see that.

His stomach rumbles, and he realizes he could really do a burger. As soon as he drops off the supplies back at the restaurant, he can go get a bite. But the traffic is slow, man! Inching along, in the heat, Matt looks around, distractedly. His tape has stopped, and he turns it over. The Violent Femmes, "Blister in the Sun". Matt taps the wheel, but this time in rhythm to the song. He can see Eve's hotel up ahead on the right. They obviously have a bit of cash – nice place to stay. An image of her flashes through his mind. She was pretty, in a European way, she had massive eyes. She had another couple of massive assets as well, and he chuckles to himself. But it doesn't make him feel lustful any more, not since he started reading his Bible again. Besides, he doesn't like the feel of titties that big, if they are real. They feel squidgy. He likes them hard these days.

He hasn't been to church for a few years, ever since that whole cult thing, and his parents dragging him back from Wyoming, from the group. It was just a phase, but his Mom got all histrionic about it. He was really only staying with a group of friends, and the head shaving was just for fun. The group sex was a little strange at first, but then David, his mentor and leader, quoted him seventeen passages from the Bible where Jesus had condoned orgies. That wedding at Canan, there had been group sex after that, after Jesus had made wine out of water. And the last supper, when Paul had arranged for the prostitutes to come in after the consecration. Matt clearly remembers Judas getting a blow job before he hung himself. It is a different version of the Bible that he has found in his room, it doesn't have those bits in it, but David mentioned at the time in Wyoming that some Bibles censored the good news. As long as you weren't married, you should partake in free and joyous love to give your thanks unto the Lord. As soon as you were married, this had to stop. Apart from in certain cases, when you were a leader of a religious group, and then apparently you could carry on. Matt wasn't clear on those bits, but David seemed adamant. But his parents came and got him anyway, and Matt was at least partially relieved – more than anything he was exhausted! David was very angry, but when Matt's dad threatened to 'beat him from here to Kansas City' he actually helped Matt pack.

Matt knows he isn't the brightest spark in the box, but he would have left eventually, his parents definitely overreacted. He kind of knew what was going on, but he was eighteen, and there were worse things to do with your time at eighteen.

The traffic is inching forward now, and Matt realizes he has been shunting forward in auto-pilot. He needs to pay attention to the road. The last thing he needs is to rear-end somebody now.

High

Stella and Ken have cocaine. My karaoke partners, the quiz show kings, the toga lovers, the Derby socialites. We are having lunch. I still can't find Henry, and I wanted to celebrate my annulment, divorce, weird experience, whatever. Stella spotted me sitting in the bar at our hotel and invited me to lunch with her and Ken. They are flying down to Texas tomorrow, but they have had a wonderful time. They are up two thousand seven hundred dollars on the betting front, which is something that hasn't even occurred to me the whole time I have been here. I wonder if Henry has been betting. I could have had a miserable time but still made some serious money on a pontoon table.

We are in a diner opposite the hotel, where all the waitresses have roller skates and little skirts, and Ken has been unashamedly eyeing up their arses! We have been looking at photos of their new patio at home, they have just had the whole garden landscaped. Don't you look at photos when you get back from holiday? But there were photos of the quiz team with their sherries at Christmas, and a huge dog that looked like it would have your arm if you tried to stroke it, but which Stella referred to as her baby. There were photos of their nephews and nieces – they have no children themselves, Stella said – she has never wanted them. Ken didn't say anything.

'So where is your nice young man?' Stella asked me as if she was seventy as opposed to fifty.

'Oh he's out sorting out some bits, at the chemist, sending some postcards. You know the sort of thing.'

Stella gave Ken a knowing yet concerned look, which frankly didn't bother me in the slightest, because we all knew it was a lie. I just didn't see any need to get into it.

Stella has a fantastic figure for a woman her age. She is just wearing trousers and a sleeveless top, but she doesn't seem to have an ounce of fat on her arms. There is no jelly under her upper arms like my mother's, or mine for that matter. I realized why when she ordered a salad without the dressing, and I ordered a hamburger with fries and onion rings. Ken loved it though, and kept saying 'get stuck in girl'. Obviously years spent with Stella not actually digesting has made him feel guilty about eating decent amounts of food himself.

'I like to see a woman get stuck into her food, go on girl, have some mayonnaise. Do you think you'll have kids then, with Henry is it?'

'Oh that's thinking ahead, Ken, I don't know, but yes they are part of my plan. You know when you look ahead and picture what you'll be doing, I see kids in the picture. Ken, share my onion rings I can't eat all of these.'

'Ken, don't have too many, she said share not take them all.' Stella turned to me,

'But it throws your whole body out of shape, darling, you know that, don't you. And stretch marks. Do you know I don't have a single stretch mark on my entire lower body! Something to be proud of at my age. I know Ken appreciates it don't you, Ken? It wouldn't be like that if I'd had children. Men just don't understand that.'

'Oh Stella, I've got stretch marks already, I don't think it'll make that much of a difference!.'

'You'll see.'

I looked away, as did Ken, as Stella examined her salad. And we sat in silence for a moment.

I think Ken's great. He must be about sixty, and he reminds me of Sid James, he has a laugh just like him. And the way he kept eyeing up the waitresses just made me laugh even more. I wanted to ask him if he'd be my uncle – not my dad though. I couldn't take my dad eyeing up other women in front of my mum. But Stella seemed oblivious, she just kept chatting away about where they had been, who they had seen (Tom Jones apparently) and what they were going to do in Texas. They bought matching cowboy hats yesterday and I half decided to go and get me and Henry a couple, after lunch, and if he didn't want his, he could just throw it in the bin. Suddenly, I wanted us to be more like Ken and Stella, wearing matching hats.

That is until Stella got the coke out. I burst out laughing at first; I couldn't grasp what was going on.

But now Stella grabs my arm.

'Quietly, darling, we don't want to draw attention to ourselves. I have enough for all three of us, would you like some?

I can't very well cut a line here at the table, but we could sneak off to the ladies lavs, and then give Ken his share. It'll be fun, just us girls.'

'Oh Stella, I don't think so' and I can't stop laughing.

'Oh it's just an afternoon pick-me-up! We do it before every quiz don't we, Ken, and look how well we've done! Sylvie at home got us on to it, she found some in her son's bedroom when she was tidying.'

This is bizarre, I feel like I'm in *Cocoon*. I don't have a clue what to do. I haven't done coke for ages, and I hadn't even done much then. I don't like the idea of it, or the way people look snorting it. It's ugly.

'Oh Stella, thank you for the offer, but I always feel like I'm going to be the unlucky bastard who snorts 98% detergent. But thank you, I really appreciate it.'

'No, honey, Sylvie's son gets it for us, and he's such a good boy and never passes anything on unless he's tried it himself.'

I cannot believe the peer pressure from someone old enough to be my mum. I say no again, but she says go on. I say I'll leave it for them, she says they have plenty for all of us. It's as if I'm being offered a cup of tea, not class A drugs.

I am sitting deliberating when I see Henry, at least I think it's Henry, crossing the road outside, going into the hotel, and it makes up my mind. Henry isn't a drugs fan, and any slim hope of talking to him would be out of the window if I am fucked on Ken and Stella's Derby charlie.

'Stella, thanks all the same, but I have to go.'

'Will you at least rub a little on your gums for me?'

'Stella, I really have to go now, I haven't got time to go to the toilets.'

'Oh no don't be silly, you can do that here. You're not depressed are you? Will you just have a little bit?'

'OK fine, just a tiny bit.'

Stella opens up the foil under the table, and I wet my finger and dab it in, taking the tiniest bit to appease her, and rub it on to my gums. There is barely any there.

'Oh have a little bit more.'

'No honestly, Stella, that's more than enough. But thank you both for a lovely lunch, have a great time in Texas, but now I have to dash.'

I kiss both of them goodbye and throw some dollars on the table, and bolt from the diner, narrowly avoiding an accident with a waitress and three beers on rollerblades.

I am still marvelling at what has just happened, laughing to myself and shaking my head as I come out and start to cross the road, which is why I don't see the truck. Something hits me in the shoulder and the hip. Suddenly I am on the floor.

Sloosh & Sling

I don't pass out, everything just goes a little blurry for a matter of moments. I'm lying on the ground face up, and I can make out activity above me, a person I think, I just can't discern quite what it is. But I know exactly what has happened, I'm not confused. I was crossing the road, not looking where I was going, and a truck hit me. There was a lot of traffic, and the truck can't have been going that fast, because I feel like I have been hit by a really good rugby tackle, as opposed to a two ton motor. Somebody else is above me now, talking to the first person, reaching down towards me. I can hear them speaking, but not what they are actually saying.

Two things concern me most, in these first seconds. Number one: can I feel my legs and twiddle my toes. Actually I am doing it anyway, I have a condition whereby my toes are moving constantly, my big toes just moving up and down, and flicking off the other toes. There is a name for it apparently, but I have never looked it up. It's not as if it affects my life, although it does annoy Henry if we are watching television and my bare feet are in his line of vision. I have to move them, or put slippers on, he says it is so distracting. My frame of reference is always Henry; how what I do affects him, what he thinks about this, what he said when that happened. I always refer back to him. And yet our relationship is ending, I am about to end it for good. Well I was. I can't actually do anything much right now, but my legs are working so that's one thing.

My second anxiety, after the one about being wheelchair-bound for the rest of my natural life, is the drugs I have just rubbed into my gums.

On Stella's bloody insistence I have put her damn cocaine in my mouth, and any moment now an ambulance will turn up and determine I am a class A drug user and sentence me to death row. I will be electrocuted, in Texas, and have to wear a drab blue dress, grow my hair into an unfeasibly wild style, and speak with a southern American twang. I will be on a BBC2 documentary called *Brides of the Chair* or something just as harrowing. I'll be discussed in sociology classes the world over.

One of the men above me is saying something strange to me, loudly. It sounds a lot like 'sloosh'. Oh dear God, I must have distorted hearing from the bang on the floor. Something has happened to my eardrums and from now on whenever anybody talks to me I am going to hear strange onomatopoeias instead of words! He is trying to talk to me and all I can hear is 'sloosh'. I decide to try and sit up, and this man is holding the back of my head and just saying 'sloosh, honey, sloosh.' But honey is a word! I can make that out.

'For the love of God, sip some of this water and sloosh!'

Oh my God it is Ken, and he is forcing water in my mouth and telling me to spit. Wonderful Ken wants me to get rid of the drugs! The other guy is standing over him and telling him not to move me, but Ken is ignoring him. Good for Ken! I sip the water, don't taste any blood in my mouth, and gargle.

'That's it, lovely, swill it round, get that bad taste out of your mouth.'

The other guy is trying to pull Ken off.

'You shouldn't give her anything, man, they might have to operate, it could be going down all the wrong tubes, she could be fucked up inside!'

But I'm still slooshing. I don't want to be executed, and neither does Ken as my official supplier. They'd give him more volts as well, for dealing.

I spit.

'Have some more, just in case.'

'What in hell is going on, man? Stop giving her water, she might be hurt!'

'Oh fuck off', and I literally spit the words at him. Ken has seen the whole thing, grabbed the first glass and just come running. I wonder if he was watching my arse as I left. No matter. He is my hero.

I can't hear any sirens though. Where is the damn ambulance? I'm guessing somebody has called it. I try to stand up and the other guy, whose voice is vaguely familiar, tries to force me back down.

'Jesus, you could be hurt for Christ's sake, will you stop moving!'

'I'm fine, honestly.' I focus on this source of panic.

'Oh Jesus, Matt, what the hell? How are you here? Are you stalking me? We got the divorce!'

'Annulment!'

'Whatever! Thanks, Ken, you are my saviour. Matt, why are you here?'

'You hit my truck! I knocked you down. You just walked straight out you crazy bitch!'

'There is no need for name-calling, young man.' Bless Ken.

'Matt, Matt? How fast were you going?'

Matt has tears in his eyes. I'm sure he must look worse than I do. He is very pale, and looking wildly around, running his hands through his hair.

'Matt, how fast were you going, because I don't feel that bad to be honest.'

'I don't know, not fast. It's a traffic jam, for God's sakes!'

I notice a couple of people stopping and staring around us, and cars are beeping their horns behind Matt's truck, but who cares. I feel a twinge above my stomach as I shift my weight from one foot to the other to make sure both my ankles are OK. There's the twinge again.

'Ken, how fast was he going?'

'Barely moving, about five miles an hour.'

'Five miles an hour! Jesus, it's not even an accident! It's a nudge! Skateboarders go faster than that. Bloody hell, no wonder I'm fine, honestly I'm fine.'

Matt looks like death, Ken looks relieved. I have no idea how I look but then I'm distracted by the sirens coming my way. Thank God I've got health insurance; for the first time I am actually going to use it. I've always paid, never needed the damn thing, and was considering not bothering any more. Hurrah! Not a waste of money after all. The ambulance is weaving its way through the traffic towards us.

'Matt, are you OK? Do you want to sit down?'

'No I'm fine, it's you that got hit. Jesus, this is weird.'

Matt looks a little wide-eyed, and I'm starting to get scared, edging towards Ken for protection. Where is Stella? Probably high as a kite in the diner wondering where Ken got to.

'Matt, you know you really have to start avoiding me, we're not doing good things for each other.'

'I wasn't anywhere near you! I never thought I'd see you again. I hoped I wouldn't anyways. Jesus, you are a nightmare! Oh my God, your boyfriend is gonna kill me this time!'

'Henry? What? No, he'll be fine. I might not even tell him. Well I won't tell him it was you anyway. Hey when is your girlfriend flying in?'

'What? Why? What the hell are you asking me that for?'

'Bloody hell, Matt, I'm just trying to be nice, seeing if you've got it all sorted out, what you're going to say. Jesus, there is no need to be so funny, you did hit me after all, even if you weren't really moving. And for a Christian you swear a lot! Hey whose is the truck anyway, that's not your car. God you haven't stolen it?'

'For crying in the night, of course not! It's my boss's. At Gerard's, the restaurant remember?'

Ken pipes up,

'Oh Stella and I were going to go there, is it any good? She thought it looked fattening.'

'No it's alright, Henry liked it, nothing special though. Matt works there.'

The ambulance is pulling up, and a nurse guy jumps out, or a paramedic. Do they even call them the same thing in America? I decide to take the lead.

'Hi, I'm the one you're after. I have health insurance! I'm on holiday, but that's not an issue, because I have insurance! I walked into this man's truck, it wasn't even moving but I wasn't looking where I was going. Anyway I just fell over, but I think I'm fine, apart from I'm getting a bit of a twinge in my ribs when I twist.'

'Ma'am, we should do the examination. Kindly sit in the back of the van so we can make sure you are OK. You shouldn't have moved really, Ma'am.'

'I only fell over, for Christ's sake. It would hurt more falling off a bike, and I bet you don't check all the kids that do that.'

'We do if an ambulance is called, Ma'am.'

'Fair point, I'm sorry. Let's get this over and done with. Ouch!'

I get the twinge, actually it's more of a real pain in my side again. Bollocks, I think I have hurt myself. But there is no need for Matt to get involved.

'So there was no incident here, Ma'am?'

'No literally I just walked into the side of his car. It could just as easily have been a lamppost.'

'Ma'am, you should watch where you are going then, because we have a thing called jaywalking here, and you can get a ticket for it.'

'Oh I'm sorry, I have no idea what that is because I am foreign you see. I am on holiday. But thanks for the advice and I won't do it again.'

We walk over to the ambulance thing, which looks more like a post van, and I shoo Matt off. Reluctantly and with the most confused look on his face he gets back in his truck. Ken walks back to the restaurant very casually. My paramedic pokes me in the side at which I yelp, and he tells me I have a broken rib. Then maybe he shouldn't poke so hard! Bloody great. I will have to go to the hospital after all, and have a more thorough examination, just to make sure everything else is OK. Whatever, I get in. I'm not going to call Henry, he'll only take over and look at me like I've done it on purpose or something, to get him to forgive me. Like people who fake being burgled and hit themselves over the head so that it won't really hurt. And I've already decided that I don't want his forgiveness anyway. I have to remind myself of that one.

The paramedic gets in the back with me, and his partner drives. I sit on the stretcher-bed and try to get comfortable, and not twist my body too much. The paramedic looks at me with disdain, which I think is uncalled for. He is head to toe in bright white, but with a Day-Glo tan. He just sits and stares at me for a while, and I look away, at the needles, and the bandages, and the drugs! Shit, I forgot about the drugs. I think Ken's water dash has probably done the trick, and if it hasn't, drinking more water now won't make any difference. But being sick might.

This is not as easy as it sounds however. I don't think my orange buddy here is going to let me stick my fingers down my throat in the back of his spotless state of the art van. I need diversionary tactics! I need to think like the Dukes of Hazard. To battle the authorities, I need a plan.

We hit a slight bump in the road, and I bounce on the

bed, and take this as my key. We hit another slight bump and I throw myself forward onto the floor of the ambulance, and jam my foot under the stretcher-bed. I scream out,

'Arrrrrrr! Arrrr the pain! Oh my God!'

The medic is on his feet and trying to pull me up off the floor, but I make my body go dead, and put my arms out in front of me, helping him as little as possible. He starts screaming at his partner,

'Randy, stop the van goddammit, we have an 818, Randy, stop the van!'

I carry on screaming,

'Arrrrrr! The pain! My leg! It's stuck under the bed, I think it might be caught on something sharp! Don't move me, you'll rip the flesh from my bone goddammit! Arrrr stop the van, I need air, I can't take the pain!'

Randy screeches over to the side of the road, as Day-Glo Florence Nightingale tries to put an oxygen mask over my face. I can't throw up with that on! I push it off

'Arrrrr, not oxygen, I need fresh air!'

'Ma'am, it can't be fresher than this – it's from the bottle, it's a thousand times fresher than the air outside. It's pollution-free!'

'Arrrrr, the pain! No, I need to hear the birds, I need to smell the sun . . .' I even confuse myself with my answer. Not the best impromptu reply I have ever heard, but I can always claim delirium caused by the pain.

Florence doesn't understand, and starts trying to force the mask under my head which is still face down on the floor of the ambulance. My rib is actually starting to hurt from all this mucking about. I scream again,

'Randy, pleaseeeee! This guy's a madman! I need to see

the sky, Randy! Randy, he's trying to break my neck – oh my God!'

Randy flies from the front of the van and springs the door open behind me.

'Jesus, Chad, what are you trying to do?'

'I'm not doing nothing, man, I'm trying to get the oxygen mask on her – she said she needed air!

'Chad, are you freaking out on me again man?'

'No, Randy, I swear I didn't touch her, I was just trying to get her some air!'

'Chad, can you hear your mother, Chad? Can you hear the voices now?'

'No man, I can't hear the voices, I was just trying to help.'

I have no idea what this whole fucking pantomime going on around me is about, but I seize the moment of confusion to stick my fingers down my throat unnoticed. The trick is to use your index finger, and your middle finger only, and make a 'V' sign, and ram them as far down your throat as you can. I learned it from a bulimic.

Randy has hold of Chad's shoulders squarely, and is shaking him, as I start to gag.

'Chad man, don't leave me now, man – we've come too far man. Chad, get control!'

Randy is starting to cry above me as I yank myself out from under the bed, and just make it out of the van before I throw up on the road. It doesn't take long, but is exhausting as always, and my rib starts to give me real pain. It occurs to me that we were headed to sort that rib out. We were going to the hospital, before I landed Chad in it, but by the sound of it he's not the most balanced guy at the best of times. Randy and Chad are holding each other in the back of the ambulance – they seem to have forgotten all about me.

But no matter. Randy had the good sense to pull over into the ambulance lay-by at the hospital. It looks more like a massive Spanish holiday complex. It is completely symmetrical. The palm trees outside seem to be planted exactly twenty metres from each other, and even the nurses and doctors moving in and out of the hospital appear to come in identical pairs. I walk in the main entrance and am dazzled by the marble. This is not the NHS. But then it's only because I have insurance that I can even afford to walk through the doors. That is *why* it is not the NHS. Illness in America is strictly for the upper classes, which is of course bizarre, because they are in a position to afford prevention. It's the poor who generally end up needing the cures. Heart surgery in the States means re-mortgaging the house. Oh we have so much to be thankful for, that just passes us by.

I sit in the minor injuries section, which has large leather chairs, and stargazer lilies in huge vases. I pick up *Time* magazine and flick through. I am one of only two patients waiting. My fellow sufferer, a guy of about forty-five, is not sitting but leaning casually against a glass wall, perusing a copy of *Variety*. He notices me staring at him absentmindedly and smiles. I smile back, nod my head and say a hushed 'Hi'.

He smiles back, and offers an explanation,

'I can't sit down, I have a ten thousand dollar casino chip up my ass.'

'Fair enough,' I say, smile, and make the face that says no explanation needed, we've all been there, no need to go on.

He raises his eyes to heaven in a look that says 'silly me', and then carries on reading the magazine.

The sunlight pours in through the window. There is no smell of disinfectant, no dozing old people abandoned in random pyjamas and wheelchairs. A beautiful black nurse in her fifties brings me a large glass of water with ice. Her nurse's cap is squarely placed on her head, her traces of make-up perfect. Her bright white pumps make no noise in coming or going. She has no visible creases or unsightly bulges in her uniform. A youngish, incredibly good-looking Asian doctor in steel spectacles approaches the man with the chip up his arse, and talks to him softly. They both nod to me as they leave, the doctor walking slowly in front of the man who hobbles off like someone who, frankly, has a gambling chip stuck up his arse.

Five minutes later, approximately fifteen minutes after I entered the hospital reception, an incredibly professional Chinese female doctor approaches me, stethoscope swinging gently around her neck, pushes a strand of gleaming black bobbed hair behind her ear, and asks me to follow her into an examination room.

They let me out an hour later, with confirmation that I have, in fact, a hairline fracture of one of my ribs, but there is nothing they can do other than let it mend. They put my arm in a sling and I just feel bloody stupid and completely fraudulent with one perfectly good arm resting in a bandage like a con man. But I keep the sling anyway. In the cab on the way back to the hotel, I watch the town go by through the window, the splendour, the grime, the prostitutes, the money. The heat, and the space, and the desert, and the wasted time.

I'm Ready for My Close-Up

Sometimes it's easier to see things from a distance, to view them from afar. In this media age that can mean only one thing: this is not really happening, this is a film. I take this whole sorry mess, and I place it on the screen, and sit in the audience, and decide how it will end. For I am the producer, and the director, and the star. One of the stars at least. But what I want to see on screen, and what I feel now, are two very different things. For a start it would be terrible to have anybody this introspective in a film – how would you push the story along without one of those terrible voice-over narrator types? As soon as the lights go down, and you hear somebody's voice booming out in stereo sound, you know you are in for an hour and a half of bollocks.

There are exceptions of course, *Goodfellas* being the obvious one, but you will have to get somebody good in to play me, if you want to make me more likeable. But then you just get somebody beautiful, and that usually does the trick. Yes who would play me? I would like Elizabeth Taylor circa 1960, but I'm not going to get her. And no actress these days actually carries any weight. And I don't mean presence, I mean hips. There is nobody on screen weighing in at more than eight stone, and you are going to have add a few pounds to that to get anyway near to believability with me.

And my God I don't want them to whinge, and feel sorry for themselves. I don't want self-indulgence. I'm sure Henry would love to be playing this ridiculous soap opera opposite somebody a little thinner and a little less sarcastic. But he lucked out and got me.

And would it be a crime to make them just a little intelligent? I don't mean a nuclear physicist, just not some whimpering bag of neuroses who doesn't know her arse from her elbow as soon as a man walks into the room. And much as I would like to think it, I am no vamp. You couldn't just stick me in red lipstick and hope for the best.

And Henry? Who would play Henry? Can I have Paul Newman forty years ago? I mean seriously, not to play Henry, can I just have Paul Newman in *Cat on a Hot Tin Roof*? The man was a god. I can't think of an actor today with that kind of quiet, moody sheer manliness. Richard Burton had it, but he wouldn't play Henry. He would have just thrown a bottle of whiskey at my head the minute I started playing up, and walked out. Nobody too pretty either. Henry's charm isn't in his cheekbones, it's in his strength. His size, and his hands. Henry has massive hands.

Actors today, the popular ones at least, all seem to resemble teenage girls, and Henry would have a fit if he saw one of those on screen, pretending to be him. I'm sure they would make his character cry, and Henry would end up punching the projectionist, and that would be the end of everybody's viewing pleasure.

The thing is, on a film screen, you are fifty foot tall no matter what. You are massive, and have a larger than life presence, merely because your digital pixels, the dots of colour that make you up, have been exploded to that size. When you see these actors in real life, they seem like caricatures of their larger selves. They just don't seem right. You can't imagine them living their lives, this small, and people not pointing and laughing. And people don't point and laugh at Henry. For a start, he might hit them. But he has a presence, a larger than life presence, without the aid of the big screen. I don't think there can be an actor working in Hollywood today with hands as big as Henry's.

I am assuming Hollywood. Of course it could be some little British independent, who shoot us on hand held cameras, and make us both look rather grainy and depressing. I don't want to be grey, that is my main proviso. Don't let them make me grey. I don't want to look all washed out, and have the action relocated to goddamn Gretna Green instead of Vegas to save on budget. I want to be studio made, because at least they'll put me in better outfits. Of course there is always the possibility then, that they will have an American playing my part, affecting some terrible accent that results in me sounding South African. Worse yet, they could just make me American! All of a sudden, that British independent is looking a lot more appealing. Just don't make me a Yank, please God, leave me my pride!

In reality, I'm sure Henry and I wouldn't even make it to the big screen – who am I kidding? We'd have to have a lot more sex for a start, and possibly drink less. Oh, did you notice that one too? We seem to drink A LOT. I didn't even realize.

Sympathy, Deserved

'Christ, what have you done? Have you broken your arm? What's happened?'

Henry jumps up from the bed and comes running over to me, with the old Henry look in his eyes. With concern all over his face. I feel a little bad for having slipped the bandage back on, but he might not have believed me otherwise. Besides, officially I am supposed to be wearing it. I could probably ease up on the limp though, I don't know what that's supposed to be.

'Baby, what have you done, have you been in a fight?'

'Of course I haven't been in a bloody fight. I got knocked over.' I put on my deliberately pathetic voice, 'I got hit by a truck.'

'Jesus! And is that all you got, a broken arm?'

'Well my arm is OK, actually. It looks worse than it is. I broke a rib.'

'A rib?'

'Yes.'

'So why is your arm in a sling?'

'They did that at the hospital. They said it stops you moving that side of your body so much, and that will make the rib heal quicker.'

'What?'

'Well that's what they said alright. I can't tell them how to do their job.'

'Hon, I've broken ribs before playing rugby. And finished the game.'

'Well you should have been wearing a sling.'

'They just tell you not to play the next game and try not to laugh too much.'

'They told me I needed a lot of rest.'

'You remember when we went to Center Parcs for the weekend. I had a cracked rib then.'

'So?'

'I'm just saying, that luckily, it's not that serious.'

'Oh fuck off, Henry, I've been in a road accident. I think that's a bit more serious than some rugby game.'

'Are you concussed?'

'Not really, I didn't really bang my head.'

'How did you not bang your head? Did you even hit the ground? Did the truck hit you, and you managed to stay on your feet?'

'No, arsehole, I hit the ground, just not that hard.'

'How fast was it going, the truck, when it hit you?'

'I don't bloody know, I didn't have a speed gun. I was too busy being knocked down!'

'I'm just saying that the truck couldn't have been moving that fast when it hit you, if you didn't really fall that hard.'

'I'm just saying, I'm just saying . . . stop bloody "just saying". There was a lot of traffic.'

'What do you mean, "a lot of traffic"?'

'What I say. A lot of traffic. So he wasn't moving that fast.'

'So it was like, a 'traffic jam'?'

'Do you think this is funny? I'm in pain.'

'Baby, I'm just trying to work out what happened, and you seem a bit confused. Did the truck hit you, or did you . . . hit . . . the . . . truck, if it wasn't moving after all?'

'Henry, it was bloody moving! It was going at five miles an hour.

Shit. Shit! I didn't mean to say that bit.

'Five miles an hour? A truck hit you at five miles an hour. Did you even notice?'

'Yes I bloody noticed! It threw me to the ground!'

'Were you drunk?'

'That is the worst thing you have ever said to me.'

'You were drunk.'

'Henry, I was not drunk.'

There is a knock at the door thank goodness. Saved from Henry's derision for a minute at least. I bet it's bloody Pedro. Lovely Pedro, wonderful Pedro. Henry moves to answer it.

'No, hon, don't you move, you have to recuperate. I'll get it.'

I think Henry may be sniggering. Bastard. He opens the door. Shit, it's Ken and Stella. In their cowboy hats. Henry looks a little taken aback.

'Well, little lady, you gave us quite a fright, are you alright? You seemed OK earlier, otherwise I wouldn't have left you.'

'Thanks, Ken, I think I'm going to be OK with a lot of rest.'

Stella pipes up, all wide eyes and concern,

'But we feel terrible, I didn't even realize until Ken came back in and told me.' Addressing Henry,

'She kept saying no, but I made her have a little bit of my stash, and then she gets knocked over. I knew it was pure, but I didn't realize it was that strong.'

Henry is looking confused. I have to make them leave.

'Actually, Stella, I should get some sleep, but please don't feel bad, it was nothing to do with you.'

I roll over on the bed, and hope they will get the hint and leave. But Henry is really confused,

'Stash? Of what?'

'Oh Sylvie's son at home lets me and Ken have a little bit of charlie for our quiz nights, you know just as a little boost. And we brought some with us, just for fun you understand. Anyway, your lovely Eve said she didn't want any, but I could see she was tempted, so I made her rub a little on her gums, and then she hit the truck.'

I spring up, and feel a twinge in my side.

'The truck hit me, actually, Stella.'

Henry is looking at them in disbelief. They could not look any straighter. They look like they have matching jumpers at home. They look like the quiz night folk that they are, but without the coke lines in the village hall toilets beforehand. You should never judge a book . . .

'Well you should get your rest. Just checking you were OK, Eve. We might not see you now before we go down to Texas, but I've popped our number on the back of this postcard and I'll leave it with you, for when we all get back.

Remember you promised to come up for the start of the quiz season. Both of you with your university degrees, we should do ever so well.'

'Thanks Stella, have a lovely time in Texas. Bye Ken, thanks. Take care.'

'You too, dear.'

And Henry shuts the door. He stands with his back to me, hand on the door knob, for moments, as I lay waiting for his tirade. Nothing happens. Maybe he's not going to say anything after all. Maybe he understands that I'm in pain, and that the last thing I need is a lecture. Maybe . . .

'Well I'm going to have a quick sleep, Henry, so . . .'

'You were on drugs! You were high as a kite and walked in to a car, and I'm supposed to feel sorry for you! You're having a bloody laugh aren't you? Serves you right! What were you thinking, doing coke, out here? It's one thing at home, but out here? Did they take a blood test? Didn't it show up?'

'No, Ken made me sloosh in time, I must have got it all out. I'd only just done it. And it was a tiny little bit to appease bloody Stella. Get off your high horse, Henry, it's not like you've never bloody done it.'

'Not here I haven't. Not in bloody America, where they carry guns, and have the death penalty! Eve, are you mad?'

'Oh Henry, I'm not going to get death row for a harmless bit of coke on my bloody gums.'

'Well fine, stupid square fucking me. You can take your bloody rave scene, and your drug-taking with a couple of middle-aged junkies, and shove them up your arse! I'm not carrying your bloody bags to the airport!'

With that Henry storms out, again. Everything ends in an argument these days. It's for the best, that we're calling it off. I'm calling it off. Maybe Henry thinks he already has.

The Bit I Forgot to Mention

Joanna, Tim's now fiancé then girlfriend, had organized it. We all groaned about how sad Center Parcs was, and yet how expensive, but we all wanted to get away for a long weekend, and it was easy to drive there, and it was eighty degrees under the dome! It was about eight outside. Henry would drive me, him, Scott, and Phil. Phil's girlfriend couldn't come because she worked weekends, as a broadcast assistant on Radio One. We all got dedications, all the time, for the worst Celine Dion songs, just so she could fill up her quota, and it was funny actually. But she couldn't come, which was both a good thing and a bad thing. The bad thing was I got on with her really well, the good thing was Scott would have been the only single one there, and Henry and I secretly suspected he was gay. If he didn't want to draw attention to it, neither did we.

Tim and Joanna were driving up in their Metro that didn't have second gear, with all the bags. I only had three overnight bags, one of which contained a load of Henry's stuff, but all the usual jokes were made, 'is one of them just for your make-up?' Ha bloody ha. Of course Joanna only had a rucksack. Of course it was a rucksack! All the boys loved it. And no, she wasn't wearing any make-up, as per usual. But I wouldn't look any good without make-up, so I had to wear it, and it wasn't my fault. It was nature's fault.

We raced a couple of times on the motorway, with Henry driving his company Alfa which could outrun Tim's Metro any day. But Tim somehow managed to get ninety out of it before it visibly started to shake, and we all decided, via the mobiles, to slow down. Scott chatted away in the back of the car about some girl he liked at work, and we were all really enthusiastic, as if we actually believed it! I had told Henry before we left to talk to him about it, as he had known him the longest. Henry had said it wasn't the kind of thing men talked about if they also played rugby together. I said they were all repressed homosexuals anyway, with their scrums and their communal showers, and got the *Sunday Times* thrown at me for my pains.

We drove up on the Thursday night, and were staying till the Sunday. Me and Henry and Joanna and Tim got the two bedrooms, and Phil and Scott got the double sofa-bed in the living room. Phil looked a little dubious, but Henry just told him to shut up and sleep in his tracksuit trousers.

Tim was sporting a black eye from their rugby game the weekend before, and Henry had bruised his ribs or something. Tim kept asking me if I would kiss his eye better, at which I offered Scott's services to shut him up, and stop me blushing.

On that first night we just went to one of the restaurants and got hammered, cycling pissed all the way home, barely missing trees. We didn't split up into boys and girls. I got the impression Joanna found me a little irrelevant, a little too girly, and she much preferred being with the lads, which was fine by me. It was her loss, and besides it was her boyfriend flirting with me, not vice versa. My occasional comments in her direction, such as, 'I wish they really were drowning each other,' when they were furiously dunking in the swimming pool, got ignored. She would look at me with disdain, and then front crawl off to dunk someone herself. Unfortunately I had never been that strong a swimmer, and so it wasn't as much fun for me, as I never got to dunk anyone. It would often end up with Henry just holding my head under the water while the rest of them pissed themselves laughing. Oh the hilarity! Joanna always found it particularly hysterical.

For the most part I read, dome-bathed, and concentrated on keeping my breasts within my bikini which was a couple of cup sizes too small. They'd all come padding back from the pool, splashing me, and saying I was no fun. Then Joanna would invariably shout 'last one to the rapids is a queer', and Scott would go bombing off without thought for life or limb. Most of these times, Henry would stay with me, claim to be exhausted, and we would just lay for a while, chatting and laughing and trying to keep my breasts in my bikini top, until he got dragged away by the boys again.

On the Friday night, we were all aching from playing tennis during the day, but we went bowling anyway. Scott had got chatting to one of the lifeguards and had gone for a drink with him, which pleased me at least. Henry and Tim both looked uncomfortable, and kept saying things like 'as long as he doesn't bring him back to the chalet.' Phil was just relieved at the prospect of a safe night's sleep on the sofa by himself. They were all a little homophobic at heart I suppose, which annoyed me, but there was little point talking to them about it. Who Scott had sex with or not had nothing to do with them I said, he didn't vet their chosen bed partners, or think worse of them for whoever they picked, so why should they? They weren't sleeping with him, they didn't have to watch him have sex, what in hell did it have to do with them? Did it affect their conversations? Did it change his personality? Did it mean he talked about baking instead of rugby? Did it in any way make him different from the friend they had always had? Didn't they just want him to be happy? Besides which I got much better birthday presents if Henry took Scott shopping with him.

Surely that was the point. Everyone deserves as much happiness and fulfilment as they can possibly get. And as long as Scott was having sex with a consenting adult, where was the harm? Who got hurt by something that was making Scott happy? Nobody.

But it was the same old bollocks. If Scott was gay, he must fancy one of them. I said I doubted it very much, seeing as I was a straight woman, and I wasn't finding any of them remotely attractive at that point. Of course in my head that argument fell down when I admitted that I was in love with one, and would have liked to have sex with another. Phil was short, so he didn't count.

Joanna, poor thing, had pulled a muscle playing tennis, although God knows how because I hadn't seen her do anything of any worth on the court, and was all tuckered out. She was going to get an early night. Not proving to be quite so much fun now was she, with her massive rucksack and her no moisturizer rule. I personally was ready to rock until dawn. So it was just me, Henry, Phil, and Tim on the bowling alley.

Tim and Henry got carried away with their whole competitive thing, again, taking it all a little too seriously. Phil and I just mucked about, laughing at people in other lanes who were just as bad as us, and drinking copious amounts of beer. I think Phil would have got into the whole competitive thing if he had been any good, but it wasn't going to happen. He was worse than me. In twenty balls he knocked just twenty-three pins down. We took the piss out of Henry and Tim who were arguing about how to do the scores, and how it would only take two more strikes for one of them to be completely clear of the other. They were dull, but it was fun on the whole.

Henry won on the last go, and I ran and kissed him in celebration. He, however, was more concerned with smirking at Tim, from which I was clearly distracting him. Bastard. I wished Tim had won instead. So much for loyalty.

They had a tiny disco by the bowling alley, filled with fifteen year olds who hadn't quite worked out how to have fun yet. We took to the dance floor, which wasn't very big, but we were the only people actually moving. Our audience, about a score of kids, just looked at us like we were freaks, the oldest and possibly the most stupid people they had ever had the misfortune to observe, and these were kids who spent every day with their parents! I did get my arse pinched by a boy of about thirteen, however, which is always encouraging.

Tim and Henry forgot their differences and went off on a dancing marathon. I loved the way Henry danced, I always had done since that first night. Tim was good as well, running all over the place, doing a chicken thing with his arms. Phil, bless him, could not hold his drink, and after half an hour of tequila slamming he staggered in the direction of the toilets to throw up. Tim and Henry were ordering another round of shots, so I went to check on Phil.

'I'm in a bad way babe, I've been a little sick. I think it best for all if I head back now. Do you want to come, or are you woman enough to last the distance with these two monsters?'

'Sweetie, I'm going to stay if you're going to be alright getting back on your own.'

'Yes yes, I feel better already, sobering up by the second. You're an angel though, I'll see you tomorrow.'

Phil stood on tiptoe to kiss me on the forehead,

'Have you got your mobile? I want to phone Natasha. Can I take it back with me?'

'Of course, I'll see you tomorrow, Phil. Take care.'

I gave him my mobile, connected him to Nat's number, and he staggered off. I heard him shouting as he was walking off, 'Natasha, I'm in a club! I'm in a club! No, I've been sick, I'm fine. I love you. I love you! No, I love you! Nat, can you hear me?'

Phil was adorable, and not caught up in the macho bullshit that Tim and Henry had going on. Everything was a competition. I'd never really had it explained. When I'd quizzed Henry about it, months before, when they had ended up arguing again at the end of the evening, drunk and abusive, he had only half told me. They had always just been competitive, he had said. Surely there was more to it than that, and it was obviously a girl, I had said. Yes, there had been a girl when they were younger. Henry had fancied her, and so had Tim, and she had ended up going out with Henry for two weeks, during which he spent the entire time gloating to Tim. She had dumped him, and I could see why I said, if that is how he behaved. She had then gone out with Tim for nearly a year, in which time he had been continuously unfaithful. Apparently Henry had really liked Susan, to which I replied that he should have been a bit more mature. It was a difficult time at home he had said, and I had let it lie. They had been sixteen. Sixteen for God's sakes and it was still going on!

The boys had moved back on to pints, and I was on the red wine, not quite feeling sick, but well aware how utterly trolleyed I was. We carried on dancing to the shittest hits of the year, or whatever CD they had on repeat, until the lights came on. Both of them were slumped on a sofa giggling, when the barman came and chucked us out. We staggered and somehow found our bikes, after both Henry and Tim had tried to make off with children's bikes with stabilizers. I didn't think it was a good idea to ride the things, I was that much in control at least. But Tim got on his, so Henry did the same. But Henry was the only fool to attempt to actually move, and promptly fell off. He kept crying 'my rib!' as Tim propped him up, and I unsteadily pushed our bikes back to the chalet. Henry collapsed on the bed straight away, after assuring me he would not be sick.

'Eve, I love you, you know that don't you, more than I've ever loved anybody. No it's fine, I'm not going to be sick, I just want you to know I really love you. But you don't love me.'

'Henry, yes I do.'

'No you don't, not really. You sort of do, but you don't.'

'Henry, I do, I'm going to take my make-up off, and then I'll be back.'

'I love you.' And then he was asleep.

I pottered about for a while, washed my face, and got in to bed. But I realized that if I was going to feel in any way decent in the morning I should drink some water. I pulled on Henry's shirt, didn't bother with the buttons, I was only going to be seconds.

I slipped into the dark kitchen and could hear Phil snoring loudly in the living room. But not Scott. I would talk to him about his 'date' tomorrow even if Henry wouldn't. I was still drunk, I realized, as I had a conversation with the tap while running myself a glass of water.

'Water, that'll make me feel better in the morning, water, water, fill her up blah blah blah blah.'

I felt the hands come up from behind me and slip under the shirt.

'Henry, I'll be in in a minute, let me drink this first. You should have some too, if you want to feel OK tomorrow.'

But one of the hands reached up and took the glass from me and put it down on the work top, and someone started to kiss my neck. The neck always gets it. I turned around and kissed him easily, but he was more insistent. Maybe he could manage sex after all, I had thought he would be well past it. But it wasn't a familiar kiss, the tongue was pushing a little more softly than Henry's, and it tasted of smoke. I pulled back, knowing full well it was Tim. He didn't even open his eyes but grabbed me back into it, and I kissed him again, while his hands moved back under Henry's shirt and squeezed. He started to pull off my shirt, Henry's shirt, and I jumped backwards, slamming into the dustbin, and Phil stirred in the living room.

'Well goodnight.' And he turned and walked back into

his room. I drank my water fast, gulping it back, and ran myself another glass. I was out of breath, and had to stop for a few seconds before drinking again. I turned around and slumped back against the sink. There was a street light right outside the living room, and it was shining harshly over all our bags.

Henry and I were going to Vegas next month.

Tim didn't mention it the next day, and neither did I. But we kept our distance.

He Was Never Really a Contender

You may be wondering why I haven't told you about me. My past, I mean. Henry is explained, safely in context, and you understand why and what and how. And maybe I seem empty, and an unlikely candidate for your sympathy, and with you all so ready to give it if I could just tell you that I had been horribly and viciously wronged in my past. If I could just say that my first love had left me for my sister, or my best friend, or even another man, you could understand. Unfortunately for you, and your efforts to comprehend my behaviour, such is not the case.

But fuck it, there is never enough time for self-indulgence, and if you are demanding I take this particular microphone, and you really want to play psychiatrist for twenty minutes, then I'll oblige.

Childhood? Reasonably straightforward I think. I have two sisters, so no 'only child' spoilt tantrums. There was no bullying at school, and no poverty, and no absent parent to add to the mix. I was good at school, I mean, I could do what they asked. I had a tendency for laziness, but all exams were passed, and I wasn't the unlucky victim of familial disappointment.

I played kiss chase like everybody else – I wasn't crouching in the corner of the playground having stones thrown at me. And I had plenty of friends. Do we really need this? It's all kind of bland. Fine, I'll go on.

I suppose I should talk about boyfriends. There were a few, sweet, but nothing serious. I didn't have one of those meaty early relationships at fifteen, when you end up with somebody completely inappropriate for the sum of your formative years, before one of you buggers off to university. Then you both realize that you've had a valuable learning experience, but there isn't a cat in hell's chance of you staying together, and thank God you never got pregnant.

There was one, I suppose, who got to me more than most, and that I remember with an unswerving affection. He was a couple of years older than I was at seventeen. He had gone to university, and came home for odd weekends, summers and Christmas. His name was Stanley George. Stanley was an unfortunate name, as I am sure you are aware. It's fine for your grandfather, but for your boyfriend? But then he was never actually my boyfriend. His mother had been a Marlon Brando fanatic in her youth. She had seen *A Streetcar Named Desire* hundreds of times. Brando had played the brooding, sweating, swaggering chunk of pure unadulterated Polak masculinity that was Stanley. Don't think of Marlon Brando *now* for God's sake. You could not be more wrong. In his day Brando was the ultimate, the closest to the male body beautiful you are ever likely to see. Couple this with his instinctive talent and intelligence, and you had a minefield of testosterone, probably resulting in the vast explosion of a man he has become today. At some point, he was going to have to get fat. His muscles strained to get out of his skin even then, and there was too much chemistry and magnetism in his tightly packed form, that something had to give. But back then, and as the doomed Stanley in Tennessee Williams's play, he was the definition of Man. Of course the fact that in this particular emotionally charged two hours of southern hell he was a wife beater and rapist was studiously ignored by Stanley's mother when she chose to name her son after him.

Now some children never manage to overcome the stigma that their stupid bastard parents sentence them to, when they think not of their child, but themselves, during the naming process. And as we all know, children can be so cruel. But Stanley was good at football, and that's about all it takes for a young boy to be considered cool. Furthermore, he spent his early years telling anybody who would listen that he was named after Stanley Mathews, the former Blackpool and England player, and all-round football god. This made him an even better footballer in many people's eyes. Stanley therefore side-stepped that childhood minefield, and emerged as a teenager, almost completely unscathed.

Of course it didn't hurt that he was a gorgeous-looking boy as well. By the time Stanley hit puberty, he was one of the popular ones. He was confident, charming, incredibly sweet, and still bloody good at football. It was during his fourteenth year, while pushing his blonde hair back from his eyes, and finding himself skimming six foot, that he realized girls were just going to like him too. The football boys, his mates, his older brothers, his friends' mothers, all of them noticed he had a way with the women. And where it happened he wasn't quite sure; it could have been on the pitch, or at the youth club, or in the pub too young, that he went from Stanley to Marlon. It had previously suited him to associate himself with a legendary footballer, but now, in this time of sexual exploration, and in the race to lose your virginity, it made more sense to align himself with one of the century's great heartbreakers.

And soon it caught on with the boys as well. For the first couple of weeks, Stanley looked bashful and embarrassed when they heckled him with a round of 'Marlon's up to his old tricks again' as he chatted to pretty blondes in the pub. But every man on a football pitch needs a nickname, and this became his. And he loved it.

It stayed with him, so that when I began to see and chat to a seventeen-year-old Marlon in the pub, as I turned fifteen and moved into the right social echelon, I had never heard of Stanley George. Only Marlon. I knew very little about him at all, and though of course I could see he was good-looking, and funny, and comfortable to chat to, I had never thought any more of it. If I have to be painfully honest I suppose it had struck me that I liked him more than most. I think possibly the night in the pub when he had made me bend backwards and open wide to show him my lack of newly removed tonsils, I felt a twinge, and not in my throat.

But there was no overwhelming crush, or sleepless nights, or tears into my teenage pillow. I just didn't do that whole phase. When he left for university, it made little impact on my life.

He reappeared mid-way through my seventeenth year. He had come back from university for the summer. It began . . .

strangely. I was going through my own tiny rebellion at the time. My disillusionment with my social circle had just reared its head. I had begun to question whether I wanted to go to the same pub every Thursday, and the same club every Saturday, with the same people, doing the same things, drinking the same drinks, throwing up in the same spot halfway home. We were still having the same conversations, bitching about the same people, and all wearing the same things. It had never occurred to me before that this was not the right thing to do, only in fact that I should be thinner, and do it better. But for the first time it struck me that I would like to talk about something else, speak to somebody different instead of dismissing anybody new merely because we didn't already know them!

And as it happened I had gone to the pub that night, with (shock, horror!) a couple of people from one of my classes at college. Not my friends! Maybe you have every idea how revolutionary this was, or maybe it just seems bizarre to you that this should have been such a big deal, but it wasn't the done thing. Unfortunately, though, my lofty plans for some sort of conversational utopia were not coming to fruition. It transpired that these 'new' people talked about exactly the same things, but without any of the humour of my friends. In short, I was bored witless, and coming to the depressing realization that everybody was the same, in my small town at least.

I had noticed Marlon in the pub about half an hour before, but I hadn't gone and said hello. It's not that it would have been uncomfortable, or inappropriate, I just didn't see the point. If I bumped into him, I would say hi, but we weren't childhood pals or anything. Bizarrely, he came over to me.

I say bizarrely, and you probably need to understand why. I didn't have looks men fought over. I like to think now that I was still growing into them. It took another couple of years before I realized I was pretty. I wasn't really comfortable in my own shoes back then. For a start I had a perm. Not a bad one by the time's standards – corkscrew was where it was at. But looking back now, and not just at the strange clothes my mother let me wear, I didn't look at all relaxed.

Marlon came over then, and looked incredibly pleased to see me, which was something of a surprise. He sat himself down, giving me a perfect excuse to ignore the boring bastards I had chosen to spend my evening with. He was bored with his friends too. He was feeling chatty.

'So, Eve, how are you? I haven't seen you for ages, you look really good. Nice corkscrew, by the way, very fashionable.'

'You can save the finger in the socket jokes as well, Marlon, before you even start. How are you? How's university? Are you enjoying it? Where are you, Nottingham?'

'Yeah it's great, I love it. I wish I didn't have to come back for the summer though, it makes this place seem bloody awful. I can't believe how boring it's got, and I used to spend every night in here! Where are the rest of your little crew tonight anyway, do you still see them?'

'Oh God yes, I just fancied a change, you know how it is. I just wanted to talk about something else for a night, but' in a whisper 'I don't think I chose particularly wisely with this lot. At the last count, they will have been talking about estimated grades versus required grades for forty minutes.'

'Nightmare. Shall we go somewhere else?'

'Oh are you heading off with the boys? I don't really fancy a club. But it was nice to see you.'

'No, I meant both of us, go to the cinema or something. I'm not really in the mood for drinking, and I'm skint. I haven't been to the flicks in ages. Come on! It's better than this.'

So we went to the cinema. He drove his dad's big white family car, and I noticed for the first time, that his hands were shaking slightly. It wasn't me you understand, it wasn't nerves. His hands were just shaking, which is slightly unsettling when you are doing eighty-five in an old banger about to surrender to a heavy rust problem. When we came out of the cinema, and isn't it terrible that I can't remember what we saw, I noticed it again, when he lit my cigarette. He held up his lighter, and I had to bob and weave to get the damn cigarette lit. Neither of us acknowledged it, although it was obvious when he singed my fringe. Similarly I ignored him taking three attempts to light his own cigarette. You know, I never asked him why. I ended up spending the entire summer with him, first as friends, and later as, well still just friends I suppose, but I never asked him about the shaking. Maybe it was because I was only seventeen, and at that age it seems rude to draw attention to something like that, as opposed to being concerned. Now of course, it would be the first thing I'd ask. I have no idea what caused it, but he shook all summer.

He phoned a lot at first, and we just started spending our days together. Neither of us were working, and we just began to occupy each other's time. We went to the cinema a lot, we went out for pizza, we went to London for the day. We sat around and watched videos. It wasn't exactly a whirlwind of excitement. And nothing happened, sexually. It was all completely innocent. We stayed completely, perversely away from each other, physically. We never touched. I didn't push him or smack him in fun. He didn't hug me, or touch my arm to get my attention. It was strictly a verbal thing.

Every time he came around to my house, he brought me a pack of cigarettes. I know it seems like a strange thing to bring, like 'ere are love, choke on these', but it actually seemed sweet at the time. I never asked for them, he just brought them anyway.

This went on for about six weeks. It doesn't sound like very long at all now, but back then, it seemed like an age. We seemed to spend years together.

Two days before he was due to go back to Nottingham, I stayed over at his house. His parents were visiting his brother, and I went to his house to watch videos and do nothing. I can remember what we watched that night more clearly than anything else that happened. He put on *Monty Python and the Holy Grail*. He was disgusted that I had never seen it. It was the funniest film ever, he said, and I had to watch it. This was obviously his student phase. I smile when I think of how mature it seemed at the time, such a grown-up film, and yet what a cliché it is, and just how young we both were. Everybody eventually goes through the 'Holy Grail' period, and Marlon was having his. He took my Monty Python virginity at least.

We were sitting watching the beginning credits, which I found bizarre, and when the film comes on, as you probably know, all you see is a grey sky, and the sound of horses galloping closer. Marlon was in hysterics, and I just didn't understand. He kept saying, 'just wait, just wait', and collapsing into fits of laughter. I was getting bored with it by the time the guy with the coconut shells actually turned up.

Marlon was a weeping wreck on the floor unable to breathe. God, I've got old. I haven't thought about it since, not properly, and it is your standard student reaction. But at the time of course, and for me, it was peculiar to him.

We watched the film, and by the time it finished, and my stomach hurt from laughter, I realized that our heads were only inches apart. I was lying stretched out on the sofa, and he was just in front of me, sitting on the floor, leaning back against the sofa.

'That is one of the best films ever. Did you enjoy it?'

'It was so funny. That part, with the French guards!' and I was laughing again.

He was looking at me then, as I laughed, and instantly I felt naked, completely self-conscious. I felt suddenly . . . uneasy.

'I should phone my dad to pick me up. What time is it?'

'Quarter to twelve, you can stay if you want. You can sleep in my mum and dad's bed.'

'Oh. Well I could I suppose.'

'Do you want to phone your dad and tell him then?'

'Sure.'

And that was that; decision made. I got up to use the phone, and instantly felt my nerves kicking and screaming inside of me. I didn't feel excited. It felt . . . ominous. I used the phone in the hall, and as I hung up the receiver, he was standing in the doorway of the lounge.

'I'll show you which room it is.'

I had always assumed he didn't fancy me. I thought our inability to touch each other up until now was a symptom of his complete non-attraction to me It was just my teenage stupidity, or naivety, or hopeless innocence. Not that I was particularly innocent. I had lost my virginity the year before, and though not exactly a sex professional, I was basking in the false impression that I knew what I was doing, and was maybe even proficient. But I was innocent enough to believe that if someone actually wanted to touch you they would, and no matter the circumstances. I didn't realize that maybe I had to give a signal too. Or that Marlon assumed, as I had given him no indicator of my interest, that I just wasn't interested. Because as interested as I was, I thought I had to wait for him to jump on me. I didn't understand the outskirts of attraction at all. And so I followed him upstairs, nervous at my own longing, but not for a second believing he would actually do anything. Hoping of course in my own childish way that he might, but safely cocooned in the knowledge he wouldn't, because he just didn't fancy me.

He opened the door for me to go in to his parent's room, and I dashed in. It was your stock magnolia and peach nightmare, with pastel paintings hanging in bad frames on the walls, dying wardrobes, and just enough room for one person to walk around the bed. There was a laundry basket in the corner, and even though the rest of the room was perfectly clean, the basket was full of dirty clothes, creeping out of the top. This basket, full of his parents washing, made the whole room seem grubby, and I had experienced a sudden flash that I wouldn't enjoy sleeping on these sheets, or putting my head on these pillows. Marlon came into the room with a T-shirt for me, and I took it. I tried to smile and relax but he seemed nervous, which I interpreted as anxiety that I might leap on him. Of course put me in that room now, and we would have been on that bed and rolling around on those grubby sheets before he could say 'dirty old woman'.

I took the T-shirt with me to the other side of the room, and said goodnight from there. He said goodnight, and left, closing the door behind him. I shouted out after him,

'Marlon!'

He opened the door straight away, and came in,

'Can I use your toothbrush?'

'Of course.'

'Thanks. Night.'

'Night.'

And he left again.

I got changed, and could hear him moving about downstairs, turning off lights, and the TV. I put the T-shirt on, I think it said 'The Doors', and went into the bathroom. As I brushed my teeth, and washed off my make-up, I heard him coming up the stairs, and his door open and close.

I turned the light off in the bathroom, and had my hand on his parents' bedroom door, when he came out of his room, in his boxer shorts. I tried to look away, look deliberately up at his face.

'Night, again.'

He walked up to me, and stood over me, too close, for a second. Then he kissed me, softly. I could taste my own toothpaste, and his cigarettes. Amazed as I was, I kissed him back, and I felt his tongue push and squash heavily into my mouth. It was a ten second kiss. He pulled back, and said he could taste his toothbrush, but all I could feel was my hand on the thread of hair running vertically down his chest. I didn't know what to do with my hand. I felt like I should move it, but I couldn't. He walked past me into the bathroom, and I turned around to face him as he went in. He smiled, and closed the door. I went into his parent's room, and sat on the bed nervously waiting to hear the bathroom door open. He was in there for five minutes, which seemed like an hour. I heard the bathroom door open, and I caught my breath, and I feel sure he must have heard, it was so loud. It was more of a raspy gasp. I heard him pad past my room barefoot, and close the door to his room.

I was breathing heavily, and the effort was moving my shoulders, and my head was bobbing. I felt my lip start to quiver. But it stopped and I crawled under the covers, and went to sleep.

The next day, a Saturday, I bolted from his house at seven fifteen a.m.

He phoned in the afternoon, asking if I wanted to go to the pub that evening. He didn't mention it, and neither did I. It was his last night at home. He turned up early, and chatted to my parents while I finished getting ready. We walked to the pub, and sat and talked and drank for the whole evening, while my emotions pretty much ran the gamut. But we got on better then ever. There was no reference to the night before, and we relaxed as the drink kicked in. I didn't touch him.

We walked back to my house at midnight.

'So have fun. I bet you can't wait can you, to get back to Nottingham?'

'It'll be good to see everyone. When are you back at college?'

'Next Tuesday. Did your parents mind me staying in their bed?'

'I don't think they even realized.'

'Oh OK. Good. Well take care.'

'You too.'

He leaned in, and hugged me for a couple of seconds, then tried to kiss me again. This time, something stopped me, Christ knows what, and I pulled back. I filled the silence with my version of goodbye.

'Take care, lovely. I'll write to you.'

He seemed a little confused, a little surprised. But he squared up, and took a step back.

'Yeah, I'm crap with letters, but I'll give it a stab!'

'See you later.' The Essex sign off.

'Bye.'

And he walked off, up the road.

I did write to him, that weekend. I got a reply about two months later, a stupidly short letter talking about magic mushrooms and some film he had seen. I wrote back the next day, but didn't get a reply. I phoned him that Christmas, but there was no reply at his house, and I found out from one of his friends that he had gone to stay with his grandparents. I started seeing somebody at college, somebody he knew actually. It didn't last. Marlon did an exchange year that summer, and went pretty much straight from Nottingham to Kansas University. I went away to university that September. He took a year out and went travelling the following year, apparently. I went back to uni. His parents moved to be near his grandparents. I went away on my gap year. I didn't see him. I got a birthday card that year, sent to my parents' house. My twentieth birthday. He was long gone. I rarely thought of him any more, and I was seeing somebody else, a little more seriously by that time.

I don't really know what happened there. It was a strange time, and I think he was maybe just filling an otherwise boring summer. And even though I have had boyfriends since, and 'relationships' that have lasted much longer, he is the one I think of with a peculiar affection.

I have no idea where he is. I haven't seen him since.

When I think of him now, I think of him at nineteen. I feel like I kept on growing, getting older, and passed him by, and now I am actually five years older than he is, instead of two years younger. I feel like an old woman, can you believe, chuckling at how impressed I was with him. It's always interesting to think what if? But I don't think I want to see him again. He's probably married, he could have kids for God's sake. Yes it could be interesting, but more credibly a massive disappointment.

Is that enough? Enough or not, you don't get any more. You don't need it.

The thing is with Henry, I don't think my actions need explaining away by some traumatic bygone, or previous underlying abuse. A shattered heart does not, in this case at least, explain anything.

I don't think I've behaved peculiarly, or bizarrely, or in any way abnormally. No this is not the stuff of fantasy. This is not supposed to be a romance novel. Henry is no lord of the manor, and I am no serving wench with a drunken father, and a questionable upbringing, but a lovely set of milk jugs.

I've had my fair share of boyfriends, mini relationships, one-night encounters, friends who have become lovers, and vice versa. But nothing where I have ever even entertained the notion of permanence. I have liked some men more than others, as you have seen, and some romantic interludes have lasted that bit longer. I haven't deliberately run away from intimacy, but I haven't forced it either. I have spent my time with the people who meant most at that time, and whose company I enjoyed for a sometimes brief period. But I have just always known that things haven't worked out, or won't work out, or that I would like to spend my time with someone else now thank you very much.

I haven't always been the executioner in my relationships. I have been told it's him and not me a few times as well, but I have always somehow agreed. I have never held on too long, and maybe I have let go too easily.

This is certainly uncharted water for me, you see. The prospect of losing somebody I don't want to lose. Of having the rug pulled from beneath my feet, when I was actually quite comfortable, and had a future mapped out. This is not an instance when I could ever look back and smile. I think this is why it doesn't seem entirely real to me. I don't think Henry and I will actually call it quits, because I don't feel I am ready to. My mind's eye sees quite clearly that we would still like to spend quite a bit more time together, so why should it end?

So no, I cannot explain my actions, and I will not give you a pair of rose-tinted glasses to view me through. I haven't hurt Henry on purpose, I haven't taken my vengeance against man, and acted upon impulses driven by a deeper torture. I just did it. I just spent the night with Matt. I just (and God knows this bit stumps me as well) married the fool. It's not like I planned it. I just got drunk and made a mistake.

And maybe it would be easier to understand if my heart had been broken before, because at least then I would know what I'm dealing with. But unfortunately for us all, Henry is the first.

A Very Real Pain

I wake up that night, roused by a pain in my side as I roll over. On Henry's side of the room a light is on, and I can see that the clock reads 9.30 p.m. Twisting painfully, rubbing my eyes to get accustomed to the light, trying to see what Henry is doing. He is packing. I have been asleep since he walked out, for over five hours. The accident must have taken it out of me. Of course I have done no packing myself, and we are leaving in hours. I pull myself up, and Henry flinches, realizing I am awake, but doesn't turn around to face me.

'Would you have woken me, or just left me here?'

'I was going to do your packing for you. I would have got you up. I'm going to have to carry all the bags anyway. You just have to walk.'

For some reason, we are talking in whispers. Both of us, barely audible, speaking gently to each other, cushioning blows to come.

'When do we have to leave, Hen?'

'I've booked a cab for 11.30. You've still got a couple of hours.'

But he is distant, cold. This is the time to do it. We've dragged this on long enough, without saying anything. I at least need to put it to bed. We've spent the last few days avoiding the subject, avoiding the fact that one of us has to say, out loud, it's over. But we both know it. I clung on there, for a while, to a hope that he might not hate me, to a chance that we could work it out somehow. But Henry is right. Two people cannot do this to each other, can't put each other through a gamut of emotions like this and kill each other's trust so much, and survive it relationship intact.

It isn't my moral code that I seem to think I should be living up to, but it is a code that we both know. You aren't unfaithful. You don't admit it if you are, and want to stay together. You don't have these doubts. None of these rules are realistic of course. It's starting to dawn on me now that they mean nothing. If you are lucky enough to be in a relationship that is really working, that is somehow making your life worth living, and not killing you both, then you pat yourself on the back and get on with the day to day of life. You just keep getting through the day together, and giving each other something to look forward too. You will invariably find someone else attractive, sometimes you'll do something about it, and sometimes you won't. Sometimes you'll just do it because you are drunk. But all you have really done is break this mythical code that we are supposed to live our relationships by. It hasn't changed the way you feel about the person you are with. But the guilt is enough to drive you apart. Or the feeling that you have been wronged, if you are on the receiving end, whether you actually feel wronged or not. You end up walking away because you have been conditioned for years to think you should.

I don't think everybody lives their lives like this any more. I think people have this realization, and I have just had mine; you do what you can to get by, and that is the end of it. But Henry? Henry has not had his realization, and it is a long way off. Henry has been fashioned by his childhood and his father, and the destruction he has seen along the way. Henry's code is a code for himself, he will be a better man, he won't cause the pain he has seen others cause. He won't tolerate it from others himself. He wants trust and to be trusted. He wants a promise, and a guarantee. He wants an assurance that he won't be the cause of someone's tears, but he needs someone else to provide this for him. Henry is tearing himself up inside because of the fear that he himself can't be trusted. Henry hasn't realized yet that that's the way it works. He'll hurt someone one day. He's hurting me.

All my bollocks, my philosophizing about love, about the 'one', is nothing compared to how I'm feeling now. I need somebody to get me through the day, and make me smile in the evening. Someone to talk to, and to hug me at night. And someone who makes me a better person, who makes me see things differently. Somehow, strangely, I had found that with Henry. It's not the way I thought it would turn out. I wish that someone could still be Henry, but he refuses to think like me. He doesn't think that's enough. Yes, Henry needs an assurance for himself and I have done too much already to give it to him. We have finished this for each other. But I have to say it.

'I'm not wrong am I, Henry, we are over?'

Silence.

'Henry? I think this is it, isn't it. I think we've killed this one off.'

'You have.'

'What?'

'You have killed us off. You ended this for us.'

'No, Henry, we have done this, together. I could carry on if I thought you would still love me. But you can't let us carry on, so we have killed this off, together.'

'You did it. I didn't marry someone else. I didn't sleep with . . .' the words stick in his throat. I can't see his face. He isn't shouting at all. He is speaking quietly. He has stopped folding things, he is just looking out of the window, at the neon outside. His side of the room is all lit up. I'm the one in darkness.

'Henry, if I thought we had a chance I'd cling to it, but we don't and that is not something that it takes just one person to decide.'

'Fine. I don't want to argue semantics. I don't want a postmortem. What you have done means I can't carry on being with you now. So yes, that is a decision I get to make, so maybe it is both of us.'

'Henry, will you look at me?'

He sits there, just staring out of the window for a long time, and I can hear the clock ticking. I can hear people walking past our room in the corridor. I can hear noise from the street. He doesn't turn around, and I stare at his back. I stare at the back of his neck, at his shoulders, the back of his arms. I will him to turn round. I want to see his face, in the quiet here, one last time on our own. This could be the last time.

He turns round, face down.

'Henry. Will you look at me?'

and there are tears in his eyes.

'I did love you. I do. I'm sorry.'

'I know, Henry, I'm sorry too.'

He turns back and carries on folding. His arm wipes something away from his face quickly.

'Hen, I'm going to have a wash. I won't be long.'

Kicking off the sheets, ignoring the pain in my side, not even really feeling it, I walk into the bathroom and close the door. I look in the mirror, at the mascara under my eyes, my nose. I look at my mouth, top lip fuller than the bottom. I look at my hair, hanging over my shoulders. And then I really look at my eyes again. I stare intensely, until it blurs, trying to see what I am really feeling. Something keeps jumping in my stomach. A frog or a fly is leaping around in there, and a slight sickness sits at the bottom of my throat. But all I can see are my eyes, big grey eyes, looking back at someone I don't really know. Someone I don't recognize. The last person you ever really know is yourself, what you'll do, how you'll make someone feel. If you looked at your face, and could see the harm you would do, I don't think you could ever really look again. I turn away. I can't bear to look any more.

Soulmates?

Am I killing you with cynicism yet, do you want to throw me against the wall? Are you already using me as a doorstop? Am I keeping your spaghetti stable, or lifting up your lamp? Or will you keep going with me? This is my life and I don't know if you care, or why you should. Or maybe you just feel sorry for Henry, and will wait until he finds himself some vapid little air hostess on the flight home who will worship him for the rugby-playing English god that he is. Except he isn't a god. He's not so hard done by. And I'm not such a bitch.

I think it will depend on the stage you are at: are you in the same place as me? Or have you been there, or can you conceive of someone who could be? Have you met your 'one' already? Are you sitting there crying out at my folly?

If you have met your 'one', the real one, then good for you, because how lucky are you? All the pieces have to fit, and they have with you. Neither of you can be too good looking or too 'unattractive' for the other, because this will cause problems as you well know. Your personalities have to fit as well, which I am sure you have found out. I mean if you have your 'one', do you believe they are your soulmate?

Do you know the most appalling thing? Soulmate comes up as a misspelt word when you type it in to your computer! Isn't that terrible. Isn't that just the one thing I don't want to hear. Are you sitting there saying I told you so? Saying stop your naivety, you loon, because we all know there is no such thing as a soulmate, and I am pragmatic and have found someone that does it for me on a daily basis and that is enough. Or are you as disappointed as me, because you are still holding out for that soulmate? Or do you know that all of this is pointless, because it is all down to fate, and you have your soulmate, because it was destiny. How did you know, I mean, that he/she was the one for you? Is it obvious? Is it completely unavoidable, and all the signs point to it, and even the most stupid among us could not fail to notice? Because I don't think I'd know. He could come up to me with a rose in his teeth, a copy of the *Guardian* under his arm, and a diamond in his pocket, cracking jokes and looking down lovingly at me from six foot two in his stockinged feet. I still wouldn't know. There would have to be something wrong with him.

Has anybody ever called you their soulmate? I've had it once. It was a man I didn't even really know. We had spent time together, and been sexual without actually having sex, and one day he just blurted it out – 'I think we're soulmates.' I was so insulted! I could have killed him. Why? It's a horrible thing to have to put down in black and white, but I suppose I should. It was because I thought he wasn't that bright. I mean, I thought I was slumming it, intellectually.

Do you hate me now? Somebody says the most flattering wonderful thing to me, and I take it as an insult, because he has less exam passes than I have. Believe me when I say I am ashamed. Although I should point out that he maybe didn't understand the gravity of the statement, not that I'm being bitchy, but I doubt that he had ever actually sat down and thought about it. He was bloody good-looking though, much better-looking than me, if that means anything.

Of course we finished not long after that; it was a mutual thing. I think he got bored with me constantly asking him to define words, to reassure myself that he knew what they meant. I got bored with the fact that he blatantly did not know. But we got on there for a while. I made him laugh, he made me laugh. We never had any earth shattering conversations. I fancied him, looks wise. I don't know what he thought really. I know that I was unlike the people he generally spent time with. I know that he had potential to be tapped if he or somebody else took the time, but I didn't bother.

I don't know what he's doing now or where he is. But he was really sweet, and if I met him now, for the first time, I think maybe we'd last a little longer. He could have been my soulmate for all I know, because I obviously have no idea what it means. I should have got him to define that one.

A Very Ordinary Break-Up

Henry's brother and his wife broke up three months after they got married.

Mikey stayed with Hen for the first couple of weeks, before he'd sorted himself out a flat, and it was a terrible time. To begin with Henry barely spoke to him, barely even acknowledged he was there. It wasn't a pleasant atmosphere to say the least. I cooked us all dinner, on the first Saturday Mikey was there, trying to be cheerful, trying to get the two of them to talk. Mikey was despondent as hell. And rightly so, his marriage had just ended. But it had been of his doing, he had walked out, which was why Henry was having such trouble looking at his brother. To say he was disgusted was an understatement. You could see absolute disdain in his eyes, and I never wanted him to look at me like that. Henry was a person who could really hurt you with a look. On the brief occasions that he allowed his eyes to meet Mikey's there was nothing but appalled disappointment.

For his part, Mikey didn't particularly want to talk about

it, and so did nothing to confront him, or argue with him, or provoke. Henry had said that he could stay because he was his brother, and that was that. He didn't have to talk to him. He didn't have to approve. There was a gulf of difference between talking and approving I said, but Henry did not want to discuss it.

Mikey had not met someone else. He hadn't cheated. Henry wouldn't have allowed him in the house if he had, we all knew that. Not that Henry particularly liked Emma, Mikey's wife. He had believed from the start that Mikey was doing the wrong thing marrying her, and he had told him so, but he wasn't saying I told you so now. Mikey had insisted that he and Emma were getting married, and Henry had dropped it. Admittedly she wasn't our kind of person. She didn't really go out, didn't talk a lot, didn't like the same films, or conversations. She was very quiet, and always nervous at dinner parties if we got the Trivial Pursuit out. She practically hid behind Mikey and refused to answer any of the questions, but never went so far as to say she wouldn't play. She was a receptionist in a dentist's in their town, and had been for years. She was more than happy to continue working there for the rest of her life, or the next ten years at least, or until they wanted to have kids. She was really very pretty, and always looked very . . . clean. That was the word Henry and I had both decided on. Her trainers were always bright white. Her jogging bottoms never had stains on them from last night's spaghetti. She ironed her jeans.

She had grown on me, the more I got to know her, the more I got out of her, and cajoled her into speaking up, dragging her kicking and screaming into conversations. Generally she would just sit and listen while Mikey talked, and spoke for her in fact. I think it was a habit they had got themselves into, him telling her stories for her. He didn't overpower her, but Henry and I could see that she did what he wanted, willingly.

She would always drive, when the four of us went to the pub, and Mikey, Hen and I would drink too much. And even when she didn't come with us, she would be waiting outside at twenty past eleven to pick us up.

And I could kind of see what Mikey saw in her, how easy it must have been for the two of them to just fall into place. They had been seeing each other since they were teenagers, when you always go for looks, and they had never really confronted the fact that they were not alike at all. It must have been easy to do, as she didn't seem the type to put up a fight over anything.

But Mikey never chatted anyone else up, took advantage of the situation. They did seem quietly comfortable together. Henry couldn't understand it.

'It must be so boring though. They have nothing to say to each other that isn't small talk, what happened today, shopping blah blah blah. I couldn't bear it, hon, I swear, I don't know how Mikey does it. They don't bring anything to each other's lives. I know they aren't unhappy, but they don't seem happy, do you know what I mean? It's a habit, an easy life, it's appalling in a way. Mikey's just being lazy, or he's not man enough to admit that it's not what he wants and he should walk away before someone gets really hurt. I think they would both be numb to it if he ended it now. It would be a relief for both of them.'

Sometimes we would sit around at dinner talking about anything and everything, and Mikey would hit on a subject that would light him up. He would become this excitable passionate other person, especially if it was American politics. It fascinated him, the whole Watergate affair, the FBI, CIA, Cold War. He could go on for ages if you let him, about the presidential right to lie, about Vietnam and Johnson, and Clinton cover-ups. He insisted Neil Armstrong had never taken a step on the moon. He wanted to go to America more than anything.

But every year he put it off, and the two of them would go to Rhodes, or the Canaries. I think he just didn't want to go with Emma, as if she would somehow kill it for him. He couldn't share it with her. It wasn't even that she wasn't interested, she just listened to him when he talked about it, and left it at that. I don't think she believed she had anything profitable to add, that she hadn't already heard from Mikey. But then admittedly, she hadn't even tried.

Nonetheless they got engaged – they were already engaged by the time I met them – and it was taken for granted that they would get married, have kids, settle down.

But two months and three weeks after the wedding day, Mikey turned up at Henry's declaring he had left her, and could he crash for a while.

He had known all the way through the engagement that he didn't want to do it he said, but he got swept along. The whole time they had just been seeing each other, he could kid himself it wasn't forever, until they had decided to get married, and he couldn't recall either of them actually asking the other, it had just got out of control. Somehow they had managed to set a date, and her parents had started throwing money at it. She picked a dress, flowers were arranged, bridesmaids decided upon. Mikey had been slowly going mad, and it had dawned on him that this was the last thing he wanted to do.

'Look at you and Henry, look at the way you get so passionate about each other, so into what you are saying. Look at how much you laugh together, and wind each other up, and just really get on!' I had felt so flattered, but at the same time so bad. I had my doubts about me and Henry, and Mikey wanted what we had!

'But Mikey, look at how we argue. You and Emma never have the steaming rows that we have. We get close to violence some days!'

'Yes, but that's the passion that I want, I'd give my right arm to have an argument with Emma the way you two go at it sometimes, like cat and dog. But it was never like that for us. We were safe, because we didn't care enough. We never had explosions. Nothing ever seemed to rock our boat. But I couldn't back out on her, after all those years, could I? I couldn't do that to her. I couldn't let her down like that. She hadn't done anything wrong. So I kidded myself it was just cold feet, the usual nerves, and held my tongue. But the wedding, oh God, that day. It was the worst day of my life. I knew it, even when I got up to make my speech. Even when I was thanking her, my beautiful wife for marrying me, I wanted to run from the reception. I wanted to walk out and do something with my life. I didn't want that to be my life.

'Look at the photos, the honeymoon photos, what a joke! You could see it then. We were in Jamaica, we were supposed to be having the happiest time of our lives, and both of us, not just me, we looked like we had been married for ten years, not ten days.'

Mikey got choked up then, but he didn't cry.

'The thing is, it's not me I'm sad for, it's her. You can grow to love someone, you can allow yourself to love someone you shouldn't, but you can't spend your life with the wrong person. I should have stopped it long ago, I suppose. That's what Henry thinks, I know. Now I've ruined her life, but life feels like it's just starting for me. I swear, I've never been so excited, never been so happy, and so fucking miserable at the same time. It's not that I want to get out there and sow my seed, it's too soon; I don't want to see anyone right now. But the prospect! The prospect of meeting someone I really like, that I can really talk to, I can't help but be optimistic. I've never felt like that before.'

'It's not always that easy,' I said.

'But it'll be alright, I know it. I can give it a stab at least.'

Henry refused to discuss it with him. Even when I told him how bad Mikey felt, he wouldn't listen. Henry said if he wasn't sure, he should never have done it. He should never have gone through with it. It was a terrible thing to do to someone, and a ridiculous thing to do to yourself. That was Mikey's life now, Henry said, and he couldn't change the fact that he had a failed marriage after three months. How did that look? I told him not to be so bloody sanctimonious, and Henry got really angry. I said Mikey was making a new start, and no matter how much he had fucked up along the way, he was being brave now, and doing something for himself. Henry should be happy for him.

'Happy? You could not have used a more inappropriate word! My family is fucked up, full of selfish men who do terrible things to the people who love them.'

Of course Henry was just scared it was in the genes.

The Beautiful People

Oscar Wilde said only shallow people do not judge by appearances. So that makes me pretty deep. And you too, admit it. It doesn't make you a bad person, it makes you perfectly normal. We all judge by appearance to an extent, because we are all aware of own faults. We know what we lack in the looks department, and assume that other people will see it too. The people with the luxury of not judging on appearance are invariably the most beautiful or handsome themselves. The rest of us, the hordes with an imperfection here and there, well we would be bowled over if Brad Pitt or Marilyn Monroe came up and asked us for a date. Would you say no?

Nonetheless we are supposed to go for 'personality' but by that we only ever mean a personality like our own – a suitable humour, intelligence, morality. This is where the 'click' is, the spark that will mean we can stay together for the rest of our lives. But if this is the aspect that will guarantee relationship success, then why do we get distracted time and again, by the height, the weight, the colour of hair, the breast size, the dick size? I believe the answer lies in the fact that appearance is often the only thing that distinguishes us from the next person. We are mostly unexceptional.

Our intelligence varies, but is rarely of genius proportions, there are in fact many cases of people who cannot even spell genius. Humour varies of course, the black, the sexist, the racist, the surreal, people who find dead bodies funny (www.rigormortis.hysterical.com) but which of us is that funny? And more importantly, who is so hard to make laugh? We all laugh at the same things most of the time, forming a consensus that certain films, for example, are very funny. The same joke can make a million people laugh, a hundred million people laugh. This in itself makes a mockery of the notion of a 'g.s.o.h.', so sought after in the personal columns. This good sense of humour equates in the end to the physical ability to laugh, and not be logging on to aforementioned sick web-sites.

The result of our perfect unexceptionality is that so many people get married in such good faith. If most people are compatible in that they have the same sense of humour, roughly the same intelligence, the same set of morals because they have been living their whole lives in the same society, then what else is there to go for but looks?

Furthermore we have taken it upon ourselves to establish an ideal of beauty which many of us spend our time foolishly chasing. We recklessly aspire to look like the 'models' of our time, and it makes our options even wider.

So you're at a party, and you see someone you like the look of, because he reminds you of that actor in that film. He likes the look of you, because you look a bit like that singer, and have the same haircut as that actress in that sitcom on Thursdays. You chat, it's fine. He tells a joke you heard on the radio last week, and you laugh now as you laughed then. You both have some alcohol. You grab each other and go to a room, and desperately hang on for dear life, try and swallow each other up, crawl inside, get as close as you can, hanging on with your hips and lips and hands. Trying not to be alone.

You meet up in the week, if you don't already have a boyfriend and he doesn't have a girlfriend, or a boyfriend for that matter. You go and see a film that scares you both, because generally we are scared of the same things. You go to a restaurant afterwards where they serve food that you both like, and you know this because you have eaten it all your life. On the way home you kiss, and start to think about sex again. That opportunity to be half of one, as opposed to one on its own.

If he doesn't sleep with someone else, or you don't find out, and you don't go off with someone with slightly broader shoulders, and you find each other bearable on a day to day basis, then you get married.

A tragedy then, that in five years' time you will either be divorced already, or be staying together for the kids, or you'll be a little slow, and just waking up to the realization that prompts the first two. From that first desperate urge to be part of someone, you will now never have felt so alone. The cure for loneliness is not just to spend all your time with someone you happen to meet, and whose ways you happen to find endearing at the time.

I'm not saying that you don't love that person, what I'm saying is that that love has a slim chance of lasting, because you were never meant to be together. You just happened. You took the easy option.

So let's go back to those few people who aren't statues of beauty but hang out for personality anyway. They have a different definition of personality however. It is distinct in that they are looking for something exceptional. This makes them exceptional themselves. They want a depth of feeling that comes from something more than just spending a lot of time together. How do you get to be one of these people, because I want to be one. I want to hold out for exceptional, without looking like a desperate single making excuses. It's a harder route to take than just being with someone for comfort.

The other side of the coin is that occasionally you see what can grow from a chance meeting, between two people who seem to be perfectly average together at first. I think the key is passion, and I'm not just talking about lust. A deeper passion for the one you are with. To be passionate about everything that person is, what they stand for, what they do, and have that passion infuse your own life. Two people that ignite a part of themselves they didn't even know was there: that is something worth all the beauty in the world, and all of Oscar Wilde's pointless soundbites for that matter.

Joining the Army

It was a lazy Saturday, my favourite kind. I didn't have to go shopping I could if I wanted to, but I didn't have to. I had absolutely nothing planned. For once Henry was not playing rugby, as the other side couldn't get enough players together because of this terrible flu virus that had been going around. Henry had stayed over last night. We had gone to see Barry Manilow at the Arena. I kid you not.

Henry's mum had phoned me at work, and said she had the flu as well, and she was a little distraught. She had tickets to see Barry Manilow that night, and she was going to have to miss it. Of course she had tickets to see him next week in Manchester too, and then in Bournemouth, and then in Cardiff, but she didn't want to miss the London show, and the first night. She was part of the 'Barry Army'. She had made loads of friends from it, all these middle-aged women who just jacked in their day to day lives once a year when the great man toured Britain. They travelled around in a coach, about fifty of them, and went to every gig that he did. They had all the best tickets as well, because they were fan club members, and got preferential treatment. Henry liked the fact that his mum had become so much more social, and noticeably more happy. Of course I had never known her not be a part of the 'Barry Army' so she'd always seemed very happy to me. However he did admit on a number of occasions that it appalled him that his mother, for two weeks of the year, followed a middle-aged American around the country waving a sign saying 'Pick Me Barry.'

When she had offered us the tickets I had accepted straight away, but I knew Henry was going to be a hard sell. I knew a couple of songs, as my mum used to play his albums when she did the ironing when I was young. She didn't do the ironing any more. They had a woman to do it now.

When I had told Henry where we were going, on the phone that afternoon, I was, unsurprisingly met with a round of expletives.

'Oh fuck off. No. I just want a quiet night in the pub. My mum likes him for God's sakes. I don't want to see Barry Manilow, even if the tickets are free. The boys will rip the piss, I'll get slaughtered!'

'Please, please, Henry, I really want to go!'

'Eve, take someone else then, I don't mind.'

'But I want to go with you. Please?'

'I don't even know any of his songs.'

'Henry, you do, you just don't realize it. You must remember "Could It Be Magic". Henry, are you still there?'

'That's bloody Take That.'

'No, first it was Barry Manilow. Or how about "I Can't Smile Without You" or "Daybreak"?'

'Did he do that one?'

'Yes! Please, Henry, please come with me?'

'Do you really want to go?'

'Yes.'

'As long as you promise not to sing. You've got a terrible singing voice.'

'Fine.'

'Fine. I'll come.'

'Hurrah! I'll meet you outside my work at six-thirty 'cos it will take forever to get there, and it starts at eight. You'll love it, I promise.'

'Whatever. I'll see you at half past six.'

'Love you.'

'Too bloody right you do.' And he hung up.

We had the best night. To start with, the seats were unbelievable, the best seats I have ever had in my life. We were two rows from the front. I couldn't believe it as we were being ushered up the aisle, and the attendant just kept walking closer and closer to the stage. Henry didn't like seated concerts, because people behind us always complained about his height, like he could do anything about it. Not this time! This time we were surrounded by a bunch of about fifty fifty-plus women, and the odd man in a feather boa, all of whom loved Henry. Well they loved him as soon as I told them he was Joyce's son. They all knew each other, and they all had a sign to wave for when Barry sang "I Can't Smile Without You". Apparently, at every show he got somebody from the audience to sing it with him, and if you held up your sign he might pick you! Henry rolled his eyes to heaven, while I thought about nabbing the sign from the woman next to me. It was laminated and everything. No offence, but she was about seventy, and I thought Barry would have a more fun time with me. As soon as it started I could see Henry, arms crossed, desperately trying not to enjoy himself, like some Stalinist git, but his foot was tapping.

Barry was incredibly saucy with the crowd, in a gentle way, which sent shrieks flying from the whole audience every time he thrust his hips or made a 'mounting' joke. You couldn't help but laugh; even Henry laughed. When I saw him sniggering I knew he was starting to enjoy himself.

My God, can that man belt out a song – none of that lip syncing business for him. He was fantastic. He played "Mandy", and I was in tears! Surrounded by all these people that loved him, and with a voice like that, you couldn't help but get swept along.

The first song after the interval was "I Can't Smile Without You", and as they played the first few bars every sign in the arena went up. A stadium full of 'fifty years young, Barry', or 'Barry, I can't smile without you!' The woman next to me was jumping and shouting and waving her banner like she was possessed, as Barry strolled to the front of the stage, and started looking over at her. I got caught up in the excitement I think, because I started jumping and shouting for her. But Henry had other ideas. Before I knew what was going on Henry had me under the arms and was lifting me up and virtually offering me to Barry. He could be so strong sometimes, and I was more excited by that than anything else. It makes a woman feel feminine if her partner can pick her off the ground, and Henry never did it normally, because I thought I was too heavy for him. He was still holding me aloft however and, wouldn't you just know it, Barry picked me.

'Yes I think so, let's have the young lady there, your

boyfriend, is he your boyfriend? or your father, seems kind of keen to get rid of you, but I'll have you!'

Somebody, a security guard, had hold of my hand and was leading me to the steps by the stage, as I started to go red. This was shocking, how could Henry do this to me? I turned to see him crying with laughter, literally doubled up, that bastard.

I know now how rock stars, pop stars, whatever you would call Barry Manilow, get their infamous egos. I got on the stage and looked out at the crowd and froze. It was lit up, so that Barry could see all the signs, and it was an unbelievable sight. All you can see is a sea of heads. You can't make out features or faces, but all of them are cheering and waving, to prove they are actually individuals and not just a long line of dummies welded together. It makes you feel sea sick, but Barry seemed fine. He had me by the hand, and was leading me centre stage. Up close he didn't look at all like himself, the man I had been cheering moments ago. He looked like a blond forty-something man in a good suit with a large nose. I remember hardly anything of what happened next, in the way that anything strange that happens to you seems to get blocked out. I remember that he held my hand for the first verse, and I remembered the words. For the second verse, the lyrics of which completely escaped me, resulting in my just making inappropriate noises into the microphone, he sat behind me on the piano with one leg either side of me. People screamed when he did that. I hope I didn't scream.

I was given a tape of the entire experience by one of Barry's entourage so that I could cherish it. I haven't watched it yet. I'll take it round to Joyce's one night, at which point she will either love me or hate me. This whole Barry love is a risky business.

I was escorted back to my seat by security and Henry was still doubled up with laughter, managing to squeeze out between breaths what a truly terrible voice I had, and snatching the video to show everybody down the pub.

If I'm honest, I thoroughly bloody enjoyed it, and every song thereafter seemed a little bit more personal because of my brief time spent with Barry. I shan't be joining Joyce and her feathered homosexuals on the Barry bus just yet, but I'll be back to Wembley at some point.

So the morning after, Henry and I chose to do nothing. We were going to sit, and read the papers, and watch some football, and maybe an old film, and do nothing else all day. I was making the bed when I heard Henry killing himself with laughter again in the front room. If nothing else Henry was a very happy boy these days, which I saw as a good reflection on me.

I walked into the living room, plumping up a pillow, to see what was so hysterical, and make sure he wasn't watching my Barry video. But it was some football programme, showing the worst penalties ever taken. Apparently a man kicking a ball in the wrong direction, or worse, over the bar, was hysterical. Anyone laughing that much has a peculiar effect however, and you start to laugh along too, like yawning. I had been feeling a little apprehensive about the holiday in a couple of weeks. About whether this was the right time for us to be going away on some grand vacation, what with the whole Tim incident still so fresh in my mind. Of course I hadn't told Henry about the kiss, or Tim shoplifting a grope, because that would be a bad thing. We would be over, there was no doubt in my mind, and quite rightly so, which was the last thing I wanted And, given Henry and Tim's competitive streak, I could not have picked a worse person to have done it with. No, Henry and I would be finished if I ever told him.

So why did I do it? Knowing that Henry could have walked in and caught us, and we would be finished, for the sake of some seedy contact with a man I fancy but have no real feelings for. What is it about being attracted to someone physically that makes you do things that you shouldn't do? Knowing that it would hurt Henry more than anything, I had done it anyway. I also knew that I loved Henry, and I didn't even like Tim most of the time. It didn't make me love Henry any less, I just physically really wanted, really want I suppose, to touch Tim's tongue with mine, and feel him feeling me. Why? It would ruin everything. Although the real question should be why would it ruin everything? Why should it matter?

Henry took the car out later to get me some cigarettes, and a lottery ticket for himself, while I made dinner. He came back and went running into the bedroom. I couldn't be arsed to investigate, and didn't even give it a second thought until later when I went to put clean underwear on after my bath. Sitting on top of my knickers was a Barry Manilow CD. "The Platinum Collection." All his greatest hits.

Everything Gets Scrambled

The week before we flew out to Vegas, Henry's boss asked us to lunch to celebrate Henry's promotion. He had been made a Marketing and Sales Manager, and received a substantial pay rise which made us all very happy. Henry was pleased as punch to be granted a glowing acknowledgement of all his hard work and talent, and in the knowledge that all his career plans were firmly on track. I was pleased at the prospect of Henry justifiably paying for more of our social excursions. We had been on roughly the same pay before this, and it drew attention to the fact that he could live on it while paying for nearly every meal at every restaurant we went to, and I could not. I had more shoes, but this argument didn't seem to hold a lot of water with him. It also meant he could upgrade his company Alfa to a sporty Audi, and that made us both very happy. We could be shallow too. It wasn't all tortured conversations and deep and meaningfuls.

Henry's boss was from Wales, and my only instruction for lunch was not to show any cleavage, to avoid embarrassing stares from the big drunken recently divorced Welshman. Henry assured me Dai would be drunk. Probably before we even got there. The man could drink five pints for breakfast apparently, and chase it all down with half a bottle of whiskey for elevenses. And this was all on a normal day, without the trauma of a recent divorce to contend with. His wife Pauline had eventually left him after one rugby song too many at three in the morning. Furthermore, she was English, and as their eighteen years together had gone by, and increasingly every time he got drunk, he had grown to view her as the Establishment personified, and the enemy of every pit worker south of Wrexham, specifically during the Six Nations Rugby tournament.

He would break down each year as his team floundered, threaten to beat her with a wooden spoon if Wales lost again and demand a divorce. He never actually raised a hand to her of course, but she began to tire of the same thing, every year, and every time a struggling Welsh team got their arses whipped by fifteen 'public school pretty boys in make-up and tight shorts.'

Dai was living the stereotype, and Pauline couldn't take it any more. And so that year, as Dai had once again packed his Louis Vuitton suitcase after twenty pints of lager and another crushing defeat for his team in the Arms Park, and stated his intention to return to the mines whether they were open or not, Pauline had taken him at his word. He had left to sleep at his office, and she had changed the locks. Dai, shamefaced and apologetic the following morning, and trying to get back into his six bedroom house, found there was no room at the inn for this son of the valleys. Pauline had finally snapped, and applied for a divorce.

Dai was a broken man, and gave her everything she asked for, which admittedly wasn't much. They both still cried every time they met. Henry knew only too well to stay out of Dai's way if he had been out to lunch with Pauline now, as he saw the big man slump back into the office, red-eyed and crestfallen, and heard the weeping through his office wall.

They had never had any children, and as the months passed, Henry played surrogate son, and took his boss to rugby matches and the pub to try and buck him up, or at least stop him doing anything silly. Dai and Pauline still spoke on the phone, and he even spent the night with her in his old house a couple of times a month. Neither of them claimed to want anybody else, but Pauline refused to let him back, as much as she loved him. Yes, Dai was a broken man. He explained to Henry that it wasn't the sex, or the socializing, or even the companionship. It was the life. It was his life. He didn't want to see Pauline once in a while, spend Bank Holidays with her. He wanted to know where she was during the day; he liked the idea of her in their bedroom at night reading a magazine, while he watched the TV downstairs. She was his life, but he had ruined it. Dai never once tried to allocate any of the blame Pauline's way.

Dai had suggested the lunch, which Henry had wanted to keep relatively booze-free, but Dai's secretary had, on his insistence, booked us into the Brazilian Champagne Sunday Lunch Special at the Waldorf Hotel on Aldwych. The plan was therefore to get as smashed as Dai, and subsequently not notice how incredibly drunk he was, or make his drunkenness conspicuous to everybody else. We needn't have worried.

The Waldorf Ballroom is only a little spectacular. It is

glitz and chandeliers, but not massive extravagance. It is lovely, but it doesn't take your breath away. However, this little deal they have going on a Sunday lunchtime does. As you walk past the hotel, from Holborn into Covent Garden, you could not possibly imagine what lies within.

We arrived at midday, and were led into the ballroom, which was quietly humming, tables full of old couples, middle-aged couples, youngish couples, chatting quietly, all out for a pleasant Sunday lunch. It seemed reserved, calm, almost timid. Bordering on boring, if I'm being honest. There was a band in the corner, quietly playing Afro-Caribbean tunes, and a food display in the centre of the room, explosions of fruit and salmon and scrambled eggs. It didn't look like a riot. Nice, but no fun.

Henry was suited and booted, which was a rare sight. Men can nearly always be split in to two camps – those who look better in a suit, and those who look better in jeans. A suit gives shape and bulk to those who lack it, makes their shoulders square, and their stomachs flatter. But Henry wasn't in need of those things, and he had massive thighs that looked comfortable and inviting in jeans, but a little ill at ease in a suit. He looked too big for a suit, but in jeans and a jumper, my Henry could pretty much beat them all.

Physical attraction usually spurs a relationship on at the start, and then as you grow to know one another over time, it becomes less apparent, but still important. With Henry it hadn't really worked that way. I had liked him at first of course, but I hadn't been blown away with his looks. I had still been lusting after Tim, who was not as big, but had a charm about his build, and his face. However, over the months, and the years now, Henry had become so much more attractive, it was almost unfathomable. When I saw Henry now, sitting at a table across the room, or walking towards me, or guiding me through tables to our seat that Sunday, I was bowled over by his sexiness. Yes, I preferred him in his jeans and jumper, but in his suit, looking a little starched, and very business like, I just really wanted to feel him: feel his arms under his shirt, feel his thighs under his trousers, feel his back as I placed my hand on him affectionately.

I was in a jacket and trousers, and had been promptly rebuked by Henry in the cab, because he could clearly see breast. I made the point that they were kind of unavoidable, and that unless I wore a high neck kaftan, you were going to know I had a fair pair. He looked out of the cab window for about two seconds, pretended to be disgusted, and then decided that he wanted to have a snog and a bit of a grope anyway. Typical. Damned if I do, damned if I don't.

Dai was already at the table, but his champagne glass was full, leading Henry and I to glance at each other in surprise – maybe he was on the wagon. As Henry shook and I kissed our hellos, a waiter leaned over and filled up two fresh champagne flutes for us. Good service at least. We arranged ourselves, and Dai and I both lit cigarettes. Dai said 'Cheers' to Henry, *Iechyd Da* (Welsh for good health, and actually remarkably easy to pronounce) and we both watched as he downed his champagne in one. The waiter leaned over instantly and filled it straight back up. Now we understood. I took a sip, placed the glass back on the table, and the waiter silently filled it up over my shoulder. Henry caught on, motioned to me to neck my drink, and gulped down his glass in one. Back to plan A – get pissed quick, try and catch up with Dai.

We chatted about rugby for a while, and Dai suddenly went quiet. Shit, we had reminded him of Pauline, but no, it was fine, he was just trying to remember the words to "Bread of Heaven". We were treated to two verses and three choruses before he ran out of steam. I necked another champagne, and Henry asked for another glass to be filled, and proceeded to drink from both simultaneously. Dai didn't seem to notice.

'So, Henry, Eve, you two don't live together do you? Any plans to, is it?'

Henry had warned me previously that Dai finished most questions with 'is it?' A Welsh peculiarity that I didn't understand, but then who really understands the Welsh, apart from the other Welsh.

'Oh I suppose, but we haven't really talked about it, Henry, have we? We spend most of our time at yours anyway, don't we, Hen, but mine is handier for my work. I suppose we will in the future, but I don't know. We haven't really discussed it.'

Henry pretended to look distracted during my reply, gazing around the room, eyeing up the food in the middle. Dai looked down at his napkin as I spoke, folding it in half, and in half again, tapping off his cigarette in the ashtray, completely uninterested. Why ask if you don't care? Why subject me to the ordeal of having to come up with a nonchalant excuse for Henry and me not living together, when it was becoming obvious to the world that we didn't, and we should, but I couldn't actually make the decision to do it. There hadn't been any heated arguments, or now or nevers, or 'we have to take the next step's from Henry, but he had mentioned it about a dozen times recently, mainly after a few too many glasses of wine. We had never discussed it soberly. I necked another glass of champagne, and this time I felt it go to my head.

Henry and Dai starting talking about work, and I surveyed the room. In the corner was a man in grey slacks, bright red socks and a tie with a barracuda on it. He had a shocking white pompadour, and was spinning a middle-aged divorcée in red lipstick around and around to the music. A few tables along, a couple who looked like wife swappers were doing the twist. I could see, even from this distance, that the woman was trying to twist too low, to impress her man, and watched with horror, as, in slow motion, she fell on her arse. I looked away. The room had started to liven up. I felt my head start to spin slightly, and as the barracuda swirled around and around, I decided to eat some food, quickly.

An hour later, after salmon and eggs, and a beef roast, about twelve more half glasses of champagne and the introduction of a rather spirited band playing much louder Brazilian salsa in the corner, I was lashed. Henry was holding up incredibly well, just looking a little bemused while Dai sung "Land of Our Fathers". It would appear that Dai was experiencing a heavy dose of what is known as 'Welsh Guilt', when a boy from the valleys comes to England, sets up his own business, does terrifically well, and finds himself enjoying it. Furthermore he had settled in the South East, which had the lowest rainfall count in the whole country. He could not have been more of a traitor. Apparently if you don't wear a Davy lamp to work every day, you actually renounce your nationality. It would seem that all his rugby outbursts at poor Pauline were a manifestation of his guilt at loving an English woman more than life itself. Poor Dai, he was the finest specimen of a fantastic Welshman I had ever seen, apart from maybe Tom Jones, but it didn't seem to sit well in his stomach. Everybody (everybody!) has so many issues: geographical, sexual, material, emotional. It is so hard these days, just to be happy, just to get by. I looked up at Henry then, as he span me round, threw me sideways and then grabbed me back in, and realized how lucky I was.

What had I been doing with Tim for Christ's sake? I nearly jeopardized the whole thing, for some random grope with a guy whose need to undermine his best friend's every happiness seemed to determine his every action. I couldn't bear to think about Tim, about the whole Center Parcs nightmare, and how close we came to upsetting this one massive boat. I started to feel slightly nauseous, as Henry tried to lift me up and get me to kick my legs backwards. I demanded he put me down, stumbled over to the table, and necked another glass of champagne. Dai was conducting an imaginary orchestra in the Llaneii theme song, the town of his birth. It was called '*Sospan Fach*' which, translated, means 'little saucepan.' It's a rugby song, about a big saucepan, and a little saucepan, and a cat scratching a boy called Johnny. I think the symbolism goes right over my head, because I haven't got a fucking clue what that has got to do with rugby.

An hour later, two-thirty, and Dai was leading a fifty-strong conga up the stairs and around the sweet trolley. Henry was puffing on a massive cigar, and twisting from left to right like Frank Sinatra, and I was in the women's toilets, talking to the mirror, trying to get my eyes to focus. My mantra, as always was 'Get Control'. Sometimes it works. Of course sometimes it doesn't. But if you can at least register that you are hideously drunk, you are on the right path to the uphill battle of sobering up. I needed water, and I needed strong black coffee.

Stumbling back into the ballroom, just missing the conga line, I collapsed at the table. Henry stopped and stared at me, realized he knew me, and slumped down next to me, arm around my shoulders.

'Have you had fun, babe?

'Hen, I'm fucking lashed. But Dai looks like he's having fun. Congrats on the promotion, baby, by the way. I don't think I've really said it yet. You've done bloody well. Your star is definitely in the ascendant.' I always try to use long words when I'm drunk, to try to at least seem coherent. Karen says it's very impressive

'Thanks, hon. Are you going to hitch a ride to the stars then, on my coat tails?'

Henry on the other hand, gets drunk and mixes metaphors.

'Oh I think so, for the moment at least, if only for the cash incentive.' Incentive. Good word. Henry kissed the top of my head.

'I love you, hon. Eve?'

I just made it to the toilets in time.

Leaving, Delirious

At the airport we sit in silence. It's unfortunate, but Henry has hurt his shoulder from carrying all the bags. He keeps rubbing it distractedly, and I smile despite myself. He half smiles at me too.

'Don't bloody laugh, it's all your bloody make-up.'

'Oh whatever, Henry. I think you'll find it's your huge bloody trainers.'

'Possibly.'

We sit again in silence, but it is resigned, not uncomfortable. We don't have anything else left to say. I'm not thinking of the flight home, or the journey back to his to pick up my car. We'll be saying goodbye then of course. I can't bear the thought. I'm awake, so awake after my sleep, and I think my eyes must look a little wild. The airport is a little way out of town, and as we drove out the signs and the people seemed to blur into one long stream of colour. I felt more relief than ever before to be leaving somewhere. I can't imagine ever coming back, or ever wanting to.

I'm feeling a little delirious. I keep laughing at things, not even funny things. I feel strangely optimistic, elated almost. I feel higher knowing it won't last. It doesn't bring me down, it pushes me up. I'm appreciating it while it lasts. Henry thinks they gave me drugs at the hospital that are just kicking in. I tell him they didn't. He just keeps rubbing his shoulder, and I can't stop laughing. The angrier he gets, the more I laugh. Like when you are in church, or school assembly. Even if I don't look at him, windmill-ing his arm and wincing, I keep thinking about it and giggling. He is not happy about this at all.

'Look, it's not that fucking funny, give it a rest.'

This makes me worse.

'I don't see what there is to laugh about actually, unless you are just being a bitch.'

I'm not being a bitch. I don't know what I am laughing at. I'm pretty damn devastated but I can't think about that now.

'I'm sorry, Hen, I won't laugh any more.' Hysterical laughter.

'Oh fuck this, I'm going to get a paper.'

Henry storms off, and it stops me laughing. As much. It doesn't seem so funny if he's not here. I'm really going to miss him. Just watching him walk away now I feel a pang. I've buggered it all up.

I'm bloody filthy. I've got dirt under my nails. I should have had a shower, but I felt bad letting Henry pack all my stuff, so I sort of supervised and got in the way. Of course my things didn't get the loving folding treatment his did. They got thrown from one side of the room to the suitcase on the other. Dirty and clean clothes together. He claimed we were in a rush, so he had to put them in like that. Of course we waited in reception for the taxi for fifteen minutes. Whatever, I don't care. It makes me laugh again.

Henry is coming back. Where did he get that tan? He looks really brown, and I've barely got my freckles out. Typical. Just the sight of him walking over makes me laugh again. I don't know what is wrong with me, but I am really exacerbating the situation. He tries to ignore it, slumps down a chair away, because next to me would just be too close for comfort I suppose, as if I would try and mount him in the airport. This makes me laugh. I think about moving over, and sitting really close to him just to piss him off, wind him up. Touch his leg accidentally, but he would only get angry. The thought makes me laugh though.

'Oh look for fuck's sake! I'm going for a drink, I'll be back in time.'

'Oh Henry, don't go, I'll stop laughing I promise.'

He looks at me, and I giggle. He gets up and walks off. Oh Henry.

I just sit there, guarding our hand luggage, watching the people go past. I think I see someone from work, but of course it isn't her. It's funny the way that so many people look the same, or almost the same. Somewhere in the world there is someone who looks exactly like you, probably ten people who look exactly like you, that you will never meet, because they live in Perth, or Prague, or some tiny village somewhere. I'll just have to find one of the ones who looks like Henry, and hope he has had a happier home life, is less of an idealist. Or a romantic. Is Henry a romantic? I suppose he is. I know he wants everything to be perfect, us to be perfect. The fact that he kissed Sarah started killing us slowly even then. He wants a blank sheet. He wants a thousand chances.

He kissed Sarah, and he admitted it. It occurs to me, would I have said anything? Would I have admitted Matt if the nasty little details hadn't forced my hand? I'd been in the room with Henry for about half an hour before Matt showed, and I had said nothing. I had claimed memory loss, pleaded ignorance of my own actions. Had I even felt guilty? I did afterwards, because I realized I had ruined my relationship, and of course Henry was there, in front of me, mortified. The guilt hit me like a steam train, and I was in tears straight away. But was Henry right? Were they tears for me, or for him, or us. Or me?

What good does it do, owning up? It doesn't make it better, it makes it worse. So I had got drunk and done something that I could barely even remember with someone I wasn't even attracted to. I had no feelings for Matt at all. Yes, he was good looking, but I didn't fancy him. I didn't know him. God knew him, we should never forget that. And I didn't fancy Henry any less, it didn't make me stop loving him. It had absolutely no effect on my feelings for him whatsoever. It wasn't a rejection of him, I didn't prefer Matt in any way. Why did it have to affect us?

So if Matt hadn't turned up, what would I have done? Tried my best to cover it up, completely forgotten about the whole night with Matt, and got on with my holiday. We would both be on our way to San Francisco now, and everything would have been alright. I would have loved him just as much as I do now.

But a year down the line he would have said to me, in the middle of some deep post-coital conversation, 'we just have to be honest with each other about everything. As long as we are honest we can last forever.' And the guilt would have hit me then instead. I would have told him, because he claimed to want the truth, and because I don't like secrets, and it would have ended then instead, because Henry did not want that kind of honesty.

'As long as we are honest with each other we can stand anything.' What complete shit. Who really wants honesty? I don't. I don't want my boyfriend or husband to come home at the end of the day all tuckered out from work and ask 'How was your day, dear?' and I would say 'Fine.' Then I would ask 'How was yours? And remember our honesty rule when you reply, honey.'

'Of course, dear, as long as we are honest. Well on the train this morning I smiled at a girl who was probably no more than eighteen. Then at work the receptionist's top was really tight, and I thought that she had a really nice pair of tits. Then I saw a dress in the window of a shop and thought that you were too old for it now. I saw this woman with a short skirt on, and she had great legs, much longer than yours. On the train home, I sat next to this girl who smelt really nice, and it made me quite randy, as did the ticket inspector, who obviously went to the gym a lot. I realized I was having those bisexual feelings again, which turned me on even more, so I considered coming home and knocking one off in the bathroom if you weren't here, but if you were here we'd have a quickie and I could think about either the girl in the short skirt or the ticket inspector. I love you. As long as we are honest.'

I definitely do not want that. But for some reason when we talk about wanting complete honesty, people don't mean thoughts, they mean actions. Admit what you did, and not what you thought, and we'll be fine. It would seem to me that that is completely the wrong way around. A one-night stand or three months of thoughts that you don't want to be with me. Or that you are bored with our sex life, or my conversation. I'll take the one-night stand any day.

But people don't think like that. Because it becomes more about how you are seen as a couple, how you are seen to behave towards each other, how you are seen to be treated. And those torturous thoughts at the end of the night when you can't sleep, those doubts and confusions that nag away at you, waking and sleeping, they don't need to be aired or shared. We keep them to ourselves, and that is fine. Just don't tell me. It is a recipe for disaster.

But it is probably the reason that at least one in two couples aren't divorced. Would anybody last a week in a relationship with complete honesty? Or maybe it would be the wake-up call to how it actually is that we all need. Maybe we need a healthy dose of mutual honesty to shake us up and see all those little sexual indiscretions for what they really are. All the petty attractions and misconducts mean nothing, if at the end of the day you can turn around and say honestly to your partner, 'I want, more than anything, to spend my time with you.'

I sit on my own, and wait for Henry to come back.

A Messenger from God

Henry can't seem to find a coffee shop in the airport; many, many bars, but no coffee. He is aware that he is wandering further and further away from Eve and the bags, but he doesn't think he should have another drink, it will only make him maudlin. He is depressed and she is in hysterics – so much for the broken rib healing, it will take years if she keeps laughing at this rate, but he won't be there to take the piss out of for years. Just tonight. She can find some other mug to amuse her. The thought of her with another man makes the seed of jealousy still in him expand and fill his stomach. But the thought of being with her, with no trust, makes him feel worse . . . almost.

Henry is just sick of feeling anything. He wants to be numb, to not have anybody hold this emotional power over him, with the ability to plunge him onto this rollercoaster of despair, and depression, and even elation.

Henry walks into a bar and asks for an Irish coffee, the closest he can get to a soft drink he tells himself, while ignoring all the painfully obvious soft drinks available.

He sips at his coffee and thinks about what lies ahead. He doesn't have the heart to ask for a seat away from her on the plane, even now he doesn't want to upset her. And if he is being honest, he wants these last hours with her. Even if they don't say a single word to each other for the entire trip, he wants her close to him, if only to finish this thing once and for all. Knowing that she was somewhere on the plane, sitting next to somebody else, searching her out with his eyes, might weaken his resolve. He has to be able to say goodbye when the time comes, because to weaken would be madness. He knows deep down that leaving her is the only thing to do. But it will be so very hard.

Henry sees a man moving from table to table handing out leaflets, probably happy hour offers, and the last thing Henry needs is a happy hour. An unhappy hour he could handle. Henry sees the man making his way over to his side of the bar and necks his drink, more whiskey than coffee, and gets up to go, but the man has sensed he might lose one, and descends upon the table at speed. Henry looks down, around, anywhere but at him, hoping he will just go away without Henry having to push past. The man sticks a leaflet under his nose,

'I see that you are leaving sir, but just one moment of your time is all I need.'

'I'm sorry, I don't want another drink, I don't care how cheap it is.'

'No man, I'm not selling drinks, I'm selling salvation. The Lord. Have you ever thought about God?'

That was unexpected. Henry lets out a burst of laughter and takes the leaflet, still not looking at the man, but reading the pamphlet, 'Have you told God lately that you love him?' Henry shrugs his shoulders,

'I'm sorry, I'm just on my way out, and much as I'd like to stop and talk about this, I have to get back . . .' Henry looks up and stops. This is no fucking man of God, no fucking toga-wearing, baldheaded, tambourine-smacking disciple. This man is the root of every problem Henry has, every black thought in his head and the nightmare that has become his life over the last few days. This is the pretty boy who shagged her. The man at the door that morning. This is the fucking guy.

Matt realizes a second too late to run for it, as this massive British guy stands glaring, his face contorting into rage, that it is her boyfriend. Henry's eyes are beginning to bulge.

Henry cannot believe the nerve of this guy, handing out leaflets on God for Christ's sake, giving it all holier than thou, when he has ruined Henry's life!

'What about extramarital sex? Eh? What about fucking another man's girlfriend? What about getting married for a laugh? These don't seem like godly acts to me, are they on your fucking leaflet?' Henry is poking him in the shoulder, prodding each point home.

Matt is horrified. He cannot believe his luck. If there is a God, and this is seeming increasingly unlikely, he is fucking with Matt's head big time. He is trying to preach the good news, but it looks as if it may get rammed right back down his throat. He is trying to make amends, repent his sins, and the sins just won't leave him alone. Matt is now a dedicated Anglophobe. What is it with these people? Matt does not feel God on his side. He only took the leaflets thirty minutes ago, from a man at the entrance of the airport, who was having no luck distributing them. Matt was two hours early to meet his girlfriend who was flying in from New York, and he decided to spend his time profitably, making amends for his actions over the last few days.

'Look man, I'm just gonna go, OK? I don't mean you any harm, you've made it up with Eve, let's just let this one go.'

'Let this one go? Are you fucking insane? And no I haven't made it up with my goddamn girlfriend for your fucking information. We are finished, relationship over – the woman I love, that I wanted to marry, have kids with – it's all fucked! And it's your fault! And you're talking about God! What are you a comedian? Is this some kind of sick joke?'

'Look man, I'm really sorry, but there's nothing I can do about this now, I am truly sorry, but what can I do? My girlfriend is flying in tonight, and I have to explain the whole thing to her, and it's not going to be easy. I don't know if we will be the same again, but with God's help . . .'

Matt is silenced by one massive British fist landing square on his jaw, and flooring him. He feels blood in his mouth, his head clouding over. The last thing he sees are two enormous feet stepping over him, and heading out of the bar. Then he passes out, leaflets floating all over the room.

Henry couldn't help it. He was not going to stand there and listen to a lecture on godliness from him of all people. Forgive that, you freak.

Henry leaves the bar, shaking out his fist, but surprisingly feeling a hell of a lot better. His resolve strengthened, he thinks he can do this. He will be able to say goodbye to her now. He doesn't want to, but he can. And he will.

True/Love.Com

Matt had never actually seen his girlfriend. They had spoken of course. That is if by speaking, you mean e-mailing. But they knew everything about each other. Matt had known within hours that she was the one. There was nothing fickle about this relationship. It was deep, and personal, and involved. They just hadn't actually met.

In his first few days in Las Vegas, Matt had been . . . well he had been lonely. Scott was off doing his own thing, and the job promised to him on arrival had not materialized. He had spent his first couple of days trawling the town, trying to get meetings with agents, but few of them would actually see him. Those who had let him in mostly wore toupees, ill-fitting suits with sweaty patches under the arms, and big fake smiles. Two of them offered him porn, one of them offered him gay porn, and the last one offered him a blow job.

And so it was that Matt had found himself stuck in his newly rented apartment with little food, less furniture, and no company. More importantly, he had no money to blow, and what do you do in Vegas with no money? On the fourth day, alone in his apartment, he had found himself talking to the bath, and decided he needed to get some fresh air.

He was trying to steer clear of the booze. His capacity for drink had recently hit rock bottom, for no explicable reason. He kept having blackouts, and winding up in unfamiliar places, with unfamiliar faces, unsure of his activities the night before. But what is there to do in Vegas with no money, and no alcohol? He had left his apartment with the intention of finding himself a waiter's job, to tide himself over until an acting job came up. However it seemed that waiters' jobs were harder to get than acting jobs. After a particularly demoralizing afternoon being turned away from every bar within a five mile radius because he couldn't name a single Frank Sinatra tune (they asked the same goddamn question everywhere!), he found himself drowning his sorrows in coffee at an internet café.

Matt hadn't understood all the computers at first. He thought he had walked into a particularly cool stationery shop that happened to serve drinks, until he tried to order a coffee, and was asked at which terminal he would be sitting when they brought it over. He laughingly explained that he didn't actually work there, he just wanted a coffee, and the waiter filled him in – you pay a certain amount and you get two hours unlimited access, more so if you decide to stay on, and depending on how busy it got. No child porn, and no dead people were the rules, and Matt tentatively agreed.

He had a little trouble to start with, but after twenty minutes the waiter came over and turned the computer on for him. Within two hours Matt was not only an expert, but an addict. Bizarrely, most of the people there seemed to be e-mailing people they didn't even know. He was desperate to talk to somebody out there. You pick a subject – Matt of course picked acting in New York – and you find a 'chat room'. Here you join in conversations with people from all around the world, all typing at once, and all with the Big Apple as their common interest. Matt was bowled over! There were a hell of a lot of directors logged on, looking for actors to star in new big budget films, and more than half of these were apparently young blondes. Two birds with one stone! He couldn't believe his luck.

Within twenty minutes he had found her. Her name was Raquel Weich, and she lived in New York. She was blonde, and an actress, but not a director as well, unfortunately. But two out of three ain't bad!

They just seemed to click, a subject they joked about later – using a mouse, clicking, double clicking. Similarly there seemed to be an 'electricity' between them! Oh how they laughed. Matt actually typed the laughter, to let her know how funny he found her. Paragraph after paragraph of ha ha ha ha ha ha ha ha ha. Never a dull moment. She was exactly on his wavelength. They talked about Grand Central Station, and how the weather was getting hotter in New York already; Greenwich Village, and Bloomingdales. Matt pined for home, and Raquel answered all his questions, even offering some great cooking tips! They talked a lot about Demi Moore, and her progress from *Saint Elmo's Fire* to *Striptease*. She was Matt's favourite actress. Raquel preferred Meryl Streep. They had soon dumped the chat room, and its constant interruptions. He only wanted to talk to Raquel, and besides, they had both got sick of the frequent requests for anal sex from someone pretending to be Steven Spielberg.

Within days Matt had forgotten all about finding a job, had got himself a Hotmail address, and was at the café at 9 a.m. sharp each morning, nervous and excited at the prospect of a day's typing. He had never been any good at writing at school, but now he found himself sending pages and pages of thoughts and feelings, dreams and hopes and everything to this woman down an Internet line.

But Matt soon realized that not every rainbow has a silver lining. On his thirteenth consecutive day at the café, he reached into his wallet to pay for his coffee, and nothing came out. He was broke, and his rent was due next week. He had completely neglected to get a job, and he had run out of money. The situation was desperate. With tears welling up in his eyes, he sent an e-mail to Raquel to explain that he would have to find himself a job, and wouldn't be able to e-mail during the days any more.

Raquel was not happy. She could only e-mail during the day, as she worked in a bar in the evenings, and all day Saturday and Sunday. They would never be able to sustain the level of intimacy they had achieved if they were merely replying to e-mails at odd hours, and couldn't actually converse with the immediacy they had now. She begged him to try and get a night job too, and he said he would try, but he had heard of a job at a fancy restaurant 'Gerard's, on the strip, through Scott, and he knew it required him to work some days. He suggested she call him, but she had refused. She said she didn't want to dispel the uncomplicated, unembarrassed closeness they had developed, and that as soon as they spoke, their nerves would get the better of them, and it would all fall apart. If she was going to actually speak to him, live, she would want to be within touching distance, and be able to reach out and stroke his hair, hold his hand.

Matt had cried that night. He was an emotional man anyway, and given to breaking down at the odd television advert, but that night he had bawled like a baby. He had taken the job the next day, and though it paid barely anything, it would be enough to just cover the rent.

Desperate to get back to the café, but unable to get a shift off in the daytime, he phoned and pleaded with the manager of the café to open all night. The manager told him to 'stop obsessing' and see a counsellor. This was not the answer Matt was anticipating. He finally got into the café four days later, and logged on this time with nervous anxiety instead of his usual excited anticipation.

There were three messages from Raquel. The first hoped his job was going well, and said she was already missing him. The second pleaded with him to e-mail her. The third concluded that he had obviously found someone else. Matt typed away furiously for an hour and a half. He typed that he loved her, and that he couldn't find someone else, because she had his heart. He told her that nobody had ever come this close to him before, and that he wouldn't be able to breathe until she was here, in Las Vegas, with him. He felt like he was suffocating without her constant communication. He even wrote a poem. It took him twenty minutes to think of a word that rhymed with Raquel, until the waiter suggested 'real swell'.

Her answer was terse, and abrupt. Unless he was prepared to put in the effort, they had no future.

The same day he received a joke about Humpty Dumpty,

signed Jack, aged five, from Raquel's e-mail address. He didn't understand – was she calling him childish? That night he had gone to work with a heavy heart, and a lump in his throat: how would he ever work this out? When would he see his Raquel? Furthermore, he had been forced to take a second job, as a . . . dancer, in a dubious bar, in an equally dubious part of town. The situation was getting worse. Even Matt had to acknowledge he was no dancer, he was a drag queen. He had started drinking before work at the restaurant that night, and when he had switched from waiting tables to the bar, he had laid into the whiskey with vengeance, charging all his drinks to some drunk tourist girl, who moaned about her boyfriend all night. The next morning, of course, he had woken up in his car with her. With Eve.

He had put a brave face on it, but inside he was dying. How would he ever explain this to Raquel? But of course that wasn't the worst of it. He had married this Eve, this tourist girl, and even though they were getting it annulled, and it could not have meant less, and he didn't even like Eve, who was far too short at five foot seven, and carrying about twenty pounds too many for his liking, he would have to tell Raquel. The only saving grace was that casual sex was allowed in the Bible, although he was sure he had found something in his new version about monogamy, or something. Tentatively he had e-mailed her that day, after spending hours in the town hall making sure he could cancel this thing out before it had even begun, and explained everything. Surprisingly Raquel had e-mailed back straight away. She had been angry, but sympathetic. Everybody made mistakes she wrote, and sometimes people get married to the wrong people. It was better that he had realized his mistake, and was fixing it, rather than spending twenty years of his life with this woman, before finding himself in a loveless marriage. Matt was shocked, but broke down with relief – did this mean that they were OK? Was she still his girlfriend?

As Matt's heart had leapt in his chest, he read her e-mail saying that they should sort this thing out properly, and that she would fly down to Las Vegas in a couple of days to see him, and see if they could make this work. She was leaving New York, and she would stay with him.

Matt's unbridled elation manifested itself in a peculiar state of nerves in the hours after receiving this news. Was it too early for them to meet? What if she wasn't a natural blonde? So many questions that needed answers, and the only way to answer them was for Raquel to join him here.

The next two days were his hell on earth. Things just seemed to spiral out of control, and any luck deserted him as he ran into Eve's boyfriend, and then literally ran into Eve herself, in his truck. The only thing that had kept him going was a copy of the Bible he had found in the chest of drawers in his bedroom, the only piece of furniture in there. Matt was sure, deep down, that with the help of the Lord, and the love of his woman, his Raquel, everything would be OK.

And this is how he came to be standing now, at the gate for the just-landed flight AA436 from New York to Las Vegas, with a bag of ice pressed against one side of his face, and blood still trickling from his nose onto his shirt. In his other hand was the sign – 'RAQUEL WEICH'. Exhausted, bruised, nervously keeping one eye out for raging Englishmen who punched like a wrecking ball, while the other eye scanned for Raquel.

As Matt surveyed the crowds for single young women, it

occurred to him that he had no idea what she actually looked like. He had a picture in his head, of a blonde, tall Demi Moore type, wearing sunglasses at night, and a pair of faded jeans. But nobody seemed to resemble this woman at all. Matt's nervous exhaustion began to take over, and as his mind started whirring with visions of Raquel not taking the flight after all, not being able to leave his beloved New York, his eyes focused on a woman standing right in front of him, smiling. She was radiating a loving warmth he had not felt for an age; a non sexual warmth only achievable by women the same age as his mother. He guessed her age at fifty.

Yes this woman was blonde – well blonde white. She was dressed in brown velour slacks and a T-shirt with a flower on the front, with pink glass stones where the petals should be. Her hair was pulled back with what looked like an elastic band. She wore no make-up, and her glasses, with their milk bottle lenses, made her eyes comically huge,. She carried two plastic carrier bags in each hand, and a pair of old trainers stuck out of one of them.

With an intuitiveness Matt had never previously experienced, he knew this was Raquel.

'Raquel.'

'Matthew?'

'Yes Raquel, I'm Matt.' His shoulders collapsed under the weight of his absolute naivety, and equal stupidity. Why would a sexy young blonde actress living in New York fall in love with a man over the Internet? On the other hand, for a middle-aged housewife like Raquel with a lot of spare time on her hands, a husband at work all day, and her little boy's second-hand computer, it was perfect. He felt the blood come rushing out of his nose afresh, as he slumped to the ground. He felt the cold vinyl floor against the side of his face, as his blurred vision rested on the cheap sandals with the old woman's toes sticking out of them. Just before he passed out, he thought he saw a corn.

Matt came round to the sound of a lullaby, and a dry slightly wrinkled hand stroking the side of his face. He felt the velour pants beneath his head, as he looked up into the milk bottle glasses, and saw Raquel cradling his head in her hands, singing to him softly. As he looked into those magnified eyes, the tears began to stream down his cheeks, and every part of his body went limp, a dead weight of fatigue, and relief, that the search was finally over.

'Thank God you're here, Raquel. At last.'

But as her face seemed to zoom in to kiss him and Matt lost consciousness again he felt a strange sensation. It was his stomach turning.

Reversing

Oh we are business-like about the bags. About the trolley, about getting to the car. There's no snapping, no joking, no conversation at all. There is no argument about who will drive. It's his car now, from tomorrow I won't be insured any more. Henry gets in the driving seat without question. I sit in the passenger seat without question. We belt up.

Henry drives fast, all the way home. He does ninety-five on the motorway, he corners in third, at forty mph, as we get nearer to his house. He doesn't turn the radio on, and neither do I. He doesn't make conversation, and neither do I. I want to say 'Henry please', but I don't. I don't know if he wants to say anything, but he doesn't. We sit at the Chiswick roundabout for an age, waiting for a gap. I stare out of the window at the dark, at lights coming on in houses, at other cars. I just stare at the window itself. I think I may cry, or rather I could let myself cry, but there is no point. It would make both of us feel worse. Or maybe Henry wouldn't even say anything, ignore it, and that would be too much to bear.

Henry shoots out on the roundabout, fast, barely missing an oncoming van, almost killing us both. He is driving like an arsehole, but I don't say anything. I remember the first time I asked Henry to do the reverse test. It had become a benchmark of attractiveness for men, and determined sexiness . . . or not. It had always been a quirk of mine, finding a really good, confident driver sexy, and part of it was the way a man reversed. I had shared it with Karen, and Alice, and Rachel at work, and it had become a test that we did on men that we knew, that we had just met, that we have never spoken to and we wanted to break the ice. It has to do with the way a man actually, physically, reverses a car into a parallel parking space, but also how willing he is to do it in the first place. The men that say 'What? I don't understand, why? What?', are the men that fail straight away.

So this is how you do the reverse test. There should be two of you girls at least, and you say to your unsuspecting male friend,

'Matthew/Mark/Luke/whoever, I need you to show me how you reverse, and it could be the key as to whether I ever want you in a sexual way. It is very important, so do not make light of this . . . take it very seriously.' It is always good to intimidate them a little at this point.

'Now Matthew/Mark/whoever, here is the scene. You and the lovely Karen here have been to the cinema, you lucky dog, and she is deciding whether to ask you in to her house for a little post-cinematic discussion, and sex. However, first she needs to see . . . how you reverse! Do it right, and that sex is yours. Do it wrong, and frankly she'll be gone before the engine stops running. In short, there will be no goodnight kiss, no goodnight anything for you, and this is Karen, who we both know . . . well, anyway. At this point you have to at least pretend that you find Karen attractive. Do you see what we are doing? It's like role-play.'

Now if your man asks what you have just seen at the cinema this is a good sign. It means he is getting into it. We applaud this, and it should be encouraged. Always suggest a raunchy film, so he knows in the mood, *Betty Blue* is a good one, or *9½ Weeks* if he isn't into arthouse, or gets a headache from subtitles, as I do.

'Now you have pulled up outside her house, and you are about to park, reversing into a space whereby the passenger seat will be nearest the kerb, is this clear? Now you sit here, and Karen sits next to you.'

At this point you have to move the chairs so that they are in the appropriate position. It is very important that he feels he is actually in the car.

'Now reverse. Parallel park that car!'

And they do. Of course there is a right way and a wrong way, but to do it completely right and get full sexy driver and therefore I will sleep with you status, there are a number of stages he must complete.

Firstly, he must slip off his seat belt.

Secondly, he must put the car in reverse.

Thirdly, the most important, he must place his arm on the back of your seat, and look over his shoulder.

Finally, he must make a palm with his hand, place it in the centre of the make-believe steering wheel, and palm the wheel until you are 'parked'.

When Henry did it, no questions asked, without any

remarks that it was stupid, or having to be badgered to do it, it was perfect, and we actually screamed. It was the first time someone had done it spot on, without coercion. I could have slept with him right there and then, but it was only our second real date, everybody was there, we were in a crowded pub, and I just wasn't in that 'sex in the toilets' mood. I slept with him that night of course. Karen had said, 'she's loving you now', and it was true. Henry had looked part relieved, part smug. Of course it helped that he had downed a few pints already that night. Never do the test on a completely sober man, they don't get into it.

Now we have a chart in out heads as to who did what. Our friend Pete started shouting loudly at traffic to hold on, which we loved. He actually had an argument with a make believe Ford Escort, and won points. Our friend Dan was chastized for not removing his seat belt, but justified it with the fact that he doesn't wear a seat belt on minor roads. This is neither big nor clever, but it excited us all no end. It was a good answer.

We pretty much use it on every man we meet these days, and Karen uses it on prospective boyfriends all the time. It has become bizarrely important, and what was once just my quirk is actually some sort of Soho mating ritual. If he does it right, believe me, you'll notice. It has to do with control, if you hadn't already guessed.

Henry is parking the car now, and he does it right of course. I look away. No chance of a post-reverse quickie now unfortunately, and we've had our fair share of those in the past. He gets out of the car. I see my little Golf parked over the road, intact, after my ten day absence.

Without my realizing it the moment has crept up when

I will have to say goodbye, and I have no idea how to play this, or what to say. Do I get to kiss him? If we are being amicable then yes, otherwise no. And it will have to be a peck, a proper kiss is out of the question. When am I going to see him? Will he call me? What do I say, here, now?

I get out of the car, and he is already carrying my bags over to the Golf. I am shocked, having gone so long without conversation, when he speaks, softly,

'Are you going to be all right, driving, with your rib?'

'What? Oh I'll be fine.' Wrong answer. It should have been no, can you drive me home and carry my bags in and get caught in a deep conversation, and not be able to say goodbye, and stay with me?

'Open the boot and I'll put the bags in. Are you going to be OK lifting them out?'

'I'll get Daryll to do it.' Wrong answer. Daryll, my sexy neighbour, bad thing to say.

'Fine.' A slight bristle? My imagination I think.

The bags are in the boot. I have my keys, and we are standing on the pavement, I am by the driver's door, Henry is standing by the back wheel.

'Well I should get going, Henry.' I take a step forward. Please Henry, say something, it's up to you. Please Henry.

'It's cold, so I'm going to go in. See ya.'

He turns and walks away, and that is it. The end. No kiss. No lingering goodbye looks. Nothing. He doesn't look back. He just unlocks his front door and goes inside. I get in my car, feel a pain shoot up my side, possibly my rib. I start the engine, and drive home in silence.

It would appear that is it.

Pulling the Trigger

I'm back in my flat, and I am terribly organized. As soon as I got in I tidied up. I did the washing-up that had been left before the holiday. I vacuumed the lounge, polished the television. I cleaned the sink, and the bath, and made a two-week-old unmade bed. One load of washing is already spinning, another one is ready to go in. The washing machine whirrs in the background as I sit on my bed and survey a spotless bedroom.

I'm not in work tomorrow, they expect me to be away for another five days. It is too early to think about the hundreds of e-mails that will have been ignored in my absence. I cannot think of speaking to anyone on the phone, without telling them about me and Henry, and I don't have the will or the strength.

I slept for a while on the plane, and woke up to find I was resting my head on Henry's shoulder. He didn't have his arm around me to make it more comfortable, he sat upright, as if I wasn't there. I shifted in my seat, moved my head off him, but didn't sleep any more. I pretended to sleep, to myself and to Henry, but it didn't work, I wasn't comfortable. It didn't feel right.

Now I am exhausted, completely drained. Looking in the mirror, I see a strangely pale complexion looking back, considering I have just come back from the desert. I see dead eyes. I should sleep properly, in bed, in my jumper with my hands tucked into the sleeves. But I try, and I can't sleep. I can't close my eyes. It is so quiet. Everybody else is asleep, in my road, in this town. Vegas is just waking up. When I picture it now, I don't picture the place I have come from, the hotel and the diner and the courtroom, the place that I have been in for the last ten days. I picture it in films, and brochures. In some way I don't feel like I have even been away, the way you never feel like you have been anywhere as soon as you get home. But the quiet, the uneasy silence that is waiting to be broken lets me know I have been away, because it reminds me that something is missing. Something, someone, stayed away.

I get up and turn the radio on, but it is all adverts and techno. I want something different. I realize what it is. I dig to the bottom of my CDs and find my Phil Collins, covered in dust. I put it in and go straight to number nine. The piano introduction comes on, and Phil starts singing "Against All Odds".

Nope, not going to do it. I press stop. Too predictable. Too contrived.

I need something less obvious. I get out my *Romeo + Juliet* soundtrack, last track, "You and Me Song". I press play.

Yeah right, like anything is forgotten. This is making me numb. I'm not really listening. I press stop. But I need music to go to bed with. I need to open up the gates and put myself to sleep. I know what to put on. I just have to be brave enough, because it is going to do the trick. I need the trigger to start it, to break me out of this daydream. I pick up the CD, and my eyes are filling. I wipe away the tears.

I take three breaths really quickly, one after the other, and my bottom lip starts to go. I put my hand over my mouth to try and stop it. But now I'm only breathing in these short little gasps, and my eyes are blurry, and my cheeks are wet as I wipe them angrily with the back of my hand, like I'm in charge. I put the CD in, press number five, and crawl back into bed, pulling the covers up against my face.

The piano begins, big thunderous painful thumps on the keys, and I just lie there, and try to listen, dispassionately. But then Barry starts to sing,

I remember all my life, raining down as cold as ice,
Shadows of a man, a face through a window,
Cryin' in the night,
As night goes into morning, just another day,
Happy people pass my way, looking in their eyes, I see a memory,
I never realized you made me happy

I don't know if I would have cried this much anyway. I don't know why I would want to make myself cry any more than I would otherwise. And I don't know why this song, these lyrics seem to lend themselves so well to my own peculiar sadness. But no matter, I curl up tightly, and cry. I don't get to phone him tomorrow. I don't get to see him. I did this to myself.

I cry myself to sleep, and Barry finishes without me.

To Laugh or Cry

Sophia Loren said, 'If you haven't cried your eyes can't be beautiful.' If you haven't been hurt you haven't lived. You will not know true compassion, or the emotional power that we can all hold over another, unless you have had your heart broken. You are a better person for the experience. That is how I see it.

If you are the person who always walks away, who is always in control, you have never really let yourself go, or loved someone fully. But it's a strange kind of masochism to walk into such a painful process knowingly, isn't it? You wonder why we put ourselves through it. Is it precisely because of what Sophia said, and you are not the person you could be if you have not felt the loss of love? Is it only in knowing how that feels that we can possibly treat others' feelings with the respect that they deserve? Is it the only way to get that kind of love back?

Mark Twain said 'Against the assault of laughter nothing can stand.' That was a little more optimistic, and typical of the sexual divide. Men are thinking of having a laugh, women are thinking about how their eyes look.

I read once that men and women must surely be the bravest animals in creation, for every day thousands more of these two warring tribes attempt to form unions and banish the centuries of fighting. The remarkable hope of any two individuals when they put aside all the reputed differences and say we shall be together for the foreseeable future, and make of it a happy union is foolish optimism perhaps.

If you address the differences between the sexes on any level, it does seem presumptuous of any of us to think a heterosexual marriage could ever work. All accounts detail our differences, not our similarities. Of course discourse on the subject varies massively, but I think these differences are partly genetic, partly social. We are different, and we learn to be different as well. We only get it right when we revel in the differences, and not fight against them.

One example is the very sketchy scientific theory that men and women biologically think differently. I am not talking about the subjects they entertain, but how they entertain them. A man supposedly thinks with only one part of his brain at a time. If he is thinking about football, to really take this to a sexist peak, then football is the only thing on his mind. However women are said to think with many different parts of their brain at once. So a woman could be thinking about football, and cars, and cookery, and clothes shopping, and woodwork as well. At the same time as she thinks of all these things, she can put them in many contexts. So, a woman can be thinking about football, and how her boyfriend assumes she knows nothing about it, and doesn't even take the time to listen and how much of an ignorant pig this makes him. Simultaneously she can think about the new shoes that she has seen, and how nice they would look as long as she can walk in them properly, and they are not going to be too uncomfortable. She can then flip to what she will be making for dinner, and just as quickly flip back to the shoes, and what her boyfriend said about how much the last pair cost, and the Imelda Marcos jibes she keeps getting. During this entire time, our man will still only be thinking about football. Or maybe sex.

This is a possible reason for men believing they are superior at any activity that requires great concentration, because their thinking is so blinkered. It may in fact make it easier for them to concentrate but often results in a narrow-mindedness of sorts, which leads to their complete inability to understand women when they argue.

When women argue they will invariably bring up the past, the future, and many different perceptions of the present. Men just argue the point that they are making. For instance, you could be rationally discussing with your boyfriend that you would prefer it if he did not stare at the barmaid's breasts at your local pub. As a valid point in this argument you can bring up the time that he stared at that girl on the train in the cropped top. It is the same thing. But you see, to him, it is not the same thing, because he is only thinking about the barmaid, and it is too much for him to jump back to the girl on the train, even though he has probably thought about her since then. You will then identify his looking at other women as a consistent problem, whereas he will insist that we are only talking about the barmaid in the pub, and that does not a consistent problem make. At this point he will call you irrational for bringing up something that has nothing to do with the point in hand. You will retaliate with the absolute relevance of the train girl to this discussion. He will get frustrated by your inability to discuss the matter in hand, and call you a 'typical woman' like it was some kind of insult. I personally will always take that as a compliment.

The possibilities for misunderstandings and name-calling are therefore endless. The trick is not to care.

What we have to learn is that being a 'typical woman' is a good thing, and being a 'typical man' is just as good, although it pains me to say it. Enjoy the disparities and we have success – end of the war! Unfortunately we are not conditioned to think like this. As, in any war, there is competition, and there are casualties, and the desire to be the winner often outweighs the need for it to be a draw.

If we go back to Sophia and Mark Twain then, we have a situation where the woman is crying and the man is laughing. The problem is this is that this is the stereotype. This is what we expect and the roles we often assume. A woman will cry until she feels better, a man will ignore the problem and mask it with fake emotion, and laugh it off. I wonder how long Sophia and Mark would have lasted? Actually wasn't he her first husband . . .

How Do I Look?

Like you, I'm not particularly forgivable. I am not awash with endearing traits that make my actions understandable, or even easier to overlook. I don't expect them to be, or ask that you find me sympathetic. No more than anyone else at least. I don't deserve anything more than I do deserve it. I haven't painted myself in an unreal light, flattering or otherwise. Did you expect to have more empathy with me? Would you have preferred that I paint out the bad, and only show the good? Did you only want half the story, leading you not necessarily to understand, but to like me at least? Did you need me to lie?

The problem would seem to be that we expect more of other people than we can ever deliver ourselves.

We expect relations to be more than they are. We say we don't want fireworks but we do. We say that we love people when we don't, we say we want things to last forever, and then one day change our minds. We break hearts, we create emotional baggage for everyone we get involved with. We make failures of ourselves and each other.

But what is the alternative? A day to day of comfortable living with someone who enables you to just get by emotionally and physically, a relationship dressed up as the 'mature reality of love'. Completely unexceptional relationships hiding behind a knowing cynicism that 'love just works out like that in the end', that sounds patronizing, makes me feel small when I hear it, but is in fact just a massive compromise. Never project your disappointment, your boredom, onto me as the way 'it should be'. I'd rather keep trying for something better. Great expectations are the only ones worth having. It's no expectations that are the real problem.

Just because you don't sleep around behind your partner's back doesn't mean you've hit the jackpot. Maybe we have both made mistakes, that doesn't mean our relationship is any lesser than yours. Because we are both looking for something amazing, and we fuck up, but we know what we have, and we keep trying. We go through the risks and the pains, because we want something greater. You? You're just safe. Something has to signify it as distinctive, as exceptional – well does it? Are you at least still smiling?

I think the real answer is always twist, never stick. Twist on nineteen and hope for a two, twist on twenty and hope for an ace. Keep pushing until you get it. If all you ever seem to reach is sixteen, where's the excitement? Where is the risk? You can bust with the same player, but agree to deal again, and this time it might work, if you both know you still want to be at the same table, playing together. I'll keep playing my hand until that magic twenty-one. Or until one of us leaves the table. Ahhh, the language of Vegas. And I didn't even play cards.

If you can honestly say that it is still fun, and nobody is

being cheated, then that is all you need. Settle for less, and you are just not playing fair.

You'll look back and see there was no point playing at all.

Have I Really Bust?

I'm sitting in the pub, waiting for Henry. Don't get excited, it's not the next day, or the next week. Tim passed on the things I had left at Henry's in my first days back at work – a bag full of half empty shampoo bottles, a couple of CDs, underwear, a pair of jeans, my wok, even a pack of cigarettes with two left in it. Henry had done a pretty good job of clearing me out. Tim looked a little embarrassed, suggested that I talk to him anytime if I needed to, but I haven't bothered.

No, Henry and I haven't spoken since the holiday, and that was nine months ago. No, I haven't had a baby either, nothing so dramatic. Through a grapevine that looked remarkably like Tim, I have heard that Henry has had some dates here and there, but nothing serious. Of course I don't know for sure, I don't know what he is thinking. No we haven't talked.

I'm moving house. I was packing, on my own, putting all my stuff in boxes. I found a camera, one of those Kodak throw-aways. I had buried it in a drawer in the kitchen, and never had it developed. It was from Vegas, twelve photos used, in that first week before it all went so . . . wrong. I hastily took shots of my little flat to use up the film, for nostalgia, and had it developed in an hour the next day. Opening up those photos, I was nervous as hell, as if Henry would look out from them and see me looking, catch me holding my breath, or worse, smiling at the two of us together. Nine months is not a long time, it seems like nothing. I haven't dated anybody since. I haven't had sex since. I have only done my morning tube scan a couple of times. I haven't even kissed a man since. I wouldn't call it celibacy, which implies a degree of choice. I just haven't met another man I have wanted to be with yet. I wouldn't be celibate if Henry wanted me.

I did go out one night, with my friend Clare, her boyfriend, and his brother. Clare had been trying to set us up even while I was with Henry, and I had always told her to back off. Apparently she fancied him more than Paul, her boyfriend. But unfortunately for her lustful urges, she had fallen madly in love with Paul, which dictated that she not touch his siblings, at least not sexually. But she decided that if she couldn't have him, somebody she liked must. I had eventually been coerced into going, after her implication that looking depressed whenever I thought nobody was looking was actually giving me lines around my eyes.

We went for a lovely meal, that is the food was lovely, but the atmosphere was a little strained. We both knew why we were there. He had e-mailed me a few times beforehand, which is always bizarre. You meet somebody, you know their tone, their stories, you just don't know the face.

His name was Pete, and unfortunately he was a lot funnier when he had time to think about things and type, than when he was actually speaking. But I didn't really give it a chance. I just kept looking at him, and seeing Henry. Wishing it was Henry, wishing he would show some random characteristic that I could associate with Hen, and thus find him attractive. Look at me with mock anger, tell me to 'pipe down', not laugh at all of my jokes, move my hair off my face.

Clare tried really hard, and kept pointing out all the remarkable similarities in our personalities. But I couldn't wait for the evening to end. I don't want to start up something, with someone else, when I know that the man who is meant for me lives just the other side of the river. Pete tried hard, I'll give him that. All of a sudden, as we came out into the evening air, Clare and Paul were gone, and Pete was walking me back to the tube. We had both been drinking, me to numb the pain a little, Pete for Dutch courage I think. But when we got to the tube, and I forced myself to peck him on the cheek in thanks, he put his hand in the small of my back and tried to kiss me. I just couldn't do it. I dodged, and ran off down the steps of Tottenham Court Road tube station, shouting my goodbyes over my shoulders. I just don't want to kiss anybody else. Drunk or sober, I just want to kiss Henry. I cried to myself, a little, on the train home. I kept thinking I might see Hen, by chance, kept looking at the doors anxiously every time they opened. But he didn't come in. I knew he wouldn't. He was definitely gone, on the other side of the river.

As I looked at the twelve photos of Henry and me in Las Vegas, I saw there were seven that we had asked other people to take of us together. There were a couple of us in restaurants, one of us outside Caesar's Palace, one of Henry on his own with some showgirls looking pretty pleased with himself, two of both of us looking pretty drunk in the daylight. There was one of us standing in front of the wedding that we saw, looking like members of the bridal party. There was quite a good one of me on my own, sitting on the grass. One of Henry naked but for a handily placed bottle of hairspray.

I discarded the photos of my flat, and flicked through the American twelve again. Then I discarded the ones of us separately, and just looked at the seven of us together. I looked at them over and over again, looked at the expressions on our faces. It took me forever to realize, and when I did, I had to double-check five times. In every photo that Henry and I were together, we were holding hands. I had stopped looking and stared at my desk to concentrate – did we ever hold hands? Did we hold hands that much at least? I was always tactile with him, we both were, grabbing thighs, hugging, kissing in public. But hand holding always seemed to me to be . . . contrived, a gesture for other people to see, as opposed to you both enjoying. I had always been against it in the past. But there we were, in every shot, holding hands. That is how it must have been. Gradually, over time, we had grown together in a way that I had only realized in the last few months, as I felt the urge to speak to him more and more, a need to re-establish contact. I felt him missing in my life. And not just a man, any man, missing. I lacked him. Like some sort of deficiency that made my hair dry, or my nails weak, or my eyes well up for no good reason. Yet, I had made no fight to get him back.

I hadn't called Henry once, hadn't gone anywhere that I thought he might be, hadn't grilled Tim for information, although frankly Tim didn't need the grilling, he just e-mailed me and told me, without asking if I wanted to know. I had accepted it blindly, and without argument. I had wholly taken the blame, and the punishment.

But I have to show Henry these photos. I have to see if he will notice the hands, think it odd, or remember that we did it all the time. I have to see if he'll see it as the sign that I have. A sign really just being an elaborate excuse. I just have to see if he has missed me. I don't think I can accept the way we have left it. I just have to see him.

So I phoned him, with every intention of speaking to him, as the bugs literally bungee jumped from my throat to my stomach and the telephone rang. But he was out to lunch. I was assured by a familiar voice that he would be back in an hour, and I was put through to his voicemail. 'This is Henry, please leave your name and number, and I will get back to you shortly.' Just the sound of his voice made me feel sick, made me want to hang up. There was too much riding on it. But I was brave. Somehow I left a message.

'Henry, it's me. It's Eve I mean. How are you? Hope you're OK. I wondered if you might want to meet me for a drink tonight in the Bathhouse, if you aren't already doing anything. Opposite my work, you remember where it is, about 7 p.m. I hope you can make it, and . . . it would be really nice to see you. So 7, the Bathhouse, You don't need to phone me, I'll just see you there, if you can make it, hopefully. Bye.'

So here I am waiting. A little early for once in my life,

it's only a quarter to. It isn't busy, so if he comes, he'll see me sitting here.

Who knows?

The End . . .

Henry is standing outside the pub, at five past seven. He should just get back on the tube and go home. But then, what does one drink hurt? With her. There won't be a scene or anything like that, even if he hasn't actually spoken to her since it had all happened. Tim has filled him in on how she is looking, what she is doing, on a regular basis. She's fine apparently, and so is he really. But nine months seems like such a long time.

And he can count on Eve to even make it relaxed, to be inappropriately sarcastic despite what has happened, to put him at ease. He would like to see her very much.

But it isn't wise is it? To start the whole thing up again, when it has become so much easier over the last couple of months. He hasn't been suicidal or anything. To begin with he was still too angry. He even started seeing someone else, a friend of Joanna, Tim's girlfriend. And it wasn't like he had flashes of a different face while he was shagging her – he wasn't thinking of Vegas or anything like that. No, Henry knows that intimacy takes time to grow, as it has before it will again, and of course it wouldn't be the same this early on with this new girl. But it wasn't even close.

The sex was good, but the quiet afterwards wasn't. Henry is not so sure now that what he wants is an easy life. He's surprised that Eve hasn't phoned him once, until now. In the first few weeks he was waiting for her voice on the answer phone, the apologies, the 'let's meet up and talk', but nothing. Tim said she hadn't even asked about him, so Henry made him tell her even when she didn't ask, tell her he was fine.

She's moving now apparently, so Tim has said. Probably to somewhere too expensive, Henry thinks. She will have done some ridiculous sums and worked out that she can just afford it, and obviously not taken into account the three new pairs of shoes she buys each month, and eating out. She shouldn't be moving. Henry had the impulse to phone her as soon as he heard, and just make her tell him how much she would be paying out each month, and how safe the walk was from the tube station to her new flat. But of course he didn't.

Everybody has been a little bemused by the break-up, his family, Dai, his boss, and even Tim, who never liked her anyway. He hasn't told them the real story, just that they argued so much they had decided to call it a day. Tim has been fishing around for the details since day one, so it's obvious she hasn't told him anything either. A peculiar kind of loyalty, Henry thinks, given how disloyal she actually proved to be in Vegas. Bloody place, he can barely even remember it now. One night, months later and incredibly drunk, he trawled through his flat to find the camera from the holiday, one of those poxy little Kodak throw-aways that they had taken with them, but she must have it.

Henry is still standing outside the pub, it's quarter-past seven. He turns around and takes two steps away from the door, and stops. All the signs point in the other direction, everything is telling him not to go in and open all the old wounds, this particular can of worms. God, he needs to make a decision! Would one pint hurt so much?

It could be fine, it could hurt like hell.

I don't know. You decide. How hopeful are you feeling? What have you done, faced with the same thing?

What usually happens?

4/98